the Baker's BATTER

Sweet Romance in a Small Town

the *Baker's*
BATTER

Sweet Romance in a Small Town

JENNIFER LOOFT

To Debra!
Love wins!
1 Cor 13:13 —
Jennifer Looft

blackbird
PUBLICATIONS

Published by Blackbird Publications

Cover Design by Oh18 Creative

Author Headshot by Beatbox Portraits

Blackbird Publications logo by MagiDesigns

ISBN 979-8-218-10828-1 (print)

ISBN 979-8-9874175-0-8 (digital)

Library of Congress Control Number: 2023900623

Printed in the United States of America

First edition 2022

www.JenniferWritesBooks.com

For my mom, who never fails to set me up for success.

For my dad, who reminds me to watch for the cream to rise.

For my baseball-loving husband, who shows me the kind of love every girl deserves.

For my children, who remind me of the importance of following my dreams.

Chapter 1

Madeleine

M adeleine twisted the key in the ignition once more, her foot planted firmly on the brake of her yellow VW Beetle. *Ugh, this car. Really? Tonight is not the time to quit on me.* She listened, but heard nothing but a repetitive click, click, click, click. The dummy lights on her dash were no help, half-lit and frozen in that mid-point between a car that starts and a car that won't.

"Come on!" Buttercup, the new yellow Beetle her parents gave her on the day she graduated culinary school, had been reliable for five years. But lately, she had been temperamental, needing constant attention and forcing Madeleine to make regular visits to the local car repair shop. Thankfully, her best friend happened to own Taylor's Auto Shop, and Dillon was always at the ready when Buttercup decided to act up.

Between her car's constant need for attention and the state of finances at her bakery, The Bean and Batter, Madeleine wasn't sure she could handle much more.

One more turn of the key, another tick, tick, tick of Buttercup's stubborn engine, and a final huff from Madeleine meant Buttercup won this round. The cheerful jingle of keys as she yanked them from the ignition switch felt like one final insult from the yellow Beetle this evening. Madeleine grabbed her jacket from the passenger seat, wrapped it around her shoulders, and climbed out of the car, making sure to slam the door as hard as possible, as if it would somehow retaliate against the defiant car.

The air was chilly, and her tights were not enough to keep her legs warm as she trudged back to The Bean and Batter's back door. She jammed the key into the deadlock and twisted. This would not be the night she had planned. She was tired, ready to go home to her cozy little house, curl up on the couch with a mug of hot chocolate, and watch the latest episode of The Great British Baking Show.

With a sigh, she slipped her hand behind the shelf against the wall to flip the light switch on in the back room of her little bakery.

The familiar mix of rich coffee and sweet frosting greeted her and her mood lifted slightly. The way the sugar mixed with the coffee beans always brought back images of the eyelet lace that used to trim the edges of her mother's apron as she baked cupcakes and lined them up ever so carefully in the glass display. Madeleine set her purse on that same counter, in the same place her mother used to leave a half-empty cup of coffee sitting, which grew colder with each customer she served.

She tapped Dillon's name on her phone and waited. *Poor guy. He's probably exhausted after a long day and ready to head home.*

"Hey, Maddiecakes. What's up?" She could hear the smile in his answer and picture that same crooked smile he'd had since high school. He was the only one who ever called her Maddiecakes. Well, except for her dad when she was a little girl. But she'd long outgrown that nickname at home. For Dillon, it stuck.

"Hi. You think you could come over with some jumper cables and give Buttercup a jolt? Her battery's dead. Again." She absentmindedly scraped a tiny chunk of dried frosting off one of the keys on the old register.

"Maddie–, I told you last time you needed to replace that battery. It's toast." The tone in his voice was light, but Madeleine still felt guilty for ignoring his advice. Like always, Dillon had her best interests in mind.

"I know you did. I should've listened." She didn't want to tell Dillon how she poured every extra nickel she had into the bakery, and a car battery wasn't exactly in her budget. He'd want to give it to her at no charge, but that would mean admitting to someone else that her mother's precious bakery was failing on her watch. Saying something like that out loud would make it too real.

"Yeah, well, what can I say?" He paused a moment, but his chuckle warned Madeleine of what was coming. "Nothing, really, except *I was right.*"

"I guess there's a first time for everything," she teased. "So, can you come help?"

"Of course." A clang of metal dropping against concrete rang out in the background, followed by men shouting, then a huff from Dillon into the phone. "I can't get over there just now. With Trent quitting last week, we're short-handed and totally slammed. I'm sorry."

She sank into a chair and rested her elbow on the wooden café table. "It's okay. I understand. I can call my dad. He's probably still awake."

"No, don't bug him. If you can sit tight for a little bit, I'll see what I can do to get out of here early, okay?"

Madeleine sighed as she looked into her office. "Oh, you know I've always got plenty of work to catch up on here. Bills, baking, and then Buttercup later." The mountain of paperwork and tedious tasks might as well have been an actual summit to climb.

"You sure you'll be alright until I can get there?"

"Dillon, you're kidding, right? I'm fine."

"All right, no need to get huffy. I'll see what I can do to help soon."

The phone was silent, and her café was still. Usually full of customers, the space filled with sounds of milk being steamed, espresso beans grinding, and conversations between friends. But when the tables were cleared and the doors locked, the café felt like an empty shell, waiting to be filled up again tomorrow with people needing their lattes and croissants to start their day.

~ℓℓ~

Madeleine closed the oven door and set the timer for thirteen minutes. This recipe of apple brie scones had been sitting on her desk for weeks just waiting to be made. *I guess tonight's as good as any to bake.* Getting her hands into the dough and working the butter into the flour was therapy for her. Even the mess of baking powder spilled on the counter and the stray apple peels scattered in the sink set her mind at ease.

Her little bakery, while always busy, just couldn't seem to make any money in this small Texas town. She needed a wider pool of customers, more special orders for local events, and she really needed to quit giving her baked goods away for free, even though it made her heart happy.

Is it time to try something else? Working for a big hotel in Dallas as a pastry chef again wouldn't be so bad, would it? She knew the answer to that. It would. She'd miss seeing her regular customers every day, and she wasn't willing to give up that slice of joy in her daily life. Her mother knew that was exactly what Madeleine needed, which is why she gave her the bakery in the first place. To give up on it would be like forgetting every piece of the legacy her mother left her.

Her phone buzzed with a text from Dillon. "Help is on the way." followed by a picture of Superman flying through the air.

Typical Dillon. She smiled at his text.

She plopped down into the yellow chair in her office and rested her chin in her hands, the smell of apples lingering on her fingers. *Feels good to sit down.* She'd long since kicked her shoes off, piled in a heap in the corner next to her purse and jacket, and slipped on her cozy slippers she kept under her desk just for late nights and early morning work sessions. Among the piles of cake boxes, spools of curling ribbon, and cases of coffee stirrers, she spun her desk chair around and sighed. *Mom would never have let this get so unorganized.*

The envelope to her left caught her eye. Another note from the bank, reminding her of the loan coming due soon. If only her bank account were as full as her café each day. *Mom would have found a way to make extra money.* For the forty-seventh time that week, Madeleine racked her brain for some new idea to generate income. *Maybe I could bring in some local bands to play in the evenings?* But paying musicians wasn't in her budget, either, unless they would work for tips only. A silent prayer asking for money-making ideas slipped through her thoughts.

The knock on the café's back door cleared out the finance fog in her brain. She laced her fingers and stretched her arms above her head as she walked to let Dillon in. She glanced at the flour-covered countertops and stray measuring tools scattered around her workspace. *Looks like cleaning this mess up will wait for later.* After a long day on her feet, the chance to sit for a few minutes in her office had been worth it. Besides, Dillon already knew her messy habits and wouldn't be surprised to find her kitchen in this state. She'd been baking since high school, and he'd been sampling her recipes that long as well.

She looked through the door's peephole more from habit than worry. Anyone who grew up in this little Texas town knew better than to cause troubl because the mama's network was strong and spread news quicker than sugar burned under a broiler. The trouble you got into at home wasn't usually worth the trouble you might cause in town.

She blinked as she peered through the tiny hole, expecting to see Dillion's crooked smirk. Only it wasn't his smirk she saw. Instead, it was a man's hand, rubbing the back of his neck slowly as he faced away from the door, toward Buttercup. Judging by the missing oil stains under his fingernails, it wasn't Dillon's hand.

"Um, hello?" she called through the door. Not that she needed to worry. This was Ryleigh, Texas, where everyone knew everyone else, and nothing interesting ever happened.

The man outside turned around and stared at the still-closed door. "Madeleine? Dillon sent me over here to help you out." He held up a set of jumper cables and raised his eyebrows.

There was something familiar about the rhythm of the stranger's words, but she couldn't place what. She turned the lock on the door and pulled it open.

Oh, my stars. The man standing on the other side of the door was definitely *not* one of Dillon's guys. His jeans, cut perfectly to fit, were too clean and too new. Not to mention, there weren't any smears of oil on his perfectly crisp royal blue t-shirt.

She stood staring at this unexpected stranger for what seemed like an eternity, not sure why the room suddenly grew so warm, making it hard to catch her breath.

He tipped his chin toward the inside of the doorway, breaking the awkward silence. His crooked smile melted her like ice cream on a warm brownie. "Smells great in there. Can I come in?"

Chapter 2

Madeleine

"What? Oh, sure. Of course. Yeah, come in." *Stop babbling and get your words together.* Madeleine smiled and stood aside as the man stepped past her and into the bakery's storeroom. Mint and clove wafted in with him. *Doesn't smell like Dillon's shop, either.*

"Dillon said he would send a text to let you know I was headed over."

As if the jumper cables aren't confirmation enough.

When he turned to face her, Madeleine gasped. In the darkness outside, she hadn't really seen who was standing there. She only knew Dillon sent jumper-cable-carrying help.

Luke Taylor wasn't the help she expected. He hadn't been back to Ryleigh in five years. Dillon bristled if his older brother's name ever came up, so Madeleine stayed careful to never mention him.

Madeleine tried to collect herself before answering Luke. "Oh, yeah, I saw Dillon's text," Madeleine set her phone on top of an empty cupcake stand. "But I wasn't expecting *you* to show up." She tucked a stray lock of hair behind her ear and grinned at the sweet slice standing just a few feet away.

Luke laughed, and the rich sound filled the tiny room and squirmed into Madeleine's heart.

He'd changed since high school, except for his smile. That crooked smirk was a Taylor brothers' signature. And his brown eyes were a carbon copy of his brother's, so Madeleine couldn't miss them. Like a pool of melted chocolate, they dripped their gaze over the cluttered stockroom. But his eyes were the only thing Madeleine saw and remembered from high school. The rest of him looked entirely different. When Luke graduated, he was a small-town boy, with clean cut hair, and great arms from many months on the baseball field. But now, this man? Whoa.

His arms weren't the only part of his body that had filled out. His jeans sat just low enough on his hips to hang perfectly, but the tucked-in T-shirt made it easy to see the ridges of his abs above the waistline. He scrubbed a hand over his chin and lips, the dark, short stubble making a barely audible scratching noise.

But those lips. Madeleine looked at those lips so many times in high school and wondered what it would be like to feel them against her own. Her teenage-self rose like bread in a proofing oven, and a rush of familiar questions flooded her brain. *Why is Luke here? What if I say something stupid? Does he even remember me?*

"Yeah, I'm sorry Dillon couldn't get over here, but I stopped in his shop on my way into town, and he asked if I'd mind helping a stranded local girl out."

"Oh." *He doesn't remember me. Just another average local girl.* A twinge of disappointment took up residence in a corner of her mind. "So, um, hi. I'm Madeleine." She held out her hand, and saw it was still covered in flour. He took it before she could dust it off.

"Yep. You were Madeleine in high school, too." The way his eyebrows lifted into a high arch and wiggled at her was almost funny.

If she hadn't been so flustered.

He wiped the flour from his hands onto his jeans, leaving a powdery smear along his thigh.

Madeleine felt her ears go warm. *Get it together.*

He held the jumper cables up again. "Anyhow, I'm here to help. I assume that little yellow bug out there is yours? And she's dead?" He tilted his head toward the still-open door.

Looking at Buttercup instead of Luke brought Madeleine out of her dazed brain. "Yep. Dillon said I needed a new battery last month, but I didn't want to mess with it." *Or pay for it.*

"Looks like I get to mess with it now." His smile grew wide as he looked directly at Madeleine. "She's awfully cute to just be stuck here."

"Excuse me?" The giggle threatening to burst forth was not easy to contain, but Madeleine managed to cover it with a cough.

"Shall we?" He swept his arm toward Buttercup, jumper cables dangling from his hand. "Gonna want to grab some actual shoes, though."

"What?" She looked down at her feet, currently sporting her fluffy pink slippers she'd slid on earlier. "Oh. Right. I'll meet you out there." She raced into her office, tugged her brown boots back on, then paused to check her hair in the mirror.

Oh. My. Biscuits. Not only did her hair look like a mess of melted caramel piled on her head, she had a lovely dusting of flour on one cheek, just waiting there like it might be some new makeup trend. She grabbed an apron from a nearby hook, wiped her cheek, and took off toward the back door, tugging the ponytail holder out from her crown and looping it around her wrist. Her fingers tangled in her locks as she hastily combed it out, cursing its natural wave that never seemed to be useful in times like these.

Madeleine inhaled a deep, calming breath, then walked outside. The wind picked up, and the chilly air made her wish she'd grabbed her jacket.

Luke's black truck was already pulled nose to nose with Buttercup. "Is your car locked?"

"Nope. I've got it, though."

Luke moved into the space between the two cars.

She hastily jumped into her driver's seat, legs dangling outside the car, surveying the chaos spilled over the front seat. She stuffed a few almond bar wrappers into her bag, shoved some old fast food napkins into the console, tossed three empty water bottles into the backseat, and threw her bag over top of them. *Maybe let's not introduce my messy habits just now.* With the front seat sort of cleared, she focused on opening Buttercup's hood. One quick release of the hood's lock and Madeleine was out of the car again. *Maybe he needs someone to watch...I mean, help him.* It wasn't as if she'd never jumped a battery before. She knew how. But this way could be so much more...fun.

His hand slid side to side in the tiny slip of an opening under the hood, but it looked like he couldn't find the lever to release it. He leaned over, peering underneath for the switch.

Those jeans do fit nicely.

Luke glanced her way as she was checking out the view, and he raised a single eyebrow.

Shoot. Caught. Madeleine leaned closer, hoping he would think she was just looking at the car. "Need some help?"

Luke shrugged and let out a puff of a laugh. "Guess so." His smile was sheepish, but in that cute boyish way that made Madeleine's heart thump just a little quicker. He stepped further between the cars. "It's been a while since I did something like this."

Oh, you think, Mr. Perfectly-pressed-jeans?

"Well, it was just last month for me." Madeleine rolled her eyes playfully. "Unfortunately." The space between the two vehicles didn't leave much room for Luke, let alone Madeleine. Like a filling squished into an éclair, she squeezed in next to him, but there was no way to avoid brushing against his arm with hers. The tingle of his light touch ran up her arm and prickled at the back of her neck.

"I can't believe Dillon let any woman out of his shop with a bad battery. It's a good thing you're just outside your own place. Imagine if you'd been stranded somewhere else."

Madeleine tugged the lever under the hood, and it released. *Does he even know how to do this?* An amused grin spread across her face, but she quickly fixed it before turning to lean against Buttercup's front, her arms crossed. "In Ryleigh? I'm never more than five minutes away from anywhere in this tiny town. 'Stranded' just doesn't happen here."

Luke reached his arm around her to lift Buttercup's hood, pausing for just a second longer than needed once it was opened. "True. But I'd think you'd still want a reliable car. Maybe it's time to trade it in?" He clamped the red clip onto her battery and grounded the black one on the frame of the car before turning to his own truck.

Madeleine pressed her side against the truck's grill, resting her elbow onto the still-closed hood. "I couldn't do that. She was a graduation gift from my parents."

"Excuse me," he said as he reached around Madeleine to release his truck's hood. The air, tinged with clove as his scent wafted her way, was like a freshly baked loaf of soda bread, and she inhaled a little too deeply.

"I'm sorry." Madeleine shifted out of his way, but only a tiny bit. *I mean, I probably should stay close. He couldn't even open Buttercup's hood for sugar's sake.* Madeline stifled a smile at her own plot of 'supervision'.

"Graduation from...?" Luke clipped the jumper cables onto his truck's battery.

"Culinary school." *A little glance inside won't offend him, right? Just to make sure everything is...okay.* She rose onto her toes and teetered to peer into the truck's engine. As she did, the clamp slipped from the battery with Luke still holding it. "Oh. Can I give you a hand?"

He leaned closer to the battery to get a better grasp. "No, it's fine. I'm just..." He switched hands, leaning his side against the truck. His chest brushed against Madeleine's shoulder as he tried again.

I really should move. Madeleine laughed to herself. If Dillon could see her, making this simple task hard on his brother, he'd smirk back at her. He'd know exactly what she was doing.

Luke lingered as he fiddled with the jumper cables, just a little closer to Madeleine than necessary. Apparently, he knew exactly what she was doing as well. *Okay, so two are playing this game. I think these are rules I can follow.*

"Got it," he stepped back.

A coolness replaced his warmth on Madeleine's shoulder, and she shivered.

"You need a jacket. The temperature dropped tonight."

Tell me about it. It was a lot warmer when you were over here. "It's inside. I'm okay. We're almost done here anyhow."

"Let's get this girl started, then, so we can go back in and warm up."

We? You're welcome to come inside and warm up next to me anytime.

Luke motioned to Buttercup. "Wanna jump in and give it a go?"

"Sure." She slid out from between the cars, and Luke followed.

He climbed into his truck and started his engine. "Just let mine run a second, then see if yours will turn over," he shouted out the window to her.

Madeleine nodded, sat in Buttercup's front seat, and closed the door against the chilly night. *Well, Buttercup. Looks like maybe you didn't fail me tonight after all.* She patted the steering wheel and saw Luke flash his headlights, indicating she should start her car.

One turn of the key and Buttercup chugged to life.

Luke jumped down from his truck, a victorious smile spread across his face. The sheer pride at his accomplishment made Madeleine laugh out loud, returning his smile. Not because she was glad the car started, but because his smile was so infectious and so adorable.

He knocked on Buttercup's window. "Looks like you're good to go."

Doesn't mean you have to go.

She rolled down her window. "Looks that way. Thanks so much."

He leaned down into the window, his arms resting on the frame. "Not a problem. She's a cute car." His eyes scanned the front seat but slowed when they passed over Madeleine's lips.

I'd be offended, but I can't say I wasn't doing the same thing a few minutes ago. The attention felt nice, to be noticed. There weren't many men in Ryleigh who saw Madeleine for more than just a cute girl who baked tarts and pulled shots of espresso.

Luke straightened up and rubbed his palms over his thighs. "Well, I guess that's that. They need to run a few minutes."

Madeleine slid out of her front seat. The night air stung her throat when she inhaled.

"I really appreciate this. Can I offer a scone or something to pay you back?"

"I'm good, thanks. But you're shivering." Luke pointed to the back door of the café. "You need to get inside."

Madeleine shifted her weight to hide her disappointment. "I suppose so. I need to lock up anyhow." She hesitated, not wanting to turn away, to end the magic. Something about chilly nights made even the most ordinary situations seem special.

Luke looked back at her, his grin mischievous. "I am a coffee drinker, though. Any chance I could grab a cup?"

Madeleine smiled, and for the first time in a while, her steps into the café were light as a perfectly whipped meringue.

As soon as Madeleine stepped through the back door of The Bean and Batter, the sweet magic of Luke's help melted with the smell of burnt scones. Apple brie scones to be exact.

"Oh, sugar! I forgot about the scones." She raced to the oven and threw open the door, only to find twelve triangle-shaped lumps of black sadness. Her heart sank over the burnt scones and wasted ingredients. She grabbed a towel, pulled the baking sheet out, and slid the rock-hard scones into the trash, each one making a firm *thunk* as it hit the stainless steel. "Those were going to be tomorrow's special." *And used tomorrow's ingredient budget as well.*

She looked around her at the disaster of a kitchen, left that way after her earlier baking. The mixer sat still tipped up, the bowl laying on its side. The counter still had its dusting of flour and shadows of rolled-out scones. *Well, this is embarrassing.*

Luke looked into the sink at the pile of dirty dishes, then let his eyes wander over the rest, with bowls and measuring spoons scattered everywhere. "It looks like you have all the ingredients still out. Wanna whip something up together?"

Chapter 3

Luke

Luke picked up a crumpled towel resting next to a pile of apple peels. A bakery definitely fell outside of his comfort zone, but the way Madeleine's shoulders dropped when she opened the oven left him scrambling for a way to help. With a gentle smile, he tossed the towel toward Madeleine, who stood worrying her lower lip and staring into the trash can at the burnt scones. *Still bites her lip, huh? Wonder if she still hums when she's concentrating, too?* "You have a little bit of flour left on your cheek there." He pointed to his own cheek and chuckled.

When Luke agreed to help his brother out and run by The Bean and Batter, he assumed he'd jump a car and head out. Quick. Easy. Uncomplicated. But when Madeleine Malone answered the door in her skirt and slippers, his knees nearly buckled. She was every bit as adorable as she had been in high school. She still had that awkward sweetness, but the playful flirting was a new development since her high school days. A development Luke definitely liked. A lot.

Madeleine looked like she wished she could crawl into a hole. "And you're just now telling me this?" She brushed at her now rosy-pink cheek with the towel. "I thought I dusted that off already."

"I didn't want to embarrass you when you answered the door. But then it had been there too long for me to not say anything." He shrugged and took the towel back. "Here. I'll get it." He brushed the towel against her cheek, and he felt himself leaning just a little closer than necessary. The second his thumb swiped over her face, electricity pulsed up his arm. *Settle down. You aren't here to get involved with a hometown girl.* "That's better." He looked around at the mess surrounding them. "At least the baking ingredients are exclusively limited to...all over this kitchen."

"Very funny. And I'm not sure I should say thank you for wiping the flour off, since you let me stand around with it on my cheek for so long in the first place."

Guilt seeped into his mind for letting it go unmentioned for so long. He truly hadn't meant to embarrass her. The little dusting of flour was endearing. "I'm sorry. Really."

She snatched the towel from his hand and playfully flicked it across his chest. "You owe me, Luke. That wasn't nice."

His eyes met hers, and without breaking her gaze, he slipped the towel from her fingers and into his own grip. "I suppose I'll have to help clean the kitchen to make it up to you." He dropped his chin. "If I'm forgiven, that is."

Madeleine hesitated before answering, holding a finger to her mouth as if considering her options. "Hmm."

The way her finger tapped against her lips drew Luke's attention to them, and he wondered what it would be like to kiss her, a question that had plagued him since high school.

"I suppose, if you'll help me with these scones, I might consider forgiveness." Her tone was light, and maybe a little hopeful.

Looking around the kitchen, Luke took in a deep breath. Other than the bowls and measuring cups, there weren't many kitchen tools he knew how to use. In the city, he mostly ate out. This would definitely be a new challenge. One he hoped wouldn't be a total strike out. He let out a dramatic, playful sigh. "I guess I have to help. Ryleigh's a little town. Can't let word get out that I'm an inconsiderate jerk. Clumsy inexperienced baker, maybe, but ungentlemanly? Never."

"Nope. We certainly can't have that." She reached over to the row of hooks near the door, each one holding a different shade of pastel apron. "But you'll need to look the part. What do you think? Lavender or coral?" She held up two aprons for Luke to choose from.

He shook his head while he laughed. "Neither, thank you." He grabbed the crumpled flour sack towel from near the sink and tossed it over one shoulder. "This is more my style, I think."

"Well, suit yourself." She slung the lavender apron over her head and hung the coral back on the hooks. She reached around her back to tie her own apron, but paused. "Wanna give me a hand, here?"

Um, yes please. "You're telling me you need help with an apron? Seems a little fishy to me." He knowingly wiggled his eyebrows at her.

With a deadpan tone, Madeline lowered her voice. "We don't do fish here. Only baked goods and coffee. Just tie, please."

His hands grazed against her hips as he took hold of the apron strings. He fumbled a minute with the long strips of fabric, lacing his fingers through them as he started the first part of the knot. "Like a shoelace?"

"Yep. Just like a pair of tennis shoes."

He turned the loops together to finish the bow, and his knuckles brushed against the small of her back.

Madeleine shivered at his touch, only slightly, but he was so close to her, he didn't miss the little tremble across her shoulders. He thought he heard her take in a tiny gasp, and he let out a slow breath to calm his own bouncing heart rate. "Too tight?" he asked. He wanted to let his fingers linger on the apron, maybe even let them slide around her waist, but he let go, stepping back as she turned around.

"Nope. Perfect."

"Cute place you've got here." Luke had been so distracted by Madeleine, he hadn't really taken the time to look around much. As he did, he saw a well-worn countertop with chipped corners, walls papered with a floral design, faded by the sun streaming through the large picture windows lining the front walls. *It's kitschy and cozy, but could definitely use a fresh design. There's some potential for a project here.* Luke didn't want to think about work right now, but he couldn't help himself. After all, finding businesses just like this one was part of the reason he'd come home.

Couldn't hurt to learn a little more history here. "Wasn't this an empty building when we were in high school?" Luke couldn't remember for sure. He didn't come down Main Street often as a teen. He was either in the gym, on the baseball field, or finding trouble with the guys.

"It was. But my parents bought it my senior year. Mom wanted something to do with her time when I went away to school." Despite the smile on her face, a softness in her voice made Luke pause his digging for information. He didn't know Mrs. Malone very well, but it was clear Madeleine shared a close relationship with her mother. They had that in common. He could still hear his mom's cheers ringing in his ears as he walked up to bat. She'd always been his biggest fan, even encouraging him to take this new assignment for work, especially when he'd called home and seemed unsure about it. Even though he hadn't been the best of the two brothers in recent years, Luke's mom never missed a chance to build him up.

"She certainly created a great business. Dillon says it's always busy here. Must be the pastries." *Or the cute tart baking them.* He leaned against the counter next to the sink.

"I'd like to think so. My mom taught me to bake growing up. It was my first love." She handed him the canister of brown sugar and a measuring cup. "You sure you're up for this baking job?"

Not really. "Of course. You're looking at an all-star baker here." *All star faker, but sure.*

Madeleine quirked her mouth to the side, giving him a look that said she definitely didn't fall for his overconfidence. "I need a half cup of this packed down, please."

He tried using a spoon to scoop brown sugar from the jar, but his hands didn't fit through the neck of it. The spoon barely reached to scratch some of the sugar toward the top. *How am I supposed to measure this out?* "Does your mom still help with the baking?"

Luke realized his mistake with the way her shoulders fell, and immediately a pang of regret pierced his heart. *Oh no.*

"We lost Mom last year." She took the jar from him and poured the sugar into the measuring cup and packed it down.

"I'm so sorry." He turned, and her whole demeanor had shifted. The bouncy, flirty girl had been replaced by a girl whose smile went missing. The urge to pull her into his arms with a comforting hug was hard to resist.

"It's okay." She motioned to the ingredients scattered on the countertop. "Mom always supported my dreams to bake, and this was her way of helping me succeed. She said she opened this for herself, but I know that's not the case. She and Dad did this so I would have a place to call my own." The way Madeleine straightened up and looked around at her little bakery would have made anyone smile, and Luke was not immune to her contagious joy. Even with the tired furniture and peeling paint around the window sills, he couldn't miss Madeleine's love for this place.

"I'm sure she would be proud to see you now. You've created something special here."

She handed Luke three apples and a knife. "I'd like to think so. But someday, I'd like to see more than just Texas." She started cutting butter into the flour mixture with an expertise that Luke found mesmerizing to watch. "There's a whole world out there that I haven't experienced, and so many great foods to try."

She glanced his way and tipped her chin toward his hands. "Those apples won't peel themselves, you know. *Allons-y.*"

The French phrase rolled off her tongue. *Let's go.* "Wow. Taskmaster, huh? In French, even." He pressed the knife against the fruit and started peeling. "I suppose you've enjoyed a freshly baked croissant at many little cafés on the streets of Paris, then?"

Madeleine laughed. "Top of my list. I'd love to spend some time in Europe, tasting all the rich sauces and seeing all the beautiful pastries."

Luke dropped the string of apple peel into the sink. "You've never been? It's one of the most magical cities on the planet." He loved Europe. It never got old hearing his boss tell him his next assignment would be in Prague, Florence, or London. *I can see the appeal, especially for the food.* "There's nowhere better to eat your way through than Europe."

"You've been?"

"Many times. For my job, though. But bashing around Europe doesn't feel like work."

She stopped mixing and looked at him. "What do you do exactly? You don't strike me as someone who usually hangs out in an auto shop."

His eyebrows drew together, and a crooked smirk spread across his lips. "Yeah, that's definitely not my scene. I work for Greyson Media in their production department." He came home at his boss's request, to work on a project that could mean a big promotion.

Greyson Media was looking for the perfect small town to film a reality show, and when word got out that Luke was from a little town in Texas, the bait was too good for the company not to take. So, Luke came home to scout out filming locations. But in reality, Luke saw it as a chance to get away from the hustle of his job. He needed a shift in his thinking. The pressure of the big city, the endless demands on his time, it all added up to a fat nothing except sleepless nights and constant heartburn. Hopefully, this trip home would help him refocus on his goals. Of course, Madeleine could be a distraction to that focus. But was that really a bad thing? Maybe not.

She turned to him, and as she did, her hand caught the edge of the mixing bowl. It clanged on the edge of the counter, but Luke scooped his hand around its bottom before it crashed to the tile floor.

"Whoa. Hang on, there." His hand rested on top of hers as he took the bowl and set it down. "That was almost a disaster."

She was so close he could smell her fruity shampoo. Close enough to see the flecks of gold in her hazel eyes. For a moment, he froze, not wanting to break their gaze.

"Um, this needs cream." Her voice was quiet, and had a little tremble laced in. She slipped her hand out from under Luke's and retreated to the walk-in refrigerator at the back of the kitchen.

He watched her walk away, a hint of disappointment nagging in some small part of his chest. He shook his head. *No, I can't get involved with her. I'm only in town for a few weeks. Small town girls get too committed too easily.* He knew she wouldn't be like any of the women he'd met in New York. They were used to men flirting without obligation, at least all the women he'd encountered. But sweet little Madeleine here? She'd fall too quickly, too easily, and he couldn't do that to her. Besides, Dillon would kill him if his big brother broke the heart of his best friend. Between the brothers, Madeleine was the one thing Dillon had always been clear on. She was off limits.

Madeleine stepped out of the walk-in fridge with a too-casual lilt. "So, what are you doing back in Ryleigh? You haven't been home since college."

"Actually, that's not quite true. I came home one Christmas. I remember you and Dillon watching some old movie. That one about a guy and a girl emailing each other? Kind of a story about an unexpected match?"

"Oh, yeah. I do remember. I'd come home from school that Christmas break, too, and spent the whole time baking. Dillon said he gained eight pounds that break thanks to me." She laughed, and the way her eyes sparkled made Luke smile back. "But I'd forgotten you were home then, too."

That stung. She didn't even remember he had been there. He'd always been the center of attention in Ryleigh, and he assumed she would have noticed him. But maybe he wasn't as memorable as he'd thought. His competitive nature kicked into high gear with the challenge to get Madeleine to remember that Christmas, and his part in it. *I'll have to remind her.*

He peered into the glass display counter at the empty shelves waiting for tomorrow morning's pastries. He reached in and grabbed one of the tiny signs. "Actually, I'm pretty sure you made these and brought them over that night." He held the marker up and smiled.

Blueberry Scone.

A quick chuckle accompanied her sympathetic smile. "Nice try, but they were cranberry orange scones. That was the Christmas I finally mastered the perfect amount of orange zest for the glaze."

Luke laughed and replaced the sign in the case. "All I remember is how whatever you baked made me want more. Been craving something that good ever since. You'd think New York City, with all the bakeries around, would have mastered a scone that well. But no." It was true, even though she overlooked his presence that holiday. He certainly had taken notice of her baking and wanted more. Seeing her again here tonight, though, had sparked a different craving. One for the baker, not the baked goods.

"Yeah, Dillon tells me you live in New York now." Her eyes grew wide with excitement. "I love New York." She turned the dough onto the floured counter and started kneading. "Not that I've ever been there, but someday." The longing in her voice tugged at Luke's heartstrings.

He leaned over her shoulder to watch her work the dough, her hands pushing and pulling with such confidence. The repetitive motion should have been soothing, but instead, he found his heartbeat speeding up as she pressed her palms into the floury mix. And with each beat, he felt more at home than he had felt in a long time. But home wasn't here. Not in Ryleigh. Not anymore.

Chapter 4

Madeleine

M adeleine wasn't used to kneading scones in front of an audience. *Focus on the pastries, not his…is that his breath on my neck, or am I just over-heating from kneading too much?* She lightened the pressure on the dough as she gave it another turn. "So what brought you home? Dillon hasn't mentioned you coming into town. Was it a surprise?"

"I had some business to take care of," he answered, his tone light and nonchalant. "Long story," he added, and Madeleine sensed that was all he wanted to say right now.

Oh, then that answers everything. The nagging feeling that tonight might be the only time their paths crossed made her stomach churn. She'd been hoping to be alone with Luke Taylor since she was fifteen years old. Maybe even younger. Dillon's cute older brother, always hanging around the house but never seeming to notice her, held a piece of her teenage heart.

She'd lied about not remembering the Christmas he came home. Of course, she remembered. She remembered the way he had filled out even more since high school, the way he laughed when he lost all his chips to Dillon in poker while she zested yet another orange peel, and how he always seemed to have somewhere else to be whenever she started talking to him if Dillon left the room.

She reached around Luke to grab her rolling pin, still waiting where she had left it earlier after rolling the previous batch of scones.

Before they burned.

Before Luke arrived.

Before she wondered if he would be around to help bake next weekend's special.

Stop it.

"Are you in town long?" She held her breath for the answer.

"I'm not sure. I'm between projects at work right now, and the break is nice." He looked toward the pile of dough heaped up on the counter. "I'd like to give rolling a try, if you're willing."

At first she hesitated, not wanting to share this precious tool with anyone. It had been a birthday gift from her mother the year she turned twelve. It wasn't even a rolling pin, really, but just a long cylinder of wood. No handles. "Because that's what all the best pastry chefs used," her mother said when she gave it to her.

But Luke wasn't just anyone, so she held the rolling pin out to him.

He wrapped his hands around the wood, and his fingers lingered atop hers. The flame sparked instantly for Madeline. The way his eyebrows lifted at her, his mouth tipped up at the corners made her never want to leave this moment. Her heartbeat sped, just as it had done when she was in high school and Luke came around. But something was different this time. Luke was different. It was as if he was not just looking past her, but trying to read her through her eyes. For the first time, Madeleine felt as though he wanted to really *see* her.

His chest rose and fell for a few seconds, as if he were trying to catch a breath. Madeleine realized she was holding hers and took in a long gulp of air.

He didn't let his gaze break from hers, even as she cleared her throat and pointed to the dough.

"Um, you just need to apply some pressure until you get what you want." Madeleine looked away, her temperature rising like an oven ready for a souffle. "To the dough, I mean."

"I see. I'll give that a try." Luke moved closer to Madeleine and took the rolling pin into both hands and pressed into the center of the dough. His forearm muscles rippled a bit with the effort, a fact that Madeleine didn't mind.

She stepped back and watched him work the dough with a clumsiness that made her grin. These may not be the best batch of scones she'd ever served, but they would certainly be memorable.

"Is this even close to right?" He pointed the end of the rolling pin at the dough, still nowhere close to flat enough.

"You're doing great," she lied. "Maybe just give it a quarter turn, like this." She reached in front of him and twisted the dough in a circle, just a small bit. " Keep rolling."

He pressed the pin into the center of the lumpy dough and started rolling again, his big hands wrapped around the rolling pin. "How do you work this thing? It doesn't even roll."

It wasn't easy for Madeleine to keep from laughing. "You've only seen the ones with the handles, I'm guessing. This one just takes some getting used to." She stepped in front of him and put her hands on top of the wooden pin, near each end. "Keep your palms flat." He stood behind her and watched over her shoulder. She wished she had taken time to put her hair back up into a ponytail, because she was sure her hair was flying in all directions by now.

She rolled the dough a few quick times, accomplishing more with these few seconds than he had done in a few minutes. "See? Now you try." Before she could shift sideways out of his way, he reached around her and rested his hands atop hers. His chest, flat against her back, was warm but not uncomfortable. She bit the corner of her lower lip. "Um, so, together?"

The knock on the door made her jump and drop the rolling pin onto the counter. Luke's hands were already off hers, leaving behind a cool void. "Great balls of fire," she exclaimed, hearing her mother's favorite phrase coming out of her own mouth, as it so often did.

Muffled, Dillon called from outside the back door, "Maddiecakes? Looks like Buttercup is running again."

Her heart rate slowed when she realized the stranger at the door was just Dillon, here to check on her as promised.

Luke stepped backward and looked at the door, then back at Madeleine. "We forgot to turn the cars off."

"Whoops. I guess I'd better go do that." She headed toward the door and tried to clear her head. Her behavior tonight certainly didn't fall into her normal routine. For years, she wished Luke would notice her instead of every pretty, popular girl in high school. She'd imagined what it would like to have his full attention, and dreamed of being something more than his little brother's best friend. Now, here she had that moment and couldn't believe she had been so bold. She was practically throwing herself at him. *What am I doing? I'm not his type, the girl with the perfect figure and swinging ponytail.*

She steeled her nerves for what she knew would happen next. Tomorrow he'd move on, never giving her a second thought, just as he had done in high school to all those other girls. Thank goodness Dillon showed up when he did, otherwise, who knows where they would have ended up? She definitely wasn't the kind of girl who flirted with any guy who stopped by and jumped her car for her. Then stayed to bake scones. Things like that just didn't happen to her regularly. Or ever, actually.

Sweet sassafras, Madeleine. Get your sugar together.

She opened the back door to find Dillon standing there with Buttercup's keys dangling from his hand. "Hey, Dillon. I was just headed outside to turn her off."

"I got it. She's good to go now." He called around Madeleine to his brother. "Thanks for helping her out, Luke. I got here as fast as I could. We were slammed today."

A quick "Sure" came from the kitchen.

Madeleine took her keys as she ushered Dillon into the storeroom. Her stomach twisted into knots, unsure of how Dillon would interpret her little baking party with his brother. Hoping to keep the tone light, she said, "Yeah, turns out Luke is helpful in more than one way. We were just making scones for tomorrow."

Dillon wrinkled his nose. "Smells like the first batch didn't end so well. I'm not so sure a bakery is Luke's area."

"You're probably right, but the burnt scones are on me." She stepped aside as they came into the kitchen, giving Dillon a better view of his brother. "Look at him, he's rolling out the dough and everything."

Luke glanced at Madeleine but quickly turned away before giving his brother a smile. Madeleine noticed it wasn't the same genuine smile she had seen earlier. It was darker somehow, as if Luke were embarrassed to be caught with her. Almost apologetic.

A lump formed in her throat, and she tried to swallow it down.

Dillon snickered at his brother, standing over the dough with a dish towel casually tossed over one shoulder.

Luke set the rolling pin down. "Hey man, don't laugh. I resisted the purple apron, at least."

Madeleine pretended to be offended, hoping to hide her actual stinging heart. "Only because I wanted to wear it."

Dillon didn't find the joke funny at all. He stood, his gaze shifting between Madeleine and Luke, Luke and Madeleine. He dug his hands into his pockets and finally settled on his brother. "Well, it looks like I sent the right guy to fix your car, Maddie. But I think that's probably all I meant for him to fix." He pointed at the lump of dough, still needing to be rolled flat. "I'm serious when I say you don't want Luke anywhere near that."

Or me, maybe. Madeleine suddenly didn't know who to be irritated with, Luke or Dillon. Seemed like suddenly they both needed an attitude adjustment. Everything had been fine only moments ago, and now, confused thoughts swirled in her mind.

Dillon turned toward the stockroom and called over his shoulder, "Gotta go, Luke. I'm headed to Mom and Dad's. She's made a roast for your first night home, remember?" His voice was cold. Not surprising. Dillon's anger at his brother from years of leaving him home to care for their parents always seemed to simmer just below the surface any time Luke came up in conversation.

"I'll be right behind you." Luke took the towel from his shoulder and set it on the countertop. He turned to Madeleine, his shoulders now relaxed and his smile clear and honest. "Can I offer some help getting this cleaned up?"

"I'm good. It'll only take me a minute to finish rolling these scones out, and I'll wash the dishes while they bake. It's nothing, really." Exhaustion from the long day suddenly settled into her body and mind, and she realized how badly she wished she were home already. *I'm not sure your kind of help is actually going to get me home faster.*

He grinned at her conspiratorially and leaned closer. "So you're saying you're some kind of scone rolling expert?" His voice was soft and low.

She leaned toward his ear, unable to resist him. Whispering, she said, "Yes. And you're not. But I won't hold it against you." *Sweet sugar, he smells better than anything I could've baked.* "Once I put these out, they'll fly off the shelves tomorrow."

"I'll have to come taste them. There's always good in coming back to something special. And I think that might be what we've— " He cleared his throat, "I mean, what *you've* got here." He ran a hand along the countertop and stopped with just a touch on Madeleine's hip, his eyes never leaving hers.

Good grief those eyes are delicious. She laced her fingers in front of her, hoping it would still their quivering. *Words, Madeleine. Make words. Anything.* "Um, thanks." The brightness in her voice was odd and unfamiliar. And annoying.

The jingle of his keys brought Madeleine back to The Bean and Batter. "See you around, Madeleine."

Chapter 5

Madeleine

"Madeleine, I need more whole milk when you get a minute," Becca Fairchild called out from behind the espresso machine, working it like a choreographed master. With one hand she poured milk into a cup, while with the other she placed a shot glass under the brewing espresso.

Madeleine moved just as swiftly, taking orders at the register, writing latte recipes on to-go cups, choosing the biggest muffins for her favorite customers, and washing mugs in between. "You got it. Give me a sec."

The Bean and Batter was already buzzing with her morning regulars. Once in the morning hit, the door never stopped swinging open and shut.

Madeleine smiled at the blue-eyed three-year-old on the other side of the counter whose plastic tiara, crookedly tangled in her mess of chestnut hair, looked like it had been there for a few days. "Chocolate croissant again today, Sara? Or will you try something new this morning?"

Sara's mom pointed at the bowl of fresh strawberries, their vibrant red standing out against the buttery pastries in the rest of the case. "What about some fruit this morning?" she prodded.

Sara was having none of it. She stood silently and crossed her arms. The way she wrinkled her eyebrows and jutted out her chin was comical.

The pleading look from the overtired mother made Madeleine wish she could help more. This argument happened every Saturday morning, with the mom trying to convince Sara to eat more fruit. "We aren't trying *anything* new these days." She looked back at her daughter, her voice now light and lilting.

"But those strawberries sure do look juicy and sweet. I know *I'd* choose the strawberries if I were a growing three-year-old."

An idea popped into Madeleine's mind. "Know what, Sara? I read that princesses love to eat strawberries but with fancy whipped cream for dipping. What if I made you some special, royal whipped cream to go with your fruit today?"

Sara's eyebrows unwrinkled. Only a tiny bit, but enough to give Madeleine the go ahead. With a nod, she headed into the fridge and grabbed a gallon of milk and some heavy cream. Without breaking her stride as she walked to the mixer, she passed the milk to Becca and poured some cream into the bowl.

The bell on the door tinkled again. *Whew. Glad I wore my tennis shoes today.* Madeleine looked up as Luke strolled in. He flashed a smile in her direction, sat at a table in the corner, and opened his laptop.

A fluttering excitement took up residence in Madeleine's belly, and her step quickened to finish whipping Sara's cream and greet her newest customer. She busied herself by tipping a little vanilla extract into the almost-mixed cream and took another customer's coffee order. Caramel latte, she wrote on the cup. *C-a-r-a-m-e-l L-u-k-e.* She scribbled out the -uke and changed it to *L-a-t-t-e.* *Geez, Madeleine. You already lost sleep last night thinking about him.*

In a few minutes, she spooned the whipped cream into a dish, gave it a swirled flourish and a splash of sprinkles, and carried it, along with the bowl of strawberries, to Princess Sara's table, just across the aisle from where Luke sat.

She saw he no longer focused on his laptop screen, but watched her walking toward him. The look in his eyes were a clear invitation for her to sit at the table with him, eyebrows raised in anticipation. But this morning, things were much too busy. *Royalty awaits, my friend.*

She tilted her head to the side with a regretful shrug before turning away from him and toward Sara. "One princess delight, your highness," Madeleine said, in a British accent that was anything but authentic, then gave a quick curtsy, knowing that Luke was watching her from behind. She didn't mind that he saw her being a little silly. Her work was a fun place, and his presence certainly shouldn't change things in her bakery.

Sara dipped a finger into the whipped cream and tasted it. Her smile was all Madeleine needed to see. "I'm glad you like it. If it pleases the princess, I shall go back to the scullery and wash the royal dishes." She winked at Sara and nodded toward the berries, then turned to grab a few empty mugs and plates from the next table, and nearly smacked into Luke's chest when she turned.

The aroma of fresh aftershave so early this morning was not something Madeleine was used to smelling in her café, but it certainly wasn't anything she minded as he leaned closer and whispered, "You're the scullery maid? I thought you were the queen of tarts." His laugh was kind and made Madeleine giggle along with him.

"Well, around here, I'm a little of everything these days." She picked up the dirty dishes and stacked them in her grasp. "You need some coffee this morning? A scone, maybe? The apple brie ones are on—"

"Special? I've heard." He took the plates from Madeleine. "Let me get these for you." He walked toward the counter. "Are they any good?"

Madeleine followed. "The plates?"

"No, the scones, silly. No wonder they keep you in the scullery around here." He set the plates down and leaned toward her, whispering conspiratorially into her ear, "But we both know it's an act. You're the princess hiding away with the servants, aren't you? That royal beauty is undeniable."

His breath warmed the soft patch just behind her earlobe. It would only take a slight shift upward and his lips would land in that tender place. Madeleine closed her eyes and leaned just a bit toward him. He smelled wonderful. It was all she could do to keep from reaching an arm around his neck and pulling him closer. She wanted to know this new Luke, the one who noticed her. Not the one who spent his high school days running off to the next party or date.

But a tug on her apron string broke the spell. "Miss Madeleine?" Sara's voice was sweet and innocent, making Madeleine blush at the thoughts rolling in her mind in the presence of a child.

Madeleine turned around, smiling. "Yes, your highness?"

"Thank you for the sprinkles. I like strawberries now." Sara skipped back to her mother, who never looked up from her phone to know her daughter had interrupted any sort of moment Luke and Madeleine might have been enjoying.

Luke chuckled from behind her.

He was still so close Madeleine could practically feel the vibrations in his chest rumbling against her back. Her elbow tingled where his fingers had been, only moments before. "Thank goodness she's got what she wanted."

Madeleine shook her head then called after the little girl, "Of course. You're very welcome, sweetheart." Tucking a stray lock of hair behind her ear, she turned back to Luke. "About those scones. Did you want to try out your handiwork?"

Luke looked down at his boots and shuffled them a bit. "I don't know that I had that much to do with them. The credit is all yours."

"I wouldn't say that." She'd never heard her own voice so full of flirtation, but she didn't mind the confidence it carried. "I mean, you wouldn't wear the apron, and I can't respect anyone who won't dress the part, but still. You did do all the rolling."

He smirked, and the way he shrugged as he tipped his head to the side made Madeleine smile. "I don't think the clothes make the man. At least not when we're discussing an apron." He pointed to the scones in the cake stand on the counter. "But I still would like to try what you've got."

I'd like to sample what you've got, too. The double meaning didn't go unnoticed, and it made her stomach buzz with excitement she hadn't felt in a long time. Madeleine lifted the dome off the cake stand and, using tongs, placed a scone on a plate. "Enjoy," she said, passing the plate to him.

Luke took the first bite and started nodding his head slowly. "Mmm," he said. He swallowed and looked right at Madeleine. "Apron or no apron, that is a darn good way to start the day."

Madeleine stood a little taller at his compliment and smiled. "You're not the only one who feels that way. We've almost sold out, and it's still early."

He swallowed and looked out the window. "It's gonna be a gorgeous day. Any chance you could get away later?" He turned back to Madeline. "Maybe let someone else do the cooking for lunch?"

The lightness in her chest gave way to the heavy disappointment of responsibilities. She shrugged, "I wish I could, but Becca has to leave early and I'll have to close."

Luke sighed, and the corners of his mouth dropped.

Well, that's cute. He's not the only one disappointed.

"The sign says you close at four. How long before you can be out of here after then?"

"I've got some paperwork to finish first." Her stomach twisted in knots as she thought about the bills awaiting payment. She fixed her face into a smile, hiding the worry. "Plus a little baking to do. Care to join in on that again today?" She grinned and pointed to the aprons hanging behind her.

"Tempting, but I think I'll pass. I'm not sure I'm a baker," he joked. He stepped backward a tiny bit and spread his arms wide, warily eyeing the aprons over her shoulder.

Madeleine took the opportunity to let her gaze wander from top to bottom over Luke's very perfectly crafted self. Quickly, of course, before hiding her disappointment with a compliment. "Your scones turned out okay, though."

Just then, the front door swung open. "Hey Maddiecakes. What's on special this morning?" Dillon tossed his sunglasses on the brim of his baseball cap as he approached the counter. His smile faded quickly when he took in the scene before him.

In an instant, the space between Madeleine and Luke grew vast, even larger than necessary. The electric hum pulsing between them turned off like a switch. She hadn't noticed the buzz before, but now that it was gone, she definitely missed it.

"Hey, Dillon." The over-heightened casual tone in Luke's voice might have been humorous at another time, but Dillon's frown changed the tone of everything.

His familiar scent of motor oil wafted toward Madeleine as her best friend came closer. He barely glanced at his brother. "Luke." His tone was anything but casual. Laced with daggers and poison, the message was clear. Dillon didn't like what he saw. And Madeleine didn't know what to feel about that or her desire to leave work right now and spend the entire day with Luke, even if it did make Dillon mad.

She cleared her throat. "Um, it's apple brie scones today."

"What is?" Dillon's eyes, narrowed and questioning, pierced Madeleine.

"The special. They're the ones we baked last night." She instantly regretted the mention of the word 'we'.

"Yeah," he said, his tone deepening as he narrowed his eyes at his brother. "I'll have a blueberry muffin." He looked at Becca, behind the espresso machine. Charming Dillon showed up again, all smiles and kind words. "And a vanilla latte, please."

Madeleine busied herself getting a plate for Dillon's muffin. *He's in a mood this morning.* Not his typical self, she wanted to ask him what caused his hot temper, but she already knew. When Dillon arrived, she and Luke were clearly standing closer than customer and shop owner. *He wouldn't be jealous. Just annoyed, maybe?*

She refused to let his sour attitude ruin her perfectly fine morning. Actually, it was better than fine. It was great. The café was busy, her new scones were selling out, and Luke stopped by. Her mama always said to "fix her face", so she did just that, turned to Dillon, and said, "Want it warmed up?" *Just as sweet as sugar, Mom always said.*

"Nope." He looked directly at Luke. "I think things are warm enough in here right now. This arrived at home this morning, by the way. I brought it in when I saw your truck in the parking lot." He held up a large envelope with what looked like contracts sticking out the top. "I thought it was mine and opened it before I realized it's yours. Sorry." He handed the opened overnight delivery mailer to his brother, but held onto the corner for an extra second before saying, "I hope you're not looking at this place for that project. Move on, dude. Not gonna happen."

Chapter 6

Luke

Luke looked at the envelope, edges frayed from his brother's prying hands. "What are you talking about?" He took the package from Dillon and peeked at the document sticking out of the top. The header on the front page jumped out at him. Greyson Media Productions: Ryleigh, Texas Filming Location. A burning sensation rose in his throat. The New York heartburn returned with a vengeance seeing the first few lines of the letter.

I didn't think filming in Ryleigh was a done deal. Luke looked at his brother, who stared back at him with narrowed eyes. He clenched his jaw to keep from snapping at Dillon for calling him out like this in public. "There's no need to cause a scene, little bro," he said, hoping to defuse his brother's anger.

"I read the first part of that letter before I realized it wasn't mine. So, you think you can just waltz into town and everyone here will celebrate you like the hometown hero for this?" Dillon thrust his hand toward the envelope, as if it contained some toxic poison. "You've been gone a while, *big bro.* You're not the hero anymore."

Luke bristled and shock coursed down his spine at his brother's accusations. *I'm not even sure if these decisions are done, but if it's as bad as Dillon thinks, I need to get this under control.* Luke waved the envelope in the air and put on his most unconcerned face. "Dillon, this is nothing. It's just a proposal for an idea someone in the company wanted me to look at."

Dillon still didn't look convinced, but he at least settled down a bit, allowing Luke to breathe a little easier. For now. The truth would have to be told at some point, but he'd manage that when the time came.

"Okay, but if your company goes through with that, don't expect me or anyone else in town to support it."

Just then, Becca appeared with a latte for Dillon, whose whole demeanor changed when she passed the mug to him. He softened, a tiny smile playing at the corners of his mouth. "Thanks, Becca."

Despite Luke's casual nonchalance, the weight of the envelope in his hands was heavy as was the need to sit down and actually read the contents. "Hey Becca? Could I grab a cup of coffee as well, please? Black is fine."

Madeline, who had busied herself washing dishes while the brothers argued, turned around. "Oh my gosh, Luke. I'm so sorry I didn't think to offer some earlier." She turned to the sink behind her and grabbed a freshly washed mug. "I was so busy with Sara, and then Dillon came in, and, well..."

The way she got so flustered was adorable. The flush on her cheeks made them the perfect shade of pink. He hadn't meant to embarrass her, but watching her fumble with the coffee pot made him want to slip his arms around her waist and tell her to relax. *I'm not that demanding. Just want a cup of coffee.*

She walked toward him, mug in hand, and smiled. "Here you go, sir. One freshly poured mug of black coffee." Her voice was playful again, and Luke was grateful for the distraction from Dillon's heavy attitude."Cream? Sweetener?"

I can think of something sweet I'd like. Luke shook the thought from his mind. After all, he wasn't planning to stay long enough to get involved with a girl from Ryleigh. But that little baker might be worth a change of plans.

"I'm good, thanks." The coffee smelled delicious. Strong but not too bitter. It tasted even better than it smelled. "What kind of coffee is this? It's great."

"Thank you. It's a Colombian blend today. That's the house special." She beamed as she pointed out the list of coffee blends available at The Bean and Batter. She rattled them off from memory, complete with a description of each one. As she spoke, she stood taller, smiled brighter, and seemed to almost sparkle.

The way she came alive made him wish he could watch her talk about her bakery all day. "You love this café, don't you?"

"I do. It's my happy place for sure," she said, her voice practically a sigh.

"That's obvious." The heartburn roared again.

Dillon spoke up from the other end of the counter, where he'd been chatting with Becca. "She's really done great for herself. The community loves her, and she is really good about giving back to the town. We're all lucky to have The Bean and Batter, but Maddiecakes here is the heart of the place."

Thankfully, Dillon's anger seemed to have dissipated. He was more like himself again when he bragged on his best friend.

"Yes, it's lucky you've got her." The jealousy in his voice came out before he realized it was even there, and it surprised him

Madeleine waved a dishtowel between the brothers. "Now, boys. Y'all are sweet, but I'm sure I'm not that important. I just bake up some muffins here and there."

There she goes with the pink cheeks again. Luke took a sip of his coffee, hoping that a full mouth wouldn't be one that betrayed him.

"And sometimes it seems that the biggest contribution goes to Dillon's Auto Shop, and I'm happy to do that." Madeleine said, pulling out a white pastry box from under the display case. "Dillon, don't keep these in your office." She was already piling muffins and scones into the box. "Put these out for your guys to share. I'm sending these for everyone, you hear me?"

The way she spoke to Dillon, the teasing but firm tone, was so comfortable. These two had years of history together. Luke could never compete with that relationship. That twist of jealousy reared up and surprised him again. *It's probably best I don't get involved with her, even if I weren't leaving town eventually.*

Dillon's regular, playful attitude returned as he stood at attention facing Madeleine. "Yes ma'am. I can't go making you so mad that you quit sharing with me altogether. The guys would never forgive me." Dillon drew an "X" with his finger over his heart. "Cross my heart, I'll be nice and share."

She handed the box over and gave him a stern look. "You'd better. Besides, if you eat all of those, you'll be so full, the guys'll have to roll you out of your office later. I've put an extra chocolate croissant in there for Mark's little girl. Make sure no one eats that one, and tell him to bring Eva in sometime so I can see how much she's grown."

"Okay, okay. I promise. See you later, Maddiecakes." He headed to the door, but stopped to add, "Call me later if Buttercup won't start. You definitely need to have that battery replaced."

Yep. But I guess I wouldn't mind coming back later to lend a helping hand again, Luke thought to himself, recalling the way she'd squeezed next to him between his truck and her car.

"I think she's fine, but thanks." She grinned back at Luke as Dillon left. "He's way too protective of me sometimes," she said, rolling her eyes.

Rightly so. He's a smart kid. "He's always been that way about you."

"Really?" She seemed surprised at his remark. "I didn't think you ever even noticed me in high school. You were always surrounded by..." her voice trailed off and her eyes dropped to the floor in embarrassment.

"Surrounded by...?" he prodded. He knew what she was going to say. Girls. Always surrounded by girls. As a matter of fact, Luke had very few memories of high school that didn't involve taking a girl out somewhere, unless he was on the ballfield or with the guys. *Not my best decisions.*

But he had noticed Madeleine. She was pretty but not in that 'captain of the cheerleaders, perfectly put together way.' She had always been different. Intriguing. And now, he stood before her, staring at her curvy figure, and seeing her as a grown woman, and not his little brother's best friend. And she was near irresistible.

"Never mind. That was a long time ago." She looked up at him, her hazel eyes twinkling. "So, about that invitation from earlier," she began.

It took a minute for Luke's brain to catch up. *Invitation? What invitation?* He'd been so preoccupied, first with the letter from Greyson Media, and then with Madeleine's perfectly sweet nature he couldn't remember what she meant.

He searched Madeleine's face for a hint, but it looked as though she were slightly deflating as he searched his brain for a clue. Suddenly it dawned on him. "Oh. You mean for us later. Right, yes," he stammered.

Her nerves suddenly got the best of her, as she fidgeted with the hem of her sleeve. She cleared her throat. "I mean, if you're busy, we don't have to go –"

"What? No. I'm sorry, I just..." he stammered. He needed to fix this before she thought he didn't want to go. "Since lunch isn't an option, how about dinner?"

"I can make six-thirty work."

Luke's head started swimming with excitement. The way she could make his emotions fly into high gear with so little effort amazed him. One minute he was arguing with Dillon, the next he was frustrated at his own stupidity to even consider getting to know this woman better, then feeling elated about spending more time with her.

"Great. I'll see you then."

She reached her arm around him, and he felt his heart speed up as she came in for a hug. He leaned closer to her, but she backed away before he could wrap his arms around her waist.

"Oops." She started giggling. "I was just grabbing Dillon's mug." That adorable pink spread over her cheeks again, and Luke felt his own cheeks warm.

"No problem," he managed to mumble. He chuckled, hoping to cover his mistake, but he really wished he could disappear. Where was that cool, confident Luke he'd always been around girls? The guy who never got embarrassed? No one had ever made him act this way before. He cleared his throat and tried to sound collected. "I've got some calls to make for work, so I'll just head on out."

He strode back to his table and grabbed his laptop.

"Hey, Luke. Don't forget your letter." Madeleine was on his heels with the envelope Dillon brought in her hands.

"Right. Thanks so much." *This town is perfect for the project, and I might never get a break like this again. But Dillon might be right. People around here don't like change, and I was about to pitch them a major change-up.*

Chapter 7

Madeleine

Washing dishes never ended at The Bean and Batter, but Madeleine didn't mind doing them. It was a nice break, giving her time to think. Usually, as the warm soapy water swirled around her hands, recipe ideas swirled around her mind. But today, no recipes came. Instead came thoughts of chocolate-syrup eyes, warm brushes against her shoulder, and the way Luke's arm muscles rippled as he rolled out the dough last night. *I gotta say, those apple brie scones did come out nicer than usual.*

But her next thought was Dillon. He had been by her side during all of her most awkward moments. The time she didn't have a date for Homecoming. The day she forgot to set her alarm for graduation practice.

The day she buried her mother.

Dillon seemed less than excited last night to find Luke helping out in the kitchen. That was easy to brush off as a long day after work, but their interaction this morning proved he was more than unhappy about Luke coming home. How could she choose loyalty to anyone other than Dillon? Sure, Luke melted her heart and made her fingers tingle when they touched his, but that wasn't enough to toss out an entire friendship.

I shouldn't carry on with Luke. He's not worth losing Dillon.

But really, a grown woman could make her own decisions, right? And if Luke made her happy, wouldn't Dillon be happy for her? Maybe Dillon just wasn't happy to see Luke, and it had nothing to do with her. It certainly wouldn't hurt for Luke to be anything other than a friend...for now. Just one ordinary baker and one incredibly hot...what did Luke even do?

See? This is ridiculous. I don't even know what he does for a living, much less think about any kind of relationship.

The oven timer dinged. The oven's heat washed over Madeleine, and she huffed it away from her face. The chocolate hazelnut muffins smelled heavenly and were always a good seller. Or at least that's what she told herself when deciding on that recipe. It certainly had nothing to do with the fact that the muffins were a spot-on match to the color of Luke's eyes.

She let her mind wander over what happened this morning. While Sara had been cute with the strawberries, it was Luke who stole all Madeleine's attention. The way he watched her work should have made her uncomfortable. It wasn't like anyone in Ryleigh ever noticed her. She was just the hometown girl who ran a cute café.

But Luke saw her.

And she liked being seen.

A quiet rap on the café's window drew Madeleine out of her thoughts. She stepped out of the kitchen doorway to see Luke peering in with a bottle of wine dangling between his fingers and a smile spread wide across his face. He reminded her of a kid peering into a candy shop window.

How does he get his teeth so white? They're like a perfect row of Chicklets gum. She held up a finger indicating to give her just a minute and removed the second tray of muffins from the oven. She caught her reflection in the mirror behind the counter and saw there was no stray flour left on her cheek for this visit. But her hair was messy. This morning's top knot wasn't holding up well. Locks of curls fell around her face, but the hairstyle wasn't completely horrible. It was more of a modern 'just tossed together' look she saw sometimes in the fashion magazines at the grocery store checkout lines.

She twisted the bolt on the front door and turned the knob.

"Smells sweet in here. Baking done? Because you promised me a date tonight, remember?" He leaned forward into the doorway and rested his forearm on the doorframe just above his head. His t-shirt clung to his chest, and lifted just high enough to give Madeleine a little peek above the waistband of his jeans.

Uh oh. He said date. Hadn't she decided just moments ago that this relationship was going to start as friends? Could she even call it a relationship? They just reconnected last night, for goodness sake.

"Um, I don't remember there being an actual agreement for a date." *Good job, Madeleine. Stand firm.*

Luke's lips twisted into a frown and his eyebrows wrinkled together. "Well, *date* maybe isn't the word to use." He lifted his eyes and they twinkled as he asked, "Outing, then?"

I mean, I can't argue with an outing. That's just two friends going somewhere. "An outing sounds perfect."

That smile came back across his face, and he laughed. "Oh good. I was worried I'd have to drink this entire bottle myself."

"Well, what kind of friend would I be if I let you drink alone?" She turned around to head back into the café. "Lock the door behind you, please. I've just got to finish drying some pans and wrap these muffins up before I can leave." *There. Friend zoned. Maybe he'll get the message.* If she kept saying it out loud, she'd also start to believe it. Maybe?

"I'd have to question our friendship in that case." He followed her into the kitchen and leaned over the cooling muffins. "These smell good."

"Thanks. Chocolate hazelnut." Suddenly her idea of staying late to bake seemed like a bad one. Now she would have to wait before she could leave with Luke. And she wanted nothing more than to race out of here and spend the rest of the evening with this handsome man. "They need a minute to cool, and then we can go. Sorry about that.""Why would you be sorry? You're working." He stepped closer to her and took her hand. It was so warm around her fingers, and it felt nice. "And your work is amazing. Don't ever apologize for that."

"It's just pastries. But I do love it." She felt a warmth spread over her cheeks as if someone had opened the oven door.

Luke leaned forward and cocked his head to the side, questioning. "But it's not *just* pastries, Madeleine. You are a key part of this community. Everyone who was in here this morning loved seeing you." His eyes held an intensity that made her pause.

She was flattered by his assessment of her, but she wasn't sure he had the whole picture. Ryleigh was a small town. She wasn't even that big of a fish in this pond. And right now, based on her bank accounts, she was a giant flop. She couldn't think about that now. "What about you? What fills your time in NYC?"

He stepped back and looked down with a sigh. "I'm in online entertainment. I work for Greyson Media."

"Oh, wow. That's a really huge company. They're a big deal." Madeleine knew Greyson Media. Their logo was splashed everywhere at major events all over the world as a sponsor. Sports teams, movie premieres, celebrity interviews, concerts, New York Fashion Week. If it was a high-profile event, you could guarantee Greyson Media would be involved. They'd been in the news a lot lately, but she couldn't remember why. "So you're a producer of..." she stammered, "...media?" *Oh sugar, Madeleine. Shut up. You sound so stupid.*

He smiled a charming smile, seemingly amused by her confusion. "Okay, so you know how when you go to a concert, there are banners for Greyson Media, or our logo on sports jerseys in high-profile games and things?"

When was the last time I went to a concert? She nodded her head, even though she really didn't know firsthand but had seen enough TV to know big events had sponsors. "Yes."

"Well, I'm the guy who attends those events and makes sure we get what we paid for, and that our company is being represented in a way that is consistent with the image we've built."

"So you're the image police for Greyson Media?"

He let a little puff of laughter out and tipped his head to the side. "Yeah, I guess you could say that."

"Sounds interesting." *Sounds like you get to travel and see amazing places. No wonder you've not been back to Ryleigh in so long. There's not much here to compare.* "So I assume you have been all over the world for work?"

Luke shrugged, his tone nonchalant. "I've traveled quite a bit of it, yes. But the world is a big place, and I haven't seen it all yet."

She took her apron off and hung it on the hook near the doorway. "I'd love to travel more. I've never even been out of Texas." A sadness pricked at her heart. She didn't have the means to travel. Everything she had, she poured right back into The Bean and Batter.

When she took over the café after she lost her mother, things changed. That loss hit the community hard, but no one felt it more than Madeleine. She missed her mother in so many ways, the way she worked barefoot in her office, the floral mug always sitting on the countertop filled with long-gone-cold-coffee, and the way she hummed while she mixed batter. By keeping this café running, it was the best way Madeleine could hold on to her mother's memory. But lately, that seemed to be a much harder task than she knew how to tackle.

Madeleine exhaled a quiet sigh. *Not now. Focus on this gorgeous man waiting to take you out. Worry later.* "Maybe someday Dillon and I can come visit you in New York."

A hint of amusement played across Luke's face. "Nah. You'll never get Dillon out of Ryleigh. He wouldn't leave his shop for that long." He stepped closer to

Madeleine, his chin lowered, and his voice dropped as well. "The sights there are beautiful, but not quite the same as the hometown views here."

She had to will her own two feet to stay planted where they were. She even gripped the corner of the countertop to ground herself into place instead of stepping toward Luke. The mention of Dillon reminded her of her earlier decision to stay uninvolved with Luke.

But he was so close. And he smelled so good.

He placed his hand over hers, and a tingle shot all the way up her arm. The way he ran his thumb back and forth over her wrist left a hot trail. "But I'd love to have you visit me in New York. Say the word, and I'll get you there. Anytime you want."

He'll get me there? Like, he'll buy the ticket? And what would he expect in return? That's a sticky situation I'd rather avoid. He called me the town's sweetheart, and I would like to keep it that way.

"That's a really nice offer, but I'm not sure I'm ready to just fly off to New York with some guy I hardly know." She let out a little laugh, hoping she hadn't offended him.

"Madeleine, you've known me since you were barely a teenager." He leaned forward a fraction of an inch, but it was, to Madeleine, a very giant fraction that brought him temptingly close. "I haven't changed that much."

She looked at his muscled chest, his chiseled chin, and had to bite her bottom lip to keep from laughing again. *Oh, yes you have, Luke Taylor. You've grown up.* "Yeah, but things were different back then. You were the state baseball champion. Home run king, I believe." *Who didn't have time to notice me.* "I was just that bookish girl hiding in the library most days. Or hanging out in your game room watching movies with your little brother."

She looked up to find Luke gazing at her, wandering over her face, pausing on her lips before drifting to meet her eyes. He let out a small exhale. The world slowed down and almost paused in this moment.

Shifting her weight to her other foot only brought her closer to him. He was so close, she could see the fibers in his gray cotton T-shirt, the little spot under his chin that he missed when he shaved this morning, that perfectly kissable mouth that took in a tiny inhale as she moved closer.

"Think things are cooled down yet?" His answer was soft.

Uh, nope. Just the opposite, actually. She didn't move. Not yet anyway. She wasn't sure where this was going. Last night, the flirting had been unmistakable. But today, he seemed to be confused. One minute he was backing away in front of Dillon, the next stroking her wrist. Not to mention, her own feelings wavered between wanting and hesitation.

He cleared his throat. "The muffins, I mean. Think they've cooled enough to take them out of the pan?"

Well there's a clear smack back into reality for you. "Oh. Right. Yes, I'm sure we can take them out by now." She stepped away and let out a long, slow exhale, trying to regulate her pounding heartbeat. She'd thought she wanted to just be friends with Luke, to keep it casual. But he'd made it clear he was looking for more. And her body was responding in kind.

How was a girl supposed to decide what to do with those mixed signals? *He's so distant when Dillon comes around but so close when it's just us. So. Very. Close.*

She grabbed a knife and slid it around the muffins to pop them out of the tin and onto the countertop. She didn't know whether the sinking feeling in her chest was relief or frustration. Maybe both? Luke already had the other pan emptied before she finished hers.

"Should I just put these into the display case, or...?"

"Nope. They'll dry out overnight." She tipped her chin upward toward a shelf above her head. "There's a plastic bin right up there, if you'll grab it for me."

He looked up. "The red lid?"

"Yep. There's a stepstool behind the door I always use."

"I think I can reach." He moved closer to her and reached up to the shelf. His fingers brushed the container, and only pushed it to the side a little. "Shoot. Hang on."

She stepped sideways, but he was already leaning his chest against her shoulder as he stretched higher. The bottom of his T-shirt lifted up just the tiniest bit, the same way it had when he first arrived. Now that she was so close, and he was so preoccupied, Madeleine sneaked a longer peek at his abs. *Sweet buttermilk biscuits. Those didn't come from eating too many scones.* She had to fight the urge to run her finger along the waistband of his jeans.

As Luke grabbed the container, three others came tumbling off the shelf with it. In his haste to catch the falling bins, his elbow slammed against her shoulder. "Ouch!"

"Oh my gosh, I am so sorry. Are you okay?"

She rubbed her aching shoulder where his elbow hit. "Yeah, I'm okay. It's no big deal." She leaned down to pick up the scattered bins from the floor.

Luke handed her the one bin he managed to keep a hold on. "That shelf needs lowering. It's a danger to Ryleigh's finest baker. And her muffins." He pointed to the muffins still resting on the countertop. But three of them suffered in the crash, and sat crumbling to pieces.

She started to giggle at the mess of muffins. It certainly wasn't the first time a bake went wrong in this kitchen, and it wouldn't be the last, either.

"You know, I'm starting to wonder if I should let you into this place. Last night it was burnt scones, today busted muffins." Her voice was light and teasing. She placed a hand in the middle of his chest and pushed him closer to the kitchen's door. "You can't be trusted, sir."

"I'm a menace, I know." He joked with a shrug and a grin. He took her by her free hand and tugged her closer to the door...and him. "I think it's time we got out of here before anything else happens. Got any pies? I'm sure I could drop them on the floor or something. You know, in an effort to be helpful."

Madeleine could look at his smile all day. It was just different enough from Dillon's to be interesting. The shape of his mouth was just like his brother's, but the smile? It was so much wider, more genuine. It came effortlessly. And it was contagious.

"You stand way over here, and I'll put what's left of these muffins away." She hesitated to take her hand off his chest before heading back into the kitchen. She placed the good muffins into the container and sealed the lid. She scooped up the busted ones and tossed them into the trash. "Where are we going tonight? I don't think you ever told me."

"Oh, I've got a little something up my sleeve. You'll just have to wait and see."

A ripple of excitement washed from Madeleine's head to her toes. She couldn't remember the last time someone had surprised her with anything, really. She grabbed her purse, flicked off the kitchen lights, and turned to Luke, whose hands were tucked into his pockets as if he were afraid they might knock something else over.

He lifted his eyebrows and held out a hand toward her. "Ready?"

She took a deep breath. *Maybe?*

Chapter 8

Luke

Luke knew bringing Madeleine along tonight was a risk. She would either love it or hate it. But he'd never been one to shy away from a gamble, and she was definitely worth betting on.

He'd spent the entire day convincing himself he couldn't fall for her. He couldn't commit to her. She wasn't right for him. Dillon would kill him. He drove to The Bean and Batter fully prepared for an evening of friendly conversation between two people who simply enjoyed each other's company. Nothing more. Once he got inside the bakery, though, it was like the scent of all that sugar went to his head, and he couldn't think of anything except how adorably delicious Madeleine could be.

Plus, that bottle of wine rattled against the console in his truck. And wine made him think of quiet evenings by a fire. Or under the stars. Or on a rooftop garden. With a girl.

And that girl looked exactly like Madeleine Malone.

With the debate still raging in his mind, once he watched her leaving her little café and sashaying her hips toward him, all bets were off. She was irresistible.

He opened the truck door and watched her climb in. Still wearing her jeans from this morning, she looked effortlessly put together. Last night, her hair had tumbled over her shoulders as she worked the pastry dough. But today, it was piled on top of her head with a little scarf tied around the base of the twist. He'd had a moment to drink in her appearance while she served the little girl her strawberries. She'd changed from flip flops to flats at some point today, but everything else was exactly the way she'd looked this morning. *She's not like the women in the city, all polish and sparkle. She's just so...real.*

He started his engine and turned left out of The Bean and Batter's parking lot. "You hungry?"

"A little. I snacked while I was working, so I'm not starving. You?"

"I could eat, but then again, I can always eat."

"So can Dillon. That boy can't ever get enough food in his belly. Must run in the family."

Luke bit the inside of his cheek. *Dillon again. Is he going to be the invisible third wheel all evening?* He hoped not, so he cleared his throat and forced a smile. "Well, how about some brisket?"

"If it's Joe's, sure. Best barbecue in town."

At least that's still the same. Joe used to set up his smoker outside the stadium and sell pulled pork sandwiches and brisket tacos during every varsity game for all the sports. Baseball, football, soccer, track. Didn't matter. If a Ryleigh High team played, Joe smoked his brisket. As soon as Luke pulled up to Joe's BBQ House, that smoky scent brought him right back to the days of playing ball. It was like he could feel the bat in his hands, and he half-expected to hear an ump's call at any second. "Does he still set up outside the stadium for the games?"

"Would it be a Hornets game without Joe?"

"Absolutely not. Glad to hear that tradition is still alive." Luke jumped out of his truck and hurried around to Madeleine's side, opening the door for her. The way her hand fit perfectly inside his made his stomach flip, and the softness of her skin made him smile as he helped her climb out.

The little bell tinkled against the door as Luke swung it open, and Joe's place welcomed him back home again in a way he hadn't expected. The cooler of glass-bottled sodas still stood next to the service counter. The sound of a knife pounding against the wooden cutting board, now permanently caved in at the middle from years of chopping brisket for sandwiches was music to his ears. The rich scent of hickory chips smoking filled his nostrils, and his mouth started to water.

"Well as I live and breathe, is that you, Luke Taylor?" Mrs. Brumbelow was Joe's wife, and she was already halfway across the restaurant with her arms outstretched toward Luke, coming in for a hug. "Get over here and let me squeeze your neck." Luke leaned down and kissed the old lady on the cheek as she wrapped her aging arms around him and gave him the kind of hug only a Southern mama can give.

"Mrs. Brumbelow, it's good to see you. Sure feels good to be back here again."

"Well it's certainly been long enough, that's for sure." She patted him on the back as she let him out of the mama hug, then leaned to the side to look past him. "Joe. Come over here and look who's just walked through our doors."

Luke turned to see Joe wiping his hands on a dishtowel as he swung the little half-door open to walk from behind the counter. "Well hey there, Luke. Good to see you. How've you been?" Joe gave Luke a big bear hug.

"I've been good. Busy, I guess." A pang of guilt niggled at him. He hadn't come home because he'd wanted to. He'd come home on assignment from work, and here this sweet couple was so happy to see him, as if he were here because he chose to be.

Mrs. Brumbelow swatted him with her washrag she'd been using to wipe down tables. "Too busy to come home, huh? We sure miss seeing you around here. Baseball games aren't as exciting these days."

Luke grinned. His high school career had been full of championship games, Homecoming king crowns, and more celebrating than working. It was the best time of his life, and remembering it made him laugh. "Well, I'm sure the boys playing out there are giving it their best."

He slid an arm around Madeleine's waist, an old habit from his high school charmer days, before he even realized it was happening. Being back here in Joe's, smelling the barbecue and talking baseball with the Brumbelows, he slipped so easily back into that persona. But Madeleine was different. She wasn't some high school girl who wanted to be seen with the star pitcher. He didn't want to be the hometown celebrity jock to her. Not today or ever. He just wanted to be Luke.

"And you've brought Madeleine in with you, I see?" Mrs. Brumbelow's eyes shifted to Luke's left as her mouth twisted into a knowing smirk.

Suddenly his arm felt very awkward around her waist. She fit so perfectly inside his embrace that he hated to move apart. He hesitated for a second, to see if she tensed up or stepped away, but she didn't. As a matter of fact, he thought he felt her lean ever so slightly closer to him. He couldn't stop smiling over that little extra pressure on his rib cage. But he had no idea how to answer Mrs. Brumbelow.

To his relief, Madeleine took over the conversation. "Luke hasn't been home in so long, he wanted to have some of your legendary barbecue. He was sweet enough to invite me along." She looked at Joe. "So, I'm thinking we need two chopped brisket sandwiches, please."

"Can we get those to go?" Luke asked. "And maybe some chips and a drink?"

"Anything you want, Luke," came Joe's reply. "On the house."

Luke started to object, but the little old woman's eyes twinkled mischievously before she interrupted his protest.

"But if you wait so long before coming back, it won't be on the house next time. You'd better not stay away like that again. It's so good to see you." Mrs. Brumbelow patted Luke on the shoulder before crossing to the kitchen door.

"You too, Mrs. B. I'm sure we'll see you soon." Luke waved, then turned to Joe. "There's no need to comp our dinner, Joe. I'm happy to pay." He was already reaching for his wallet.

The old man smiled. "And I'm happy to give you dinner. That's the end of it."

I've forgotten how people are nice because they're just nice. He didn't realize how much he'd missed this little town until right now.

Madeleine held up two bags of chips. "Are you a salt and vinegar guy, or sour cream and onion?" She asked the question as if it were some life-changing decision, and his answer would make or break their future together. The glimmer in her eyes and the way she wiggled her eyebrows as she asked was adorable.

Definitely not sour cream and onion. No one wants to kiss onion breath. He smiled to himself at the thought of kissing her. "Uh, maybe just plain?" *That's a safe bet.*

She must have thought the same, as she traded out the flavors for two bags of plain potato chips. "Okay, but if you tell me you're not a Dr. Pepper drinker, you can just take me on home right now because we can't be friends."

"I'm a Texas boy, aren't I? If we don't drink Dr. Pepper, they kick us out north of the Red River. Unless sweet tea is an option."

"Obviously." She grinned as she pulled two Dr. Peppers from the cooler.

I haven't seen a Dr. Pepper in a glass bottle in...actually, I can't remember the last time. Once again, he smiled at his hometown's charm that was definitely missing in New York City.

Joe held a bag out to Luke with the sandwiches. "I threw in some of Mrs. B's snickerdoodles for y'all." He leaned forward over the counter and whispered, "They're good, but we all know Madeleine's the best baker in this town." He winked as Luke took the package.

The pride swelling up inside Luke surprised him. He hadn't expected to be so attached to Madeleine so quickly, but standing next to her while Joe talked her up made him excited to be with her. Is this how people in high school felt about being with him back then? It was a nice feeling. "She is definitely a treasure in this town." He glanced at Madeleine, who rolled her eyes at him.

"Y'all stop. It's just baking. I'm not changing the world with pastries." She looked down at her shoes, but the way she smiled told him she appreciated his compliment.

"You make it sweeter, though." Luke shrugged.

"Thanks, Joe. We appreciate it." Madeleine handed the chips to Luke, who dropped them into the bag with the sandwiches.

"Anytime. Y'all are always welcome here."

Luke opened the door for Madeleine, and together they climbed into the truck.

She twisted in her seat to look at him. "So, where to? Are you going to tell me what you've got up your sleeve?"

He shifted the truck into reverse and looked over his shoulder. "Nope."

She didn't move. Out of the corner of his eye, he could see her staring at him. He chanced a sidelong glance her way. *She's awfully cute over there, with her eyes wide and her mouth pursed up like that.* "Buckle up, young lady. Time to get rolling."

When he didn't say anything else, she must have given up because she twisted back into her seat and fastened her seatbelt.

It only took a few minutes to arrive. Luke could've made this drive with his eyes closed. He'd pulled into this stadium so many times during his life that it was truly a homecoming. He looked out his window at the rows of bleachers, the giant scoreboard in the outfield, and the home dugout along the first baseline. *Same field. Same sponsors. Just some updated paint.*

"The baseball field?" Madeleine's confused tone made him look her way.

"Sure. Why not?" A pit was developing in the bottom of his stomach. "Wait. Don't tell me you don't like baseball anymore?" *Please say you do. Please say you do.*

"Of course I do."

Relief washed over him. "Okay, good. Because up until now, I thought you were brilliant. But if you were about to tell me you didn't like baseball, I was going to have to question your intelligence. Not to mention your taste in sports." He winked as he grabbed the bag of sandwiches and a blanket from the backseat. "Temperature's dropping, but I thought we could have a picnic?"

Madeleine looked out the window at the field. "In front of the pitcher's mound looks like a perfect spot for that." She grabbed the drinks and climbed out of the truck, without waiting for Luke to open the door.

He jumped out after her, and his long legs made for a few quick strides to catch up. The gates were never locked at the field. One quick flip of the metal latch and they were in. Just a few more steps and he'd be back on that grass.

The way his feet sunk into the soft ground made him stop dead. It was like biting into Mama's homemade pecan pie, with BlueBell vanilla ice cream on top. It was such a familiar feeling, and yet new all over again. The way it sprung back against the balls of his feet as he pushed off to take another step was invigorating. Almost like it was inviting him to run. He wanted to play again, to hear the roar of a crowd cheering him on.

Even in the still, quiet evening this fall, he could hear a million games from the past all echoing in his mind.

Only right now, instead of preparing for a win or warming up with the guys, he was getting ready for a different challenge. One that meant being vulnerable, exposed. If he wanted to win Madeleine's heart, he'd have to be something really amazing. She deserved that.

Chapter 9

Madeleine

Madeleine headed for the infield, but didn't hear Luke's footsteps behind her anymore. She turned to check on him, and there he stood, both feet planted on the field just inside the gate, not moving an inch. He was staring at the stands, smiling and nodding slowly. He looked more at ease now than she had seen him since he'd come home.

"Luke? You okay?"

"Hmm? Yeah, fine." He cleared his throat and caught up to her. "Kinda weird being back on this ballfield again."

"I suppose it would be. Good weird, or weird weird?"

He chuckled. "Both, I guess." He paused, not so distracted now. "But not bad weird, so that's good."

"So not bad, but weird, and that's good. Okay. Totally clear now." Madeleine knew how he felt. Thoughts of her high school days, sitting on the bleachers laughing with Kristy and trying to not stare at Luke while he warmed up before a game came rushing back. This place, along with everything else in this town, held so many memories. Everywhere she looked, reminders of some past event stared back at her. But for Luke, he had the benefit of distance. He'd gotten out, seen other places. A dull ache of longing to see more than this life settled in her chest.

He led her to the pitcher's mound and spread the blanket in front of it. He took a minute to look across to home plate, his hands on his hips and his mouth pressed into a line before sitting. She recognized that wistful look. She'd made it herself when thinking about making her bakery better. But for Luke, it looked like he wanted to be back here, where everyone chanted his name as he walked to home plate, his bat slung over his shoulder and jaw squarely set, ready for another home run.

Settling cross-legged on the blanket, Madeleine unpacked the sandwiches and chips from Joe's package. Luke twisted the cap off a Dr. Pepper and handed it to her. *This is nice, but it won't be long before I'll wish it were a hot chocolate.*

She took a quick sip of soda. "You miss being here, don't you?"

"What, in Ryleigh?"

"No, here. I mean, on the field." She popped a chip into her mouth. "But yes, also Ryleigh."

"I didn't realize how much I missed it until right now." He looked at the dugout with a faraway gaze. "That concrete bench was everything to me back then. It was where I first realized I could make something of myself."

"Looks to me like you've done just that. Working for a global company, traveling the world. Do you ever meet famous people?"

"Mm-hm," he answered, chewing then swallowing his bite. "I get to do press junkets with some of them. Most of my interviews end up as print articles for our news division, but I'm hoping to branch out into on-camera interviews soon, if I can catch a break."

"And the company pays for it all?"

He took a bite of his sandwich. "Mm-hm."

"Wow. That must be nice." *Dallas is about as exciting as I ever get. He must really see me as a small-town girl.* Her stomach started twisting into knots. It couldn't have been Joe's sandwich—she'd been eating those her whole life, and they always went down fine.

No, it was something else. She couldn't get too attached to Luke. The way he traveled all over the world, and her so tethered to Ryleigh by The Bean and Batter, they'd never work together. And not only that, she'd never be enough for Luke. His life was too full, too exotic, too...well, everything. Meanwhile, she was busy trying to keep her little hometown bakery running and her bills paid.

Luke stretched onto his side, his legs running the length of the blanket, and leaned on his elbow. "I mean, the things I get to see are great, but being back in Ryleigh is something else."

Yeah. Something lame. He was probably leaving town tomorrow to fly off to some royal wedding in Europe, the reception sponsored by Greyson Media. He hadn't been home in ten years, and it would be another ten before he returned again. By then, The Bean and Batter would have gone bankrupt, and she'd be the crazy cat lady who offered children slices of unwanted fruitcake from her front porch. Well, maybe not fruitcake. That was truly awful. Carrot cake, possibly.

"Right there." Luke said, pointing into the bleachers.

"Hmm?"

"Right there," he said again, propping himself up on one hand while pointing with the other.

"What's right there?" Madeleine squinted her eyes to see what he pointed to. By now, the sun had fallen behind the bleachers and darkness covered that side of the field.

"That's the very spot you always sat. I could count on you to be there every home game." He looked at her, tipped up the corner of his mouth and then looked down at the blanket. A tiny piece of lint suddenly became very interesting to him.

Her heartbeat began to thunder in her chest, but her lungs decided now would be a good time to stop working. *He knows where I sat during the games?*

She breathed out a tiny squeak. "What? I mean, you're not wrong, but why would you know that?"

"It's a small school, Madeleine. The stadium's not that big." He sat up and shrugged.

"Oh." She tried not to look hurt by his comment, but her short reply came out more sharply than she meant. She thought maybe Luke noticed her for a different reason, other than she and her friends had their game night routine and it never changed. But, just as she'd always thought, he never noticed her in high school. And why would he? She was two years younger than him. He was the high school hero, and she was on the yearbook committee. Granted, she was usually with Dillon, so maybe he at least knew her name, but he certainly never acted like he knew her either in the halls or when she was at his house.

"I guess we did always sit in the same spot. We did that because Kristy always wanted to make sure Jake knew where to look when he was playing."

"Jake Matthews? He and Kristy were something, weren't they?"

"They were cute together. They got married, you know."

"You're kidding?" He laughed and ran his hands through his hair.

Oh, to be those hands. "Nope. They moved down to The Woodlands a few years back. He's a lawyer now. Kristy and I still keep in touch."

"A lawyer, huh? Who would've thought that? Then I guess I'm thankful for Kristy."

"You are? Why?"

He reached over and placed his hand on top of hers. "So between innings, I could always find you in the stands."

The way his hand rested on hers felt so warm, so right. Her head wanted to argue with her heart, but she knew it would be a losing battle. Even if he hadn't seen her in high school, he saw her now. And when she looked into his eyes, she knew that this Texas girl was toast.

"Luke," she started. "I'm not sure we should—"

This couldn't continue. Or start, really. Last night in the bakery had been a fun mishap, but she didn't mean for things to land her sharing a picnic in front of the pitcher's mound with Ryleigh High's former three-time Homecoming king. She started to pull her hand out from under his, but he held on to it, and moved closer to her. *Good grief, keep coming closer and I'll lose my nerve.*

"Not sure we should what?" His voice had dropped to a murmur.

She bit her bottom lip and tried to think about what she was going to say, but the words were gone. "Um..." she trailed off. *Deep breath. Just stay cool.* Right now, she was anything but cool. Her insides quivered like a half-baked crème brûlée.

"Not sure we should do..." He paused, and traced a finger along her jawline, leaving a hot trail in its wake. "We should do...this?"

Oh, sweet snickerdoodles please do that some more. And maybe again on the other side.

"Or maybe even...this." He was so close now, she could feel his breath on her cheek. He brushed his lips just under her earlobe. One turn of her head, and his lips would be on hers.

"I just don't know that this is a good idea." There. She'd said it. Even if it had been a whisper, and probably didn't sound very convincing, her decision was made, and she'd said it out loud. Surely he would walk away. After all, he probably had women all over the world wanting his attention, just like in high school.

Luke sat back, his eyes saying everything as they dropped to the blanket. He swallowed hard and nodded his head slowly.

"I'm sorry, Luke. But I've got a life here. A bakery that I'm trying to keep afloat. My mother gave it to me, and if I lose it, I've got nothing else. I have to protect that legacy." Saying that out loud only strengthened her resolve to do anything to save her livelihood. Luke's kisses couldn't hold a candle to how much she loved that little bakery, and she couldn't afford to let anything distract her from that.

Luke finally looked up and smiled gently. "Madeleine, I'm not asking you to marry me and move to Australia or somewhere. I just want to get to know you better."

"I know. But then there's Dillon and all that comes with that. He's been my best friend since high school. And he didn't seem very happy about us this morning." She felt her anxiety rising, and she couldn't contain her thoughts any longer.

Luke let out a sigh. "You let me worry about Dillon."

Her words poured out like melted chocolate and oozed all over what started as a perfectly lovely evening. "I couldn't do that to him, though. He's been there for me during all the rough times. He held my hand while I buried my mother, Luke. Our friendship runs deep, and I can't just throw it away because you've swept into town and decided to have a fling with the small town's sweetheart." *Oh, my word. I can't believe I just said that.* She blinked and tried to take a deep breath, but she couldn't make her body cooperate.

He sat up taller and furrowed his eyebrows. "Is that what you think this is? A fling?"

A flash of sadness flickered in his eyes.

"Madeleine, I've wanted to be with you since tenth grade. You used to come over, and I was always so irritated that Dillon got to spend all that time with you, and you never even looked my way." His voice was rising in pitch with every word.

Whoa. What? Madeleine's entire body turned custard-style-shaky. Her head felt light, and she put a hand onto the blanket to steady herself, trying to stop the dizziness and quivering. The stadium was suddenly out of focus, except for one place: the dugout where Luke always leaned against the fence, his hands gripping the metal, eyes squinted, alert and watching the game. She found herself twisting the blanket between her fingers in the same way his fingers gripped that metal fence. And all at once, she didn't know whether to laugh out loud, bury her face in her hands, or squeal with delight at this news.

He had been watching *her?* She remembered the countless evenings of secretly glancing across the kitchen as he grabbed the keys to his truck to go pick up some girl for his next date and wishing it were her. That tingly feeling she felt when they were rolling out scones had been familiar, because it was the same way she felt when she used to walk past his locker and he was there. But he never knew any of those things. Because he wasn't paying attention. Or so she had thought.

Luke interrupted her thinking. "You were always so careful about leaving our house before curfew. I should probably confess, I ended lots of dates early just so I could get home before you left."

"Are you serious?" She laughed at the thought of a younger Luke leaving some girl standing on the front porch waiting for her goodnight kiss while he sprinted back to his truck. It sounded completely ridiculous, but she really did want to believe him. "Why didn't you ever say anything?"

He took a deep breath and hesitated. "Well, honestly...I was stupid."

And there was that smirk again. The one he made in every yearbook photo she'd snapped of him. The one that said, 'I'm charming, and I know it.' And as much as you wanted to be irritated about it, you liked him even more for it.

She couldn't stop her laughter. All the emotions of the evening came rushing to the front of her brain and out of her mouth in a blast of giggles. When she heard Luke join in, she only laughed harder and louder. "Luke Taylor, I wish I could say you've changed, but I'm not so sure about that," she said in between howls.

"Aw, come on. Give me a little credit," he said, finally settling down. "I am smart enough to finally ask you out."

"True."

"And you're smart enough to have said yes." He moved closer again, his lips slightly parted and eager.

"Also true." She leaned toward him, her breathing slow and shallow.

"Wanna do something stupid with me?" He pressed his lips to hers before she could answer. At least not with words, anyhow.

Chapter 10

Luke

Luke rolled over and swiped his phone alarm off, his eyes still shut. Lying on his back, his mind filled with thoughts of one thing—Madeleine. Last night, everything had gone exactly against plan, and yet it was somehow perfect. He never intended to jump into anything serious with the sweetest treat in Ryleigh, but as the evening progressed, he couldn't stop looking at her and wondering what it would be like to kiss her, to feel the softness of her lips on his. Everything changed the instant he slid his arm around her waist in Joe's BBQ House.

She had been too cute to resist, the way she twisted her fingers together with nervous energy.

Her fingers. A vision of his fingers intertwined with hers, resting on her knee as he drove her back to The Bean and Batter last night, made him smile. He wanted to know everything about her. What made her tick. What made her laugh. What made her smile. He wanted to drink in every detail of her, and he wanted it all right this second.

"I just want to take it slow," she'd told him after a few moments of really great kissing. Her lips were soft, her kisses sweet and hesitant. "I never expected this to happen."

I can respect that. I've waited this long to spend this time with her, I can wait more. He was glad to let things develop gradually, since he wasn't sure what the end game would be. Even though they were growing closer quickly, there was still the problem of actual physical distance. New York City and Ryleigh weren't exactly conveniently near enough to commute for any relationship.

Sitting there, in the middle of the baseball field, a flood of memories of high-school-Madeleine rushed back. *I can still see her sitting in the stands, eating popcorn and laughing with her friends.* The images were as clear as if they were happening right then. He could see her passing his locker on her way to lunch, her backpack slung across one shoulder and her long ponytail swinging behind her. He could see her curled up on his game room couch, half asleep while Dillon's movie droned on. Even back then, he was so tempted to scoop her up and drive her home. But she was younger, his little brother's best friend, and she seemed to always ignore him.

And last night, there she was, cross-legged next to him on a blanket, her eyes wide, and Dr. Pepper in her hands. *How would any man be able to resist that? I made a mistake in high school, not going for it back then. I won't make that mistake again.* When Dillon took her call asking for help to jump her battery on Buttercup, Luke was all too happy to head over there.

He needed to see her again today. And soon. But first, he had some things to take care of with work. Plus, there was the matter of Dillon. *I sure hope this goes better than when I forgot to close his hamster's cage, and Squeakers was lost for three weeks.*

He rubbed his fingers across his chin. *I need a shave and a shower first.* He threw the quilt off, grabbed his sweatpants, and headed toward the bathroom. *Dang. Occupied.*

Dillon's electric razor buzzed from behind the door. Luke's parents had offered to let him stay with them, but Dillon's place had better Wi-Fi, which made working from here so much easier. He kept walking past the bathroom and into the kitchen, where he looked at the coffeemaker. It was, upsettingly, one of the old-school, drip brew kind. *Dillon, come into the twenty-first century and get a real coffee machine.* Luke hadn't used one like this in years. He had one of the K-cup kinds, the one you didn't have to measure or prep. Just pop in a cup, put the mug underneath, and hit 'brew'.

He was just guessing at how many scoops of coffee when Dillon came into the kitchen. "You'll want to put a filter in there, or that coffee's just going to drip into your mug, dude." He hadn't showered yet, and his toothbrush was dangling from his mouth.

"Thanks."

"Yup. I heard you out here digging in the drawers and I figured you didn't know how to work one of these old-school, small town things." He finished brushing and spit into the kitchen sink, grabbed a glass from the cabinet, and rinsed out his mouth. "You know, I don't have a latte machine here. You'd have to go see Maddie for that."

Luke's heart skipped a beat at her name, but the fact that it was Dillon who brought her up made his stomach simultaneously drop. "Yeah, I may have to do that. This is probably going to taste like mud."

"You were out late." Dillon's eyes were narrowed, and he seemed to be standing just a little straighter than usual.

"Dillon," Luke started, shaking his head. "We probably need to talk about last night."

"You're not good for her, Luke."

"I'm not good for her? What's that supposed to mean?" A prickly defense rose up in his throat. *Is he kidding me?* He shoved a coffee filter into the basket and began counting out teaspoons of coffee. Again.

"Just that." He leaned backward against the counter and crossed his arms. "I can't watch her get involved with someone like you."

"Then you'd better walk around with a blindfold on, little brother. She's involved. And I'm happy about it." He hadn't wanted this conversation to go this way, but Dillon had given him no choice by coming in here with a growl.

What gave Dillon this kind of ownership over Madeleine anyhow? It wasn't like he ever wanted her for himself. If he had, there were plenty of opportunities over the last thirteen years. It wasn't Luke's problem that his brother had been too stupid to take what was in front of him. "You haven't wanted her for years, and now that I have her, you want her? That's nice, dude. Man up and realize you missed your chance."

"It's not that I want her." Dillon stepped back and held his open hands out defensively. "It's what I said earlier. She's too good for you." He pointed at his brother and raised his eyebrows at the accusation.

"I can't disagree there. For sure, she's too good for me. She's too good for anyone." *Maybe if I explain this better, he'll see things more clearly.* "Dillon, this isn't a quick, fly-into-town-and-notice-her situation. This isn't as new as you think."

Dillon furrowed his eyebrows and challenged, "Yeah? Care to explain?"

Luke sighed. *Here goes nothing.* "I've liked her since high school. I was just too full of myself back then to abandon the cheerleaders and actually go after who I really wanted." That felt good. Honesty was a new suit he liked wearing. He tried to fill the coffee machine with water, but the carafe leaked as he poured and water flooded the countertop. *I hate this machine so much.* He mopped up the mess with the paper towels next to the sink.

"You've been looking at her since high school? I don't believe that. You could've had any girl you wanted back then. You had girls you didn't even want sometimes. Why her? Why now?" His voice grew louder with each question.

"Do I really need to tell you how amazing she is?" Luke threw the wet towels into the trash can and started looking for the 'brew' button. "She's smart and funny." A vision of her hazel eyes flashed in his memory. He could practically feel her long eyelashes brushing against his temple when she had kissed his cheek last night before hopping out of the truck and into her car. "And, Dillon, you have to see how beautiful she is."

"Oh, I know." He reached over and jammed his finger against the elusive 'brew' button. "Such an idiot," he muttered under his breath, but loud enough that Luke heard. "You're in town for who knows how long and then you're going to leave. You'll break her heart, and I'll be here. Picking up your mess just like I've been doing for the last ten years."

That struck a nerve. Luke knew he hadn't been the most loyal son and brother, but it wasn't fair for Dillon to throw that up at him as a reason to keep him apart from Madeleine. "You know I couldn't help how things went down."

"Yep. I know exactly how it went down. You galivanted all over this world entertaining athletes, princes, and diplomats. Meanwhile, Mom and Dad had to read about it in People Magazine while sitting in the waiting room of doctor after doctor. When Dad had his heart attack, you were in Milan. Likely getting to know some supermodel who'd just left the runway hours before you bought her champagne." The rumble in his voice resonated bitterness, and he faced off against his brother.

Luke's blood boiled. *Who does he think he is, standing here and assuming things about me? He doesn't know the pressures of my work. The millions of dollars at stake. If I'm buying champagne for supermodels, it's certainly not for my own gain.* "You know what? You don't know what you're talking about. I'm not listening to this."

He headed to his bedroom and slammed the door.

Dillon yelled down the hallway, "Fine. Go ahead and run away from the hard things. Just like you always do. But I'll be damned if I let you rope Madeleine into anything you will run away from later."

"And I'll be damned if I let you stop me." Luke dug out a clean T-shirt and jeans from the closet, and as he did, the forgotten envelope from yesterday caught his eye. Dillon had either glanced through it, or read it thoroughly, he didn't know which, and it upset him.

When he got into his truck yesterday morning, he pulled the pages from the envelope and read the first few lines. With that info, he knew instantly why his brother flew off the handle: GREYSON RENOVATIONS.

Renovations? That's a new take.

Everyone had heard of Henry Greyson. Being widely recognized had recently backfired on Henry, though. Not so much Henry but his company, Greyson Media. A major New York paper released an exposé on the company, one that pointed out how out of touch the company had become with the people who read and watched all their media. Greyson Media had lost the pulse of the average American in their pursuit to become a global media superpower, focusing only on celebrities who also had no clue how the regular person's life was carried out. The article went viral, and soon there were protesters outside Greyson's skyscraper, people calling to boycott their channels and publications, and Henry's botoxed forehead started showing more wrinkles of worry.

Greyson Media was looking for a small town to feature in an upcoming promo event. Having recently taken some flak for not understanding the 'everyman' of America and focusing more on the hip, glamorous lifestyle of the rich and famous across the globe, the corporation needed to revamp their brand. Henry Greyson had this idea to find some Smalltown, USA and bring their media team to feature the businesses and citizens in a five-part series on their streaming channel.

When he'd heard Luke was from the very kind of town Greyson Media was looking for, he'd jumped on the connection. A few quick online searches, much to Luke's chagrin, and Greyson found Luke Taylor's name in multiple newspaper articles. His smile was especially salacious when he found pictures of Luke wearing his Homecoming king crown.

"It'll be great. What's better than the hometown hero going back to revamp his childhood paradise but with a major corporate backing to fund and film it all?" He slapped Luke on the back and then poured them each a glass of ridiculously expensive whiskey to celebrate his genius.

The people of Ryleigh were the salt of the earth, and Luke had connections to almost all of them. New people hardly ever moved to Ryleigh, so it hadn't changed much since he'd left. But the idea of going home was not one he relished. He'd have to face all he'd left behind, all he'd neglected. Madeleine

Malone was part of that neglect. She was a missed opportunity he wouldn't strike-out on a second time.

Chapter 11

Madeleine

Buttercup roared to life, her usual protests wailing when Madeleine turned the heat to high and headed in to work. 4 o'clock came early this morning. She hadn't been out so late in a very long time, and the alarm was not her friend today. She couldn't blame the wine. Luke hadn't thought to bring a corkscrew, a fact that she didn't intend to stop teasing him about.

Luke. Luke Taylor. The handsome, talented, and incredibly amazing man who she never expected to be kissing. But she did kiss him. And it was perfect.

What is happening? I assumed Luke Taylor never noticed me in school. Suddenly we're having picnics together? And on the very field I watched him play baseball night after night. She still marveled at how all those times she secretly watched him in high school, he was doing the same to her.

She pulled into the space behind her bakery, shifted into park, and closed her eyes. Resting her head on the seat, she touched her fingers to her lips, pausing to remember how his lips had felt there. Gentle, yet hurried. Soft, but burning. She wanted to sit in the warm car forever, replaying last night's scene in her mind, but work called.

The cool air hit Madeleine's warm cheeks like ice cubes added to freshly brewed sweet tea, motivating her to quickly turn the key in the back door of The Bean and Batter and flip on the lights. The scent of last night's chocolate muffin bake still floated in the air. She loved coming in to the bakery first thing in the morning, while it was still quiet and still. It was almost like she sensed her mother watching over her here before the business of the day started brewing.

Her purse hung on the same hook her mother once used for her own purse. She took off her rings for today's baking and set them in her mother's porcelain dish, hand painted with a bunny in the grass. It had been a gift from Madeleine's grandmother to her mother, bought on a trip to Tiffany & Co in New York. Her mother was so excited to get anything in that Tiffany Blue box. She'd saved the box, with its white satin ribbon tucked neatly inside her nightstand drawer.

Someday I'll see Tiffany's. And maybe, if I'm lucky, I'll have a blue box of my own.

On went her favorite lavender apron, and the day's baking began with a gathering of ingredients from the shelves in the stockroom. *Let's see. Today, something savory needs to be on the menu.* Lunchtime wasn't where she did most of her business, but she did like to have some fun new offerings for those wanting a quick snack.

She'd binge-watched a baking show recently and saw a new recipe she'd been holding on to. Samosas were interesting enough to want to try, but not so exotic that people in Ryleigh wouldn't be turned off. Occasionally, she thought of herself as the person who could broaden the horizons of the people in her little town. She tried something new and exciting last night, and today, she was inspired to do the same for the people who came to her little bakery. It would be a perfect lunchtime special.

The potatoes were boiled and the dough was already chilling in the fridge when the back door opened. "Hey Madeleine," Becca called out as she dropped her backpack in the little office.

"Becca, you're just in time to help stuff these samosas. Come check these out."

"What even is a samosa?" She came into the kitchen, already wrapping her apron strings around her waist and tying them in the front.

Madeleine pulled the dough from the fridge and unwrapped it. "They're Indian. The filling is already started on the stovetop. It's potatoes and spices, all sealed inside these little triangles of dough."

Becca laughed. "Been binge-watching cooking shows again?"

Madeleine smiled and shrugged. "What can I say? I'm a sucker for a good baking competition."

Becca set about stirring the filling in the pan on the stove and tasted it. "Oh wow. That's really good."

"Yeah? I thought so. It's not too spicy, though, is it?" She added an extra few dashes of 'rooster sauce' earlier, hoping the heat would be a good kick.

Becca shook her head then swallowed. "No, it's perfect."

"Awesome." She started rolling the dough out onto a flat surface. Rolling dough was one of Madeleine's favorite things to do. She loved watching it stretch and grow as she worked the rolling pin over it, and the repetition of it was relaxing.

"Want me to start filling the case?" Becca eyed the containers of baked goods Madeline set out, ready to be stacked inside the glass display counter.

"Sure, thanks."

Only twenty-five years old, Becca held a degree in Sports Medicine and left the bakery every afternoon to train and work with the high school teams once they headed to practice or games after school. Working at the bakery was good money, but it wasn't her passion. Yet she always gave it her full effort, and for that, Madeleine was thankful. Without Becca's help, The Bean and Batter would likely be out of business by now.

After Madeleine lost her mother, Becca kept the bakery running, putting in extra hours earlier in the morning to bake pastries or to place orders for products. It had meant the world to Madeleine, knowing that Becca had come through in a big way during that season. She had proven herself invaluable time and again, and Madeleine wished she could afford to pay her more. But, with a busted water pipe followed by an oven that went out, the shrinking bank account roared its hungry mouth. At least Becca understood and never made a fuss if her paycheck was a few days late here and there.

"So, I noticed Luke Taylor was in yesterday." That was more of a question than a statement and laced with curiosity. Becca never held back in getting straight to the point. Many good, honest conversations happened in these early mornings before the bakery opened, and Madeleine always appreciated Becca's candor.

"How do you know Luke? He graduated a long time ago."

Becca scoffed. "Please. His pictures are all over the field house. That championship team is legendary. Coach Levine still talks about some of the plays from Luke's senior year."

Wow. I had no idea anyone other than Dillon still thought about Luke. The topic of Luke didn't come up that often with Dillon. The way Luke left and seemed to abandon his family was a touchy subject, one Madeleine tried to avoid. But now that he'd returned home, she wasn't sure what to do. *Has he been to see his mother since he's been back?* Come to think of it, Madeleine didn't even know where Luke was staying, whether with his parents or his brother. A sinking feeling landed in her stomach. *If Luke's at his brother's, Dillon probably already knows where we were last night.*

"Yeah, he came over a few nights ago and helped me with Buttercup." She tried to sound nonchalant, but she knew Becca would see right through this ruse and it wouldn't be long before they were talking about last night's...date? Outing? At this point, it didn't matter what she called it. It had ended with a kiss and left her wanting more time with Luke.

"Dead battery again?"

"Yup. I guess he'd just come into town, and Dillon sent him over to help me out, since the shop was swamped."

"And he came back the next morning to...just say hello?" Becca grinned as she loaded the chocolate-hazelnut-color-of-Luke's-eyes muffins onto the top shelf in the case. She stood up and put the empty container in the sink and filled it with soapy water. "Because he looked like he had a lot more to say than 'hello.'"

Warmth spread across Madeleine's cheeks, and she knew Becca noticed. She distracted herself with cutting the samosa dough into diamonds and started forming the pockets, one at a time. "He was just being nice, I think."

Becca flicked some water off her fingertips and onto the back of Madeleine's neck. "Just being nice? Oh, okay then." Her sarcasm was one of the reasons Madeleine liked Becca. She always said exactly what she was thinking, but it was never unkind. Just honest with a dose of sass.

"Fine." She cut another diamond of dough. *She won't stop until I tell her anyhow.* "He asked me out." Her stomach did a little flip. Thinking about her date with Luke was one thing, but saying it out loud to someone else was completely something else.

"Are you serious?" Becca's voice rose up in pitch about three notches. "And did you say yes?"

"Of course."

"And when is said date supposed to happen?"

Madeleine turned around and shrugged at Becca, who stood with her mouth hanging slightly open. "Well, about that..."

"Oh. My. Word, you already went, didn't you?" She tossed the towel she'd been using to dry the muffin container onto the countertop. "How was it? Where did you go? It's a good thing you're telling me now. You know this gossip will be all over Ryleigh before we even unlock that front door, right?"

Oh, sugar. This kind of news is too juicy to stay quiet in this town. "Uh. Didn't take the time to think that part through." Madeleine loved Mrs. B, but she was also the queen of the granny gossip gang. She was probably on the phone to the rest of the ladies before Luke had pulled his truck out of the parking lot of Joe's.

"Does Dillon know?"

Her stomach dropped to her toes. She set the samosa she'd been sealing down on the counter and sighed. "Trying not to think about that, either." *He won't like this. I know Luke said he'd take care of it, but it won't change the fact that Dillon will feel completely betrayed.* They'd never had anything come between them before, and Madeleine didn't want that to change. But she knew how Dillon thought of her like a sister, protective nature and all.

"You'd better take care of telling Dillon before he hears about it from somewhere else."

Madeleine hoped Luke was staying with his parents. If he were staying at Dillon's, she was sure he would know about the date already. *He'd have been up reading when Luke came home.* Dillon had always been a night owl, staying up until the latest hour possible finishing one more chapter.

She picked up her phone and checked the time. Almost six. Dillon would be awake by now, since he had to head into work and be open by seven a.m. "You're probably right." The text was quick. 'maybe give me a call on your way to work, k?'

She put the phone down and finished filling the last of the samosas and packed them into a container to fry up later today around the lunch hour.

Before she could start cleaning up the extra dough, her phone rang. She swiped to answer it, her heart beating fast.

"Madeleine." His voice was flat but tense.

Uh oh. He's using my whole name.

"What do you think you're doing with Luke?"

Chapter 12

Luke

L uke threw the truck into reverse and headed into town. It was early, and not much would be open. But he needed to get out of Dillon's house and find a quiet place to work. It was almost nine in New York, and the city would be buzzing. Henry Greyson would be in his office, finishing his third cup of coffee by now, running his media empire as if the world's most famous celebrities and royal houses had no idea who he was. But in reality, Greyson Media was a household name, feeding content to the world through every streaming option possible.

Grey's 'fix' to his out-of-touch image was his chance to show that the company did understand and care about their biggest consumers. But Luke could tell things were already off track. Even here, in this tiny town, he was certain the people of Ryleigh wouldn't take kindly to a media superpower taking over.

Luke would be pinned as the one who offered up Ryleigh as a sacrifice, even though in New York he'd been a nobody.

One thing Luke found in the few days that he'd been home was that there was no laying low for him here. Everyone knew who he was. He had been sent to scope out Ryleigh before Greyson Media's announcement about their new channel went public. Knowing his hometown like he did, he thought maybe he could do some damage control before things got out of hand, but it might be too late. True to character, Greyson had moved ahead with his plans before even waiting for Luke to give the green light.

When he'd moved to New York, it was the first time he wasn't Luke Taylor the star ball player. He'd enjoyed making his own path using his intellect and drive, not just having everything handed to him because he was the town's shining star. In New York, no one cared who you were. They only cared about what you brought to the table. For Greyson Media, Luke brought an excited voice coupled with in incredibly handsome face, and they were only too happy to send him around the world to represent them. It didn't hurt that he was quick with a joke and could talk to just about anyone, whether they were musical royalty or actual royals.

But this new assignment would change things for Luke.

He took a deep breath and dialed Greyson's number.

"Well, if it isn't lucky Luke calling from America's favorite hometown," Greyson's excitement came through loud and clear.

I hate being on speakerphone. You never know who else is listening. "Hey Grey. I got your envelope yesterday."

"Good, good. Did you review the files? Get the city's mayor to sign those documents and send them back. Email them for now, but we need the hard copies overnighted. You know how legal can be."

"Right. I glanced through them, but I noticed that page about remodeling. What's that all about? I thought we were just going to feature some businesses. Do a few little special interest stories." *Careful. You don't want to blow this.* The fact that Henry Greyson put Luke on the scouting mission could lead to a big opportunity for him. He might actually get to take the lead on a project for the first time.

Grey cleared his throat. "You're going to love this. It was Emily's idea."

This morning's coffee turned sour in his stomach with every passing minute of this phone call. *How did Emily squeeze her way into this project? Oh, wait. Probably how she always does, with a fake smile and false flattery. Anything to get ahead.*

"Oh?" He tried to sound nonchalant, but Grey already knew about Luke's history with Emily. They'd worked together for four years, and dated for most of that time. But the closer he got to her, the more he saw their differences. She was all city girl, with a fast-paced career track, while Luke wanted to settle down and enjoy his work without worrying about how to get the next promotion. Her drive to get ahead always came before their relationship. He grew tired of second place, and she didn't understand his need to slow down.

When Greyson didn't offer any additional explanation about Emily's involvement, Luke pressed for more. "What's she got brewing?" *Yeah, brewing is definitely the right word. Only I'm thinking more cauldron than coffee.*

A quick flash of Madeleine handing him a cup of coffee yesterday landed square in the front of his mind. The scent of almond shampoo was so real to him right then, it almost knocked him off his game. But he couldn't think about her now. He had to be on his toes. Especially now that Emily was a part of this.

"She thought we could expand our company's name by building your little town into our own empire. Take a local business and do a makeover. You know how everyone loves those shows. We walk in to an old, run down business, redecorate, maybe bring in an expert or two to show the owner how to really step up their game, and boom. A new, successful business is made."

Luke tried to process everything Henry was telling him. *So, we're getting into the renovation business? That's a terrible idea.*

"But then, once we're done, we advertise the businesses we've jazzed up, maybe build some B&B's, and we've created our own destination for big city folks to get away and enjoy the slower pace of small town America. It's a whole new category of profits for us."

Luke's mind started ticking through the small businesses in Ryleigh. There were several, but he couldn't think of anyone in town who would want to relinquish their business to 'Corporate America'. As a matter of fact, most of them were perfect the way they were.

Or too boring to be featured on a show.

Who would want to watch a show about a remodel of Samuel Achison's tax office? "Uh, I'm not sure the town has a business that would work."

"Nonsense. We've already looked into it. Emily has targeted several businesses, and she is supposed to email those over to me. I'll forward them to you as soon as I get them."

He clenched his jaw muscles, and his sweaty palms slipped over the steering wheel. He knew what was coming to his little hometown. Or worse, who.

"Is Emily taking the lead on the makeover show?" That would mean she'd need to come to Ryleigh. Which would completely undercut part of the reason Luke had come here in the first place. He needed an escape from the...well, the whatever it was that hadn't worked between them.

"She's asked about it, yes." Henry paused. "Listen, Luke. I know the two of you haven't been exactly cozy with each other lately. But I think she's on to something."

"I'm just not sure she'll fit in with the people here." Luke was grasping at straws. This trip to Texas was supposed to be his chance to get away from her, to let his heart heal after they'd broken up. He wasn't sure he could see her without falling back into their comfortable rhythm. "What about Jeremy? Couldn't he run the shows?"

"That wouldn't be fair to Emily, and you know it. This is her baby. She has the right to run with this ball. But I'll tell you what, she had an idea to sweeten the pot for you a little."

A prickle of suspicion nagged at him. Anything Emily did was intentional and usually served her own goals. Whatever this "sweetener" was, it came with strings. "How so?"

"She wants you to be the face of the series. More than just overseeing the way we are represented to the Ryleigh community, we want you to be in front of the camera hosting all the episodes, doing the interviews, the whole thing."

Luke took in a deep breath and held it. His vision went narrow, so he pulled over onto the shoulder and put his truck in park. This was something Luke had been wanting for a long time, but he'd never asked for it. He knew he hadn't been with Greyson Media long enough to earn that kind of promotion. He ran the palms of his hands over his thighs trying to calm himself. *Emily did this. She knew I wanted to be on camera. She's dangling this carrot on purpose, so I will agree and she can take the lead.*

Greyson kept talking. "Emily thinks it would be a great image shift for Greyson Media, and I think she's right. If we build the town up, it becomes a destination spot, and we can keep everything in-house. That way our image is protected."

"Oh?" *Control the assets. Manage the company image.* Luke knew the drill.

"Grey, no one is going to care that much about some small-potatoes town."

"Maybe not, but with all the bad press we're getting lately, I can't afford even the possibility of more negativity. The board is questioning everything. You know that. Our stocks are plummeting, and our shareholders are threatening to dump their shares."

Luke did know that. Greyson had been in his office just last week getting an earful from one of them. It was yet another reason why he'd wanted to come to Ryleigh. The atmosphere in the office was turning volatile with every negative article. "I know. But, Emily? There's really not another option?"

"Man up, Luke. She's in. I'd have thought you'd be excited about this opportunity. Emily made it sound like you've secretly been wishing to be on camera all this time. She was eager to give you that break."

A momentary guilt niggled in the back of his mind. *I probably should be more grateful. I just didn't plan on seeing her so soon. And in Ryleigh, no less.* "I know, but it's not really—"

A voice interrupted him. Emily. Had she been listening to everything they'd said? "Hey, Luke. I thought I heard your voice in here. We need to get a move on if we're going to scope out the town for filming spots."

"Yep," came Greyson's answer. "Luke, I'll forward her email over to you."

"Already in his inbox. I cc'd you, Luke." He could hear her flirty smile all the way from Texas. "Grey and I agree you're the perfect face for this new audience to fall in love with Greyson Media again. Who could resist you?"

"Thanks, Emily." He cleared his throat. Her flirting made him uncomfortable, especially because he couldn't tell if she was genuine or not. Either way, she had managed to get him in front of the camera, so he at least owed her some gratitude, begrudgingly or not. "Sounds like a great project. Nice thinking." There. He'd been complimentary enough. Right?

"Wow. Is that a kind word from Luke Taylor? What a turn of events. He's speaking to me again. And nicely?"

Don't air this in front of Greyson, Em. Luke gritted his teeth in frustration. He wasn't sure how to respond without digging further into an argument with her. Which seemed to be how every conversation went with Emily since the breakup. And he didn't want to argue with her. Not in front of their boss, or on the phone, or ever.

Greyson rescued him before he could respond. "Emily, rein it in if you want to keep this assignment. Take a look at her email, Luke, and see which businesses might fit the bill. Get back to me tomorrow."

"Will do." Luke hung up, tapped the email icon on his phone, and clicked on Emily's message. The list of businesses was short. And the name at the top of the list made him want to throw up.

Madeleine's Bean and Batter was certainly not on the table.

Chapter 13

Madeleine

D illon had his arms crossed over his chest, and even though his sunglasses covered his eyes, Madeleine knew him well enough to imagine they were squinted at her as she walked toward the bakery's front door. She flipped over the sign from 'Closed' to 'Open' and unlocked the front door.

He barely waited for her to get the lock turned before he pulled on the handle to open the door. "Madeleine. This isn't a joke." He flipped his sunglasses onto the bill of his baseball cap, turned backward on his head.

"Who said anything about joking? If anything, this," she circled a finger in his direction, "is an overreaction." She kept working while she spoke, switching on side table lamps and straightening magazines. She'd only seen Dillon like this a few times before, and it rattled her. She tried to focus on the task of opening the Bean and Batter to keep her thoughts straight.

"Oh, really? So you think that you getting involved with my brother isn't something I should be concerned about?" He followed her from table to table, a gesture Madeleine found maddening. "You know, the guy who basically has a track record of scrolling through the lineup of girls awaiting their turn with the 'Home Run King'?"

Madeleine rolled her eyes. "That's not fair. He's not seventeen anymore. He's an adult." Her voice was confident, but a new thought popped into her mind. She really didn't know what kind of adult relationships Luke had. Was he still that pretty-boy-player who flipped from woman to woman, or had he grown up and taken things more seriously? She hoped it was the latter, but she really couldn't be sure.

"Oh, so let's look at his adult behaviors. How about the fact that he can't be bothered to come home and take care of his family when things get rough? Yeah, Maddie, that's exactly the kind of grown up man you would want to be involved with, for sure."

His sarcasm grated on her nerves.

She rounded on him, and he nearly smacked into her when she stopped short. "Know what, Dillon? I think you need to step back a minute and realize that I'm an adult here too."

"You think I don't see that?" He reached to take her hand, but she swatted it away.

"Then stop trying to run my life. I would think you'd be happy for me. You know Ryleigh isn't exactly teeming with men lining up to marry a nearly-broke baker." She waved her hands in the air as if she might conjure up the perfect man.

"Madeleine," His voice was low, and the way he said her name slowly made her want to throw something...specifically in his direction.

"I would be more than happy for you if you were involved with anyone else. But he's not right for you."

"See, that's where you're wrong. You just *think* he's not right for me, but really, he's not right for *you*. Just because you can't get out from under his shadow, you can't imagine I might enjoy spending time with him." Madeleine knew that was a low blow, but she was so mad and the words came out before she could stop them.

Dillon had long-suffered as Luke's little brother. Teachers in school called him Luke. When Luke graduated, the town expected Dillon to carry the team to the state championships in football just like his brother had done with the baseball team. But he didn't have the passion, or the talent, for sports like Luke. Dillon went out with girls who, while they seemed interested in him, were only looking for a way to get noticed by Luke. The shadow Luke cast was long, and Dillon hated it. And it had turned to bitterness toward his brother.

Dillon stopped following her. "Wow." He raised his eyebrows and shook his head. "You're going to fight dirty over this, huh?" The scrape of the chair legs on the floor made a horrible sound. It seemed to mirror the halting screech in their argument at that very moment. Dillon sunk into the chair and rested his jaw against his balled fist.

Madeleine stared at him, guilt seeping into every fiber of her body. Her friendship with Dillon ran deep. When she'd first moved to Ryleigh, Dillon had been the one to stand up for her at school when everyone else whispered about the new girl. The year she'd finally gotten up the nerve to ask Mark to homecoming and he'd told her no, it was Dillon who took her instead. He'd even borrowed a '66 GTO convertible from a friend in the next town over, and when that engine roared in the parking lot outside the football field, it almost stole the attention away from the game altogether. Mark's face went so pale when he saw Madeleine, Dillon, Kristy, and Jake in the car together, it almost matched the white leather interior.

Dillon had been there in the fun times too. He teased her about kissing Mark a few years later. He was the first to try every new recipe she baked. He helped her move into her dorm at college, then taught her how to do shots of lemon drops (and carried her home later). And when she'd graduated from culinary school, Dillon came to graduation and cheered louder than anyone else.

But it was during the dark days when he meant the world to Madeleine. He held her hand when her mother got sick. He came to the hospital to cry with her when the doctors suggested calling hospice. After the funeral, she spent weeks in the same yoga pants, dirty hair, and barely brushed teeth, lying on the couch at her parents' house. The Bean and Batter had become a shell of the place her mother once cared for. But it was Dillon who came over that day and pushed Madeleine to get off the couch and reopen the little café, to honor her mother.

And here she stood, in the very place he encouraged her to make a success, and she had taken out the biggest bullet in her arsenal and shot it directly at him. She wanted to throw up.

"I'm sorry." She swung a chair around the table and scooted it right next to him. "That wasn't nice at all."

He didn't move. Didn't even look her way. He just kept staring straight ahead, his jaw muscles clenching over and over.

She rested her palm on his back. His muscles were so tense. "Please look at me."

He shook his head no and closed his eyes.

Remorseful tears welled up in hers.

"Dillon, please. I'm so sorry. I didn't think this whole Luke situation through, and I shouldn't have been so quick to defend him."

"It's more than Luke, Maddie."

Oh, good. We're back to Maddie again. She let out a slow breath of relief.

"You know how he nearly destroyed our family, not coming home after Dad's heart attack. Mom is trying to forgive him, but he left us to deal with that mess without him. And Dad, he's just so glad to see him now that it's like it never happened. Those two have been thick as thieves this week, and it's right back to the way it was when he when we were kids."

"I know that's tough on you." Her arms suddenly felt like sacks of flour, heavy and thick. She hadn't meant to add to his stress. Their friendship was stronger than this, and she should have known Luke's return would have been hard on Dillon.

"Yeah. And even though my shop is always busy, and I make good money, now that Luke is back, all I've heard is how successful he is, how he's gone out and made something of himself, and how I'm still stuck in Ryleigh just doing oil changes and tire rotations." He slammed his fist down on the table.

Madeleine jumped, then took a deep breath to calm herself.

"Dillon. You can't compare yourself to him. You know that. He's doing his thing, you're doing yours. The shop is doing great. I'd trade books with you any day, one business owner to another. He may be making a different impact on the world, but you're here. You're helping your parents when they need it. They know that. And they surely know it's more valuable than some fancy trips and pictures with celebrities."

"I know. But then he waltzes back in here, flashes that town celebrity smile, and even you go all weak-kneed and melt into the president of his fan club. I need you to be on my side, not his."

I mean, maybe my knees didn't exactly go weak. But that's just because we were sitting during that kiss. But this wasn't about choosing a side. "You know if it comes down to it, you'll always be my first choice, Dillon." She took a deep breath. He wasn't going to like what she had to say next. "But I also think I have the right to see where things lead with your brother."

"He doesn't even live close by. It'll never work. He's not loyal enough to manage a long-distance relationship. You'll just be some girl that he had a fling with and then tossed aside for someone new. You don't deserve that." He looked at her, and those chestnut-brown eyes were awfully hard to resist. Just like his brother's.

"Let me worry about him." She remembered Luke said the same thing to her just last night about Dillon. "I'll be fine. Besides, how long will he be here? A week? A few days?"

"He hasn't said for sure, but I have to assume it will be a short visit. You know, bigshot city boy will have to get back to work." He rolled his eyes at Madeleine.

At least he's looking at me now. Her thoughts landed on what Dillon said. *A short visit. So really, not even long enough to get too involved.* Her heart sank at the thought that he wouldn't be here long. She'd waited over a decade to be noticed by him, and now that he'd finally looked her way, he would leave before anything could happen. *I need to talk with him myself, though, and find out what his actual plans are.*

"Is he staying with you?" She almost hesitated to ask the question, but she had to know.

"Yup."

Shoot. She was hoping to avoid Dillon watching every single detail of her time with Luke. The last thing she wanted to do was to constantly wave it right in his face

The door to the café opened and a few customers started making their way to the counter. Becca, who had made herself scarce when she saw Dillon standing outside the front door, reappeared from the office and started taking orders.

"Dillon, I've got to get to work." She hated to cut this short, but she also needed time to figure things out. What her heart wanted and what her mind said were two different things.

"Yeah, I should get going." He stood up and took his sunglasses off his cap. "I shouldn't have reacted the way I did, but I just can't stand by and watch you get hurt."

She took his hand and gave it a squeeze. "You need to settle down. I'll be fine, but you have to let me handle some things on my own. Okay?"

"I guess." He headed toward the door. "Just don't fall for that smile, Maddiecakes. It's got a long line of victims behind it." He turned and hollered, "See ya 'round, Becca. Sorry for the outburst."

"Bye, Dillon," she called after him as he walked out.

Madeleine pushed the chairs back into place around their table and headed for the register. Becca was already pouring their coffee into mugs, and the samosas still needed frying.

"Guess he'd already heard about you and Luke, huh?" Becca grimaced.

"Of course he had."

"Didn't take it so well?"

"He'll be fine. I don't think Luke will be in town that long anyhow. Maybe I should rethink getting involved with him if he's just going to leave soon."

Becca wiped down the counter. "Why would you say that, Madeleine? You know just as well as I do that you deserve to date. And if someone as cute and successful as Luke Taylor is in town and interested, you'd be an idiot to turn away."

She's not wrong. It's not like I've been on tons of dates since college. "I don't know, Becca." She smirked at her friend. "Maybe to Luke, I'm just something to do while he's here. Ryleigh's bound to be boring compared to New York."

"Well, even if that's the case, why not have a little playtime?" Her smile was laced with mischief.

Madeleine grinned, then turned to grab another gallon of milk from the cooler. Becca's idea sounded a lot more appealing than she wanted to admit.

Chapter 14

Luke

Luke stared at the papers sitting in the front seat of his truck. At every red light, they called for him to look at them once again. When he'd first read The Bean and Batter's name on Emily's list, his stomach threatened to revolt. But the more he thought about it as he drove around town, the better the idea sounded. Hadn't Madeleine said something about having trouble keeping the business afloat? What better solution than a feature series, hosted by yours truly, to drum up some business?

And at the end of it all, financial burdens wouldn't worry Madeleine anymore. She could focus on what she loved about the business, helping customers and putting out great food. *If I play this right, I might come out looking like a hero here.* He smiled at the idea of fixing all of Madeleine's business problems and helping her enjoy what she loved.

He felt light as he jumped out of his truck and strolled to the door of The Bean and Batter. He couldn't wait to tell Madeleine about this project. She'd been asking about his job, and this would give her a firsthand view of everything he did. And, as if the heavens were smiling on him, he'd be doing something new for this project. He'd finally get to be on camera as the show's host. All with a beautiful girl there to support him in this new position, cheering him on the whole way. Everything was working out better than he'd expected when he'd decided a trip home was a good idea. He'd managed to get the promotion and the girl.

If only Emily weren't involved. But surely even Emily couldn't ruin something as good as this—after all, Ryleigh was *his* turf. He'd be able to keep her in check. Probably.

As he tugged on the door to go inside, Luke noticed The Bean and Batter had only a few empty tables left. Today must be a busy one for Madeleine. It was Saturday. Apparently the weekend was when business picked up. *I'll let Emily know to plan to shoot segments during the week, but get some action shots on the weekend.*

He paused at the door, searching for one thing. She stood behind the register, reaching over it to hand someone change. The customer said something he couldn't make out, but the way Madeleine laughed was beautiful, her head thrown back in complete joy, and her hand flew to her throat and then over her mouth as she did. Her laughter was big and bold, as if she didn't care who heard her. *I want her to laugh like that with me.*

She glanced up toward the door, and he caught her eye. This time, the smile was just for him. He waved, searched for an empty table, and set his bag on the chair before heading to the counter.

Madeleine was already helping the next customer in line when Luke started eyeing the case of baked goods. Looked like the apple brie scones from yesterday were sold out. Too bad, he would've liked to have another. He was still bent over, peering into the glass, when he heard her voice.

"See anything you like?"

I do, but what's on these shelves aren't really what I'm admiring right now. He looked up at her. Today she wore jeans, frayed at the knees, and a white, flowy top with lace trimming the sleeve. The way one shoulder kept falling down frustrated her as she frowned and fixed it again, but he loved it. Her hair fell over her shoulders in cascading curls, and he wanted nothing more than run his hands through them and feel its softness slip through his fingertips.

"I do, but what do you recommend?"

"Well, depends on your mood, I guess. The chocolate-hazelnut muffins are fresh, so if you want something rich, that's a good option." She pointed to the muffins under the glass dome on the countertop. "But if you want something a little more simple and sweet, I'd go with the fruit and yogurt parfait."

It was almost like she'd read his thoughts about his current relationship status. Rich? That was Emily, with all the mess, and more than he ever wanted to take on again. Simple and sweet? Well, he couldn't think of a better way to describe Madeleine. Not that she was simple. Down to earth might be a better way to describe her.

"I like the sweet things, I suppose." He pointed to the parfait in the case and reached for his wallet.

She was already shaking her hand at him. "Nope. On me. I feel like I owe you still for jumping my car, then helping me bake. You want some coffee with that too?"

"It's fine, really. I'm happy to pay for my own breakfast."

"I won't have it. My momma always said to take good care of your friends, and they'll take good care of you. Hang on, and I'll grab your coffee."

He didn't want to take advantage of her kindness because he knew she needed the funds, but he also didn't want to offend her. His thoughts drifted back to Emily's email and the envelope sitting in the front seat of his truck. If Greyson Media helped promote the bakery, she'd be free to give as much or as little food away. Once their makeover was finished, he knew she'd have no trouble stirring up enough business to make up for the occasional free meal. He'd have to tell her soon, so she could relax and enjoy running this place more.

"Madeleine, I can't just take all your food for free the whole time I'm in town."

"Who said anything about getting everything for free every day? I'm just talking about this morning, Luke Taylor, and a real Southern gentleman would just smile and say thank you. Or have you forgotten how you were raised?" Her smile was teasing, but the reminder of how he should behave did smart just a little bit.

He smiled. "Well, in that case, thank you very much." He added a wink in her direction for good measure, but not before stuffing a twenty dollar bill into the tip jar next to the register.

With the coffee in one hand and the parfait in the other, she motioned toward the table where he had left his laptop. "I'll follow you."

"At least let me carry something. I'm not totally useless, even if I did forget my manners for a minute there." He took the coffee from her hand and started walking. "Do you have a minute to sit with me? I've got something I'd like to talk to you about." His pulse quickened with anticipation.

She put the yogurt down and set a spoon on top of a napkin. "I've got a minute or two, sure." She glanced over at Becca working the espresso machine. "Becca, holler if you need me, okay?"

"Sure thing. I'm good here for now."

He sat at a table on the far side of the dining area, facing the front of the café. Madeleine hesitated and glanced toward door.

"Oh. Do you mind if I sit on that side? So I can see who is coming in while we talk?"

Luke pulled the chair next to him out and motioned toward it. "Chair's all yours."

She let out a sigh as she sat. "Becca and I make fun of people who sit on the same side of the table. You're just asking for trouble from her later."

"I think I can handle a little bit of trouble. I've been in my share of it."

It seemed strange to hope no other customers came in, because that felt like wishing failure on her day's business. But he wanted her full attention for what he was about to tell her. It could be life-changing, and he wanted to be able to enjoy her reaction.

He took a deep breath. "So, remember the other night when you were asking about my job?"

She nodded her head. "Mmm-hmm."

"Well, that's sort of not the whole story."

She leaned against the table and looked questioningly at him.

Good grief, that little tip up at the corner of her mouth is so kissable. He took a sip of coffee to refocus. "Greyson Media actually wants to produce a show right here in Ryleigh. It's going to feature some of our small businesses and the town itself. Sort of a piece of Americana at its best, you know?" He set his coffee down.

"They want to come to Ryleigh?" Her eyes were wide and bright.

She's excited. That's a good thing.

"Not they, Madeleine. We. This means a promotion for me." He smiled at her, sharing her joy.

"That's great, Luke." She put her hand on top of his, and he turned his around to take hold of it.

The way her hand fit perfectly in his felt right. Like it was exactly how they were supposed to be. As if it should always be this way. For a minute, he wanted to linger in this moment, to make it more than just a quick celebration.

Her voice was cheery and, to his delight, she didn't pull her hand back from his. "So what does this big promotion mean? What do you get to do?"

The scent of her almond shampoo wafted toward him. "I get to be the on-camera host for the show." He smiled, remembering all the other events he'd attended for Greyson Media, standing behind the camera, watching all the action but not participating. The sting of longing had been bitter at times, but now, he had his chance to change all that. "Being on camera is something I've wanted to do for a long time. It could open all kinds of doors for me."

"That's so exciting." She leaned back, but kept her fingers laced around his. "But I'm not sure I'm excited about sharing your good looks with the rest of

America. Some crazy stalker lady might come and snatch you right from me."
She waggled her eyebrows and faked a pout.

"Oh, possessive much?" he teased, even though he loved that she declared
him as hers.

"Maybe a little." She looked down and bit her lower lip, her voice softer now.
"Does that bother you?"

"Nope." He took his finger and lifted her chin. "It's actually sort of adorable."
He brushed his lips against hers, and he felt her lean in to his kiss, pressing
against his chest. *One quick kiss won't hurt her business, right?*

She smiled, eyes still closed, when she felt him pull away. "We can't do this
in front of everyone, Luke." She finally looked at him, then her glance darted
around the café.

"No one's watching. I mean, maybe those two grannies over there, but they
look more excited to talk to each other than to watch us."

She turned to look over her shoulder at the ladies. "Oh my gosh. Do you not
know who those ladies are?" She was half giggling, half horrified as she spoke.

He looked more closely, squinting to see better. They just looked like two
blue-hairs to him. Then a memory sparked to life. He could smell the detention
room all over again just by looking at these ladies. "No. Way."

Madeleine took Luke by the hand and led him to where the grannies were
seated. "Mrs. Nelson, Mrs. Blanchardt, surely you remember Luke Taylor? He's
back in town."

Luke felt his cheeks warm and pressed his lips together tightly. This could
be embarrassing. These ladies were two of the toughest teachers in school.

Mrs. Blanchardt looked up at him. "My, my. Haven't you grown up?"

"Yes, ma'am. I suppose I have." *Please remember Luke the baseball player,
not Luke the 'toilet paper the principal's office' prankster.*

Mrs. Nelson stood, a smirk on her face. "You haven't been around any toilet
paper rolls lately, have you?"

*Of course she remembers. That was a legendary prank. It took me and Jake
weeks to figure out how to get into the school overnight.* He had to smile at the
memory. "No ma'am. Not for anything unusual, that is."

"Hmm. That's too bad. All the teachers were high-fiving in the teacher's
lounge over that." Mrs. Nelson smiled. "I even gave you some bonus points on
one of your essays just for pulling off that prank. You never knew, but I chose
to ignore your horrible comma use."

Surprise registered when he realized the teachers were like regular people sometimes and enjoyed his antics a little too much. "Thanks, I suppose. I'm still a mess with commas."

Mrs. Blanchardt looked up. "You did earn that week's worth of detention, though."

He laughed. "I suppose I did, Mrs. Blanchardt. But Coach was none to happy for me to miss practice."

"I'd imagine not. It's good to catch up. I'm sure we will see you again before you leave town."

Madeleine piped up. "Yes, these two dolls come in for their morning coffee three days a week." She shot him a smile that said she was really enjoying this embarrassment. "You can count on running into them again." She headed back to their table as she spoke. "You ladies let me know if you need anything else while you're here, okay?"

Luke nodded his head to say goodbye. "Very funny," he whispered when he caught up to her.

"Careful, or I might have to offer them a cookie on the house delivered by one rebellious baseball player."

Not one to poke a bear, Luke changed the subject. "So, about this show. I've got some good news for you."

"Oh yeah?"

"They want to do a feature spot on Ryleigh's very delicious hometown bakery." He paused, gathering his courage. This was it. The moment all her problems would be solved. Nerves made him take a bite of the yogurt parfait. He swallowed, then continued, "You can share all your best recipes, like this oh-so-perfect granola, with the world."

Madeleine's whole face lit up, and she waved her hands in the air excitedly. "You're kidding, right? This publicity is just what I need to keep The Bean and Batter afloat."

"See, I was thinking that exact thing. This could solve all the financial worries for you." His words spilled out quickly, wanting to tell her everything all at once. She looked so perfect with fresh eagerness in her eyes. *I knew she would jump on this idea.* "They want to do a makeover on a business in town and yours is the perfect option."

Her smile wavered. "What do you mean a makeover?" She scanned the room, a confused look on her face. "My mother made this place what it is. I thought they wanted to see a slice of small town. Why change what they are wanting to showcase?"

He hesitated. This wasn't how he'd imagined things going. She was supposed to throw her arms around his neck in excitement and whisper a giant thank you in his ear. He tried to pivot. "I think The Bean and Batter is great, but a makeover makes great television. Everyone loves a good update to a mom and pop shop, and that's what you've got here."

He took another bite to have something to do, but struggled to swallow. Things had taken a swift, tense turn. *I thought she would be excited to freshen this place up, make it her own.*

"I don't know, Luke. Everywhere I look in this bakery, I see Mom. Changing things up in here would take all that away." She grew quiet and looked around, her index finger tapping against the table. He'd been sure this conversation would be a home run, but she'd thrown him a curve ball he couldn't hit.

Chapter 15

Madeleine

M adeleine needed to tell her dad about Luke's news quickly. Luke didn't say anything about how soon Greyson Media would be in town, but she knew how fast news spread in this town. And this wasn't your typical "Myrtle replanted all her mums yesterday and they look terrible" or "Travis had too much to drink at the bar the other night and Ali had to drive him home." This kind of gossip was guaranteed to spread like wildfire through Ryleigh and even to the towns within a fifty-mile radius in about an hour.

The town would be buzzing with excitement over the arrival of the film crew soon enough, but Madeleine wanted to be the one to tell her dad about the series. The idea of a makeover wasn't one she relished, but the extra business she couldn't afford to turn away. Her dad would give her some solid advice, and right now, that was exactly what she needed.

She'd closed up the bakery in a hurry this afternoon, knowing tomorrow would be slow and Becca could handle the tasks she left unfinished. Madeleine always took Sunday off. Becca ran the café that day on her own, since it was only open from noon to four o'clock. Since most people went to church and then home for a family meal and a nap, the bakery stayed pretty quiet. But there were always a handful of customers that still came in on Sunday for a quick snack or cup of coffee. She never knew what to do about Sundays, because she barely made enough sales to justify paying Becca and turning on the lights, but she hated to close for the whole day. Any income was good income, right?

The screen door creaked as Madeleine pushed it open. "Dad?"

He was sitting in his office, shuffling through some papers, his glasses slid down to the tip of his nose. "Hey, sugarplum." He looked up and smiled. "What are you doing here this time of day?"

She stepped around his desk and kissed him on the cheek, the familiar scent of Calvin Klein cologne reaching her nostrils. Her mother chose that scent years ago, and he still wore it every day. Even though he was getting up in his years, no one would ever know he was pushing sixty-eight. His hair, cropped short, hadn't quite gone gray so much as it did silver. She thought it made him look distinguished. His face was round and bright, with lines etched into all the places that crinkled, but only when he smiled.

"I've got some news to share, and I bet you haven't heard it yet."

"You're probably right." He set the papers down and took his glasses off. "I've been holed up in this office all afternoon doing paperwork."

"Well," she started, perching herself on the corner of his desk and crossing her legs. Her late lunch was long gone, but she would have sworn she could feel it churning around in her belly. *Just start with the basics of the company coming to town.* "You know Greyson Media?"

"The ones who are always at the fancy-dancy Hollywood elite things?"

"That's them. Only they are looking for ways to seem more relatable." *Is my little boring bakery even relatable to anyone at all? What if I come out looking like a stupid country girl and become the next viral meme that everyone makes fun of?*

"Yeah, I've heard a few reports on the news that people aren't happy with them right now."

"Right." She had also read articles online about how the giant media company had lost touch with reality, becoming nothing but a toxic stream of Hollywood trash. As if that weren't enough, rumors of fabricating stories about celebrities and their lives were coming to light in a big way. Lawsuits were being threatened, sources were going underground, and their credibility was quickly going down the drain.

She looked at the pictures scattered on her dad's shelves behind him, a tapestry of memories from growing up in a small town. Three-year-old Madeleine holding up a freshly caught catfish, her mother's senior picture from high school, complete with 1970's winged eyeliner, Mark and Madeleine at Homecoming her senior year, where she wore her mum proudly even though it was almost bigger than she was. Their little life here in Ryleigh stayed simple and easy. Greyson Media might change that.

Nope, they definitely would change that. *Do I want to bring that kind of change to our town?*

She argued with herself, countering that she wasn't the one bringing them here. Luke was. She had a chance to be a part of a show that would let America see what makes a small town so wonderful. Not country and backward. Not to mention, she'd be helping Luke make a big career move. *Rip the band aid off. Just tell him what's going on.* "So they are going to come to Ryleigh and film a reality show. Sort of a 'slice of small town USA' piece and they are going to focus on some of the small businesses here. Trying to win back the 'everyman' viewer, you know?"

He rubbed his chin and nodded. "Sounds fun. I'm sure there'll be plenty of ladies in town who'll have something to say about being on a national television show."

She laughed, "Mrs. Brumbelow will be itching for a shopping trip to Dallas as soon as she hears. She'll need a new wardrobe for sure."

"Poor Joe. That's a lot of barbecue sandwiches to sell." He sat back in his chair. The way he grinned at his daughter, it was like he knew what was coming next. *He looks a little bit...is that excitement on his face?* Madeleine wondered if that might be the way she felt, too, but couldn't quite be sure.

He snapped his fingers in the air like he'd just been struck with a bright idea. "Maybe they'll do a spotlight on his place. That would help sell some brisket for sure."

She pursed her lips into a pout. "Dad, you've already figured it out, haven't you?" He always seemed to be one step ahead of her thoughts, even when she had a surprise in mind.

"What? I just thought a special show on Joe's would be a nice pick-me-up for his business." He spread his arms wide and pretended innocence, but his smile gave him away.

"Oh, alright then. They're wanting to do a special on The Bean and Batter."

He stood and gave her a hug. "What? That's amazing news. I would've never guessed that."

She rolled her eyes. "Mmm Hmm. Sure."

"You know I'm teasing." He headed into the kitchen. "I really do think that's great, darlin'. Are they going to pay you for it?"

She followed him, but his question took her by surprise and she stopped. "Huh. Didn't think to ask that question. I'll call Luke and find out."

"Who's Luke?" He took two glasses out of the cabinet and filled them with ice cubes.

Her heart jumped around in her chest when she realized she would have to talk to her dad about a grown man. A grown man she'd kissed only yesterday while sitting in the bakery her mother built. She grabbed a pitcher and started scooping sugar into it. "Luke Taylor. He works for Greyson Media now." *That seemed nonchalant enough.* She tossed some teabags into a glass measuring cup and filled it with water.

"Dillon's big brother? The baseball slugger?"

"That's the one." The microwave beeped as she pressed the two-minute button and hit start. "He's in town checking things out before the rest of the filming crew gets here."

"I'm surprised I'm just now hearing this. You'd think having Luke Taylor back in town would have everyone talking."

"Dad, you'd have to get out and visit with people to know what's going on."

"I get out. I went grocery shopping just yesterday. Got that sugar you're using right now."

"Did you get anything healthy, though? Maybe some lettuce for a salad?"

He wrinkled his nose. "Do I look like a rabbit?"

She dropped her chin at him. "You look like someone who may like a salad if he'd try it."

"Salads were your mom's thing. I'm good with my turkey sandwiches." They were just now able to talk about her mom without stopping the whole conversation to remember how much her loss hurt. It still stung, but at least any mention of her didn't end in awkward silence. That was good progress. Healing progress. But she did worry it also meant her mother was slipping slowly out of not just their conversations, but their memories.

"You could put lettuce on your sandwich, then."

"Yeah, I could. But then it'd be ruined."

The microwave beeped, and Madeleine pulled the brewed tea out and dumped it into the pitcher.

"Spoon?" Her dad handed her a wooden spoon, and she stirred until the sugar dissolved.

"Thanks. But back to Luke." *I don't have to tell him everything, but I will need to at least tell him that we are spending time together. He's sure to find out soon enough.* She added more water to the pitcher until it was full and gave it one more good stir.

"Right. I'd rather talk about anything other than my veggie eating habits."

"Yeah, well, the veggie conversation would be a short one, since you don't have any habits except avoiding."

"I eat potatoes and corn. What else does a man need?" He handed her the glasses.

She poured a glass of tea and handed it to her dad. *I'll make some zucchini muffins this week for him. Maybe that will convince him to eat a little bit of something green.*

"Oh, I don't know. Just maybe something green every so often. It's good for you."

"Bah. Vegetables are overrated. I'm doing just fine." He pointed toward the front door. He always liked to sit on the porch and visit. Madeleine felt the same. She always found she stayed about an hour longer than she meant to when they sat out there to talk.

The chairs outside were comfortable, like they invited you to sit and stay for a lifetime. Her parents bought these chairs when her mom got the cancer diagnosis. She'd wanted to stay and sit on her porch as much as possible, 'watching the world go by as she enjoyed it with the love of her life,' she'd said. It still felt strange sitting in her mom's chair, but Madeleine also loved giving her dad someone to visit with.

"So Luke's in town, he's filming this new show, and it's going to be about you?"

"Not about me, Dad. About the bakery."

He took his first sip of the tea, and stared into the glass afterward. "That's just like your momma used to make."

Madeleine's heart squeezed a little bit. "She's the one who taught me."

"Well, they can't feature The Bean and Batter without including you in it."

She blushed. "I suppose." *I haven't really thought about that. I guess I'll have to be on camera, too.* She wasn't sure how she felt about being on camera next to someone as gorgeous as Luke. She was sure she'd look extra plain standing by him. "I might need to schedule a shopping trip in Dallas along with Mrs. B, then." She laughed.

"You're beautiful the way you are. Don't go presenting yourself as someone you're not. America will love you just as much as Ryleigh already does."

Oh. Her heart jumped into her throat at this new thought. She hadn't taken time to realize she'd be under all kinds of scrutiny, and she could only hope it would be positive. "You're sweet, Dad. But it's still a big deal to put myself out there for the world to judge. I'm trusting Luke to make sure it's all on the up and up." And a new weight started to settle on her shoulders. *What if he doesn't do that? Or maybe he can't do that? Surely the fact that they want good press means this show will be happy and fun, right?* She hoped so, but the worry showed no signs of shrinking.

"Yes, back to Luke. You keep mentioning him."

He's already figured that little part out, too. Can't fool him even for a minute. She smiled. "I suppose." She took a sip of tea, delaying the task of going public with her...relationship? Could she even call it that? Probably not. Not yet anyhow. The inevitable task of telling her dad that she and Luke were spending time together for more than just planning the show loomed. If she closed her eyes for a minute, she could feel his lips on hers all over again.

"Anything you'd like to share that your smile isn't already sharing?"

She laughed softly. "You know me too well, don't you?"

"Your momma used to say the same thing." He shrugged. "It's my gift."

"I guess you've figured out that Luke and I have spent a little bit of time together."

"Yeah, that look on your face gave you away. Looks like your momma did when she first met me."

Madeleine rolled her eyes. "He's a nice guy. Grown up into a good man, I think."

"Seems like he must be doing okay for himself," he said with a shrug of his shoulders. "I'd imagine his momma and daddy are still pretty proud of him. I would be."

"Yeah. This gig is a big deal for him too. He's finally able to be on camera as the host of the show, so he's excited about it."

"That's good. But I guess I'd have to wonder what a bigshot from New York City would be hoping for by getting involved with you, Maddie. You might want to be careful with your heart if that boy isn't willing to stick around here."

She sighed, then took another sip of tea. The sugar spread over her tongue like balm on a wound. Her momma's sweet tea fixed everything. But it couldn't make Luke stay in Ryleigh forever. He would eventually go back to New York, and she'd be right back where she was, running a bakery and trying to find a way to pay her bills.

"I know." The answer stuck in her throat. If she were ever going to be honest with anyone about anything, it was her dad.

"And Maddie?" His voice was soft now, like he had more hard things to say. "Have you thought about Dillon?"

Yeah, I have, Dad. But he's a grown man, and I don't have to baby him.

She opted to keep that opinion to herself. Even though it was true, she didn't think her dad would appreciate the idea that Dillon wouldn't be her first priority. He hadn't exactly kept it a secret that he hoped she and Dillon would eventually end up together.

"Dad, you know Dillon and I are just friends."

Now it was his turn to have another gulp of sweet tea and think. He stared out at the front lawn, with its brown-hued leaves falling onto the grass.

"I know. I just want you to make good choices. Finding a friendship like the one you have with Dillon is rare. Don't throw it all away just because his handsome older brother came back into town."

That stung a little, the fact that her dad would even entertain the thought that she would be so flippant about her friendship with Dillon. "I know, Dad. I won't." She knew Dillon was, at best, uncomfortable with her new relationship, and he didn't deserve to be pushed aside. He'd had too much experience of being caught in his big brother's shadow already.

But shouldn't he be happy for her? Shouldn't he be glad she'd found someone who liked her for more than just her smile as she served up a croissant? Walking this line between the Taylor brothers made her feel like a dough that had been overworked. And experience taught her, better than anything else, overworked dough never rises to its full potential, no matter how warm the oven gets.

The glass was cool against her lips as she drank her sweet tea, but it offered no comfort at the hot bitterness she felt.

Chapter 16

L uke opened his laptop and clicked his email icon. Unsurprisingly, at the top sat an email from Emily. *She's never been one to stall out on a project.* It had been a long time since he'd been excited to work on a project with Emily. But today, he appreciated her drive to get going. Once she got hold of an idea, she moved forward with lighting speed and anyone else on the project could only hope to stay caught up. Getting in front of the camera, plus helping Madeleine couldn't happen fast enough for Luke now.

Her email was to the point. She needed pictures of The Bean and Batter to pass to the designers, who would start the process of ordering materials for the makeover. And could he possibly send measurements of the building space, including ceiling height, sometime today?

Even though the makeover conversation wasn't exactly a home run, Madeleine had truly been thrilled for his promotion. That was a nice change from Emily, who would have reacted with jealousy at his success. *You've got to stop letting Emily invade your mind.* It seemed like every time he had thoughts about work, Emily came hand-in-hand with them.

Theirs was an easy relationship in the beginning. She didn't work in the media department of Greyson Media. She was a project manager in the graphic design department. The night they met, she took his breath away. Standing near the door in a white fringe dress, she looked like an angel waiting to cause trouble. The length of her skirt certainly invited ideas Luke knew no angel would appreciate.

She was quick to appreciate his softer approach to life, a product of his small town raising. She was bold, always ready to drag him to the next art gallery opening or hottest new bistro. Her social media game was nothing to play at, and she loved to be seen in all the hottest locales. It never hurt that he was good arm candy for her. But he'd happily gone along, hoping the exposure would launch his on-camera career. It wasn't long before he realized she was more interested in climbing the career ladder than tending to their relationship. And, while he hated to admit it, he had used her to further his own exposure as well.

I suppose we both kept our focus on the wrong things. Using Emily wasn't something that made Luke proud, but it did open doors for both of them. Besides, she was fun to be around, always the life of the party.

He knew the party girl wasn't going to like Ryleigh. One look at Main Street and she'd spin on her designer stiletto heels and head for the nearest big city. *She'll not like the three-hour commute from Dallas.* Gearing up for Emily's arrival wasn't something Luke looked forward to, knowing she'd have to stay in town at the Lamplight Inn. He could already hear her complaints about the chintzy wallpaper and outdated furniture. It would be nonstop.

And what would happen when Emily met Madeleine? Always looking for a contest, his ex would never step to the side and watch another woman snuggle up to her trophy of a man, even if she had discarded him already. The two women couldn't be more different.

The idea of telling Madeleine about his previous relationship made his stomach flip. She was too sweet and would buckle under Emily's manipulation. If Emily caught any whiff of a relationship between Luke and Madeleine, retaliation would almost certainly follow. For Emily, nothing was off the table. She could ruin the bakery makeover, the show, or anything else that came in front of her. Their breakup had been mutual, but Emily still seemed to think she had some level of possession over him. Madeleine wouldn't be any sort of match for Emily. *I can't let Madeleine get hurt by this.*

His phone buzzed. Madeleine's name came up on the screen, and he nearly dropped the phone in his excitement.

He cleared his throat as he answered, "Hey, I was just thinking about you."

"Oh really? I was just talking about you."

"And who were you talking with?" *Please not Dillon. I still need to sort things out with him when he gets home from work.* He glanced at the clock. Seven-twenty-two in the evening. His brother would be walking in the door any minute now. And not in a good mood, either. Saturdays were always busy days at the shop, and he was bound to be tired. A lifetime of experience with his little brother had taught Luke one thing—a tired Dillon meant a cranky Dillon.

"My dad. I wanted to bounce this makeover idea off him to see what he thought."

He smiled at the light tone in her voice. Hoping for the best, he had to know more. "Well, you don't sound too upset, so can I assume Mr. Malone says it's a go?" The line was silent for a moment, causing a second of panic. "Hello?"

"Oh, sorry. I was thinking. Well, he didn't discourage it, if that's what you mean. I'm still not convinced I want to get into this, though." The hesitation in her voice couldn't be missed.

His heart went from pounding anticipation to deadened disappointment. "I promise I'll be there every step of the way, making sure it all goes the way you want."

Her sigh was so heavy, her worry came through the phone. "I want to trust that, really. But this is a big risk for me."

The front door slammed shut. Dillon threw his keys onto the table where Luke had papers spread from one end to the other. "Going to shower." Dillon's words were short, and he barely made eye contact as he passed.

Just as I expected. Grumpy Dillon. Tonight wouldn't go any smoother than this morning. Luke turned his attention back to his phone conversation.

"I'm not even sure I know what kind of look I want the bakery to have. I like it the way it is. It feels like Mom in there." The wistful tone of her voice only strengthened Luke's resolve to reassure her. If he had to battle Emily over anything on this makeover, this would be the one sword Luke would fall on.

"We can work that out together. Trust me, this is going to be great for you and the bakery. It could open doors you never thought possible."

"I suppose. But I'm counting on you to fight for my business. I don't know what I'd do if I lost it."

His throat was so dry. He reached for his lemonade and tried to swallow, but it went down like sludge. *I'm not sure I have enough clout to say this, but here goes.* "I promise, everything will be fine. Are you home yet?"

"Still driving home from Dad's."

"Okay, drive safe. Do you work tomorrow?"

"Nope. I have Sundays off."

His mood lifted, but only slightly. He could spend the day with her tomorrow, convince her that he really was in her corner. Greyson Media would be a good thing, would make things easier for her. He could be the hero in all of this if he could get her to see that.

"Perfect. Can I pick you up then? Maybe we could..." He had no idea what to do in Ryleigh on a Sunday. The town nearly shut down that day, because old Southern traditions were still strong here. Church, Sunday afternoon dinner, nap, and then leftovers for supper was standard Ryleigh Sunday agenda. That hadn't changed. As a matter of fact, his parents would likely expect him and Dillon both to come eat tomorrow after church at their house.

"Could what?" Madeleine prompted.

He laughed as he answered, "I actually have no idea what to do on a Sunday in Ryleigh."

"Ah. Well, it's not exactly the busy city you're used to."

"Not really, no." He heard the shower shut off. Any excitement he might have had about taking Madeleine out tomorrow vanished when he realized he'd have to deal with Dillon over it.

"Tell you what. You come get me around two, and I'll handle the rest. Okay?"

"Sounds like a plan. Or at least a start to one."

"See you tomorrow." At least he sounded happy. Maybe some of the dark clouds over the makeover could fizzle away eventually.

"Okay. Good night." He clicked the call off and set his phone down. He needed to answer a few more emails and send Greyson some of his ideas for episodes. But first, this business with Dillon needed to be squared away.

"Hey Dil? You busy?" He leaned back in his chair to peer down the hallway to Dillon's room. The door was shut. "Dillon?" he shouted, louder this time.

His door flew open. "What?" he shouted back, a towel tied around his waist and a shirt in his hands.

"We gotta talk."

He rolled his eyes and kicked his door shut with his heel as he retreated into the bedroom.

Wow. An actual shut out. He'd hoped for an easier start, but that was definitely not in the cards. Luke stood and started down the hallway. "I'm serious. Let's get this worked out."

"Nope. Nothin' to work out, big bro. Just like always." His voice was muffled through the closed door, but the hostility came through loud and clear.

His jaw tightened. "What's that supposed to mean?"

"Don't wanna get into it tonight, dude. I'm tired."

"Well, that's too bad. Man up and come out here." He reached for the doorknob, but the door flew open.

Dillon finished buttoning his jeans then shoved past his brother and headed into the kitchen.

Not a word, huh? Time for a different approach. "How was work?"

"Work? You know you don't want to talk about my day."

True. "Alright, fine. I want to talk about Madeleine."

Dillon slammed the jug of lemonade onto the counter. He flung the cabinet door open and grabbed a glass, then poured himself a drink. After three swallows, he looked at Luke. "I know."

"You know what?"

"That you want to talk about Maddie. But I don't."

Luke stood straighter. He had always been bigger than his brother, and even now that they were grown men, Dillon was still a good two inches shorter. "Well, that's what we're going to do. Like it or not."

"Look. I talked with Maddie, and she's not all that interested."

Luke let out a quick huff of disbelief at the ridiculous statement. "That's a load of bull and you know it."

"Okay, well, I'm not interested in seeing her get hurt."

A sharp prick of offense traveled up Luke's spine. "Dillon. You don't know what you're talking about. I've got her best interests in mind."

"What, by coming into town, sweeping her off her feet, then leaving? That sounds like a great way to protect her, Luke. By all means, I won't get in the way of that genius plan." He finished his lemonade, then set the cup into the sink.

"It's not that simple. I don't know what is down the road for Madeleine and me, but this feels different than anything else. She's different." The certainty in his voice surprised him.

"Damn right she is. She's incredible." Dillon stared at Luke with an intensity he'd never seen before. For a moment, he even considered backing down and letting his little brother have this win. But that moment was fleeting. Too much was at stake to let Dillon have his way in this situation.

He needed a different approach. "I know." *There. That's the honest truth. She is incredible, and he needs to know I see that.* "And that's why I would never do anything to hurt her."

Dillon stared back at him. "Maybe she doesn't know who she's getting involved with."

Again, the vitriol in his brother's comments stung, but Luke couldn't worry about himself right now. This was about Madeleine. "She's a grown woman, Dillon. You have to respect her enough to let her make her own choices."

Dillon pulled out a chair from the table and sat. He surveyed the mess of papers strewn into piles and picked one up and read it.

Luke waited for his response, but only silence came. He leaned against the refrigerator and crossed his legs at the ankle. *I'll wait it out.* His brother never was good with change, and to assume he'd shift his thinking in one day was a lot to ask.

Dillon picked up another paper and started reading it. Then another. And another.

Luke stood, not moving, but watched silently. The scowl on his brother's face slowly melted away, as he concentrated on each word he read.

Finally, Dillon asked, "What is all this about?"

There it is. The question I needed him to ask. "It's a new project I'm working on. Greyson Media is doing a new show about small towns in America, and they're featuring Ryleigh for the premiere season."

"Does Maddie know?" He continued to scan the pages.

"She does. I think it will be really good for the town. They're going to feature The Bean and Batter."

"And she's excited?" He finally looked at his brother, a mixture of worry and hesitation splayed on his face. "She thinks this is a good idea?"

"She does." *Well, mostly.*

"Okay then. You're right. She's a smart girl." He cracked a tiny smile, just barely lifting the corner of his mouth. "Too smart to get involved with you, anyhow. You go ahead and see if you can win her over." He stood up and crossed to Luke. With one swift punch to his bicep, he added as he walked out of the room, "My money's on her brains, not your looks, big brother."

Chapter 17

Madeleine

Church seemed to drag on this morning. Seated in her usual space, next to her dad, Madeleine tried to focus on the sermon. But instead of taking good notes, she found herself doodling flowers and vines around the borders of her Bible journal.

She trudged through Sunday dinner, and while she loved the time with her dad, she just couldn't engage like usual.

Her dad noticed. When it came time to clean the kitchen, he shooed her out of the room to go home and freshen up. She protested, albeit half-heartedly, but he insisted, saying she was "As jumpy as a cricket on a coffee bean." One quick kiss on the cheek for him and she bolted for the door.

The clock read 1:53 p.m. She'd already changed into jeans and a t-shirt, freshened her makeup, and thrown her hair into a ponytail. Now all there was to do was pace in her living room. Luke had never been to her house, and she found herself straightening the same things over and over again. She rearranged the pillows on the couch. She turned the vase of flowers another quarter turn one more time. *Oh, for cupcake's sake, Madeleine. Leave it alone.*

A knock relieved her of the flower positioning dilemma, and she half skipped across the living room before she made herself slow down. Smoothing her ponytail into a slick drape at the back of her neck, she opened the door.

There he was. His navy button-down only served to make his athletic build look even more perfect than he had in a T-shirt. And was he wearing *cowboy boots*? She always had been a sucker for a man in jeans, a button-down, and boots. Sleeves rolled up to the elbow, hands shoved into his pockets, he was the picture-perfect date.

Gracious and mercy, I'm going out with Luke Taylor. Like a real, live 'he is picking me up at my house and everything' kind of date. It still shocked her.

"You look nice." His gaze slid over her, starting at her head and working his way down to her tennis-shoe-clad feet.

Standing next to this gorgeous man, Madeleine suddenly wished she had dressed up more. At least a cute blouse, rather than a plain pink T-shirt. "Thanks." *Think fast, you can fix this.* "I rushed over from Dad's after church and haven't had time to change. Can you wait?"

He spread his arms wide. "Sure." He looked at the chairs on the porch. "Want me to wait out here?"

"What? No. I mean—" she stepped to the side. "Come on in. You can wait inside. Just in here is fine." *Shut up, Maddie.*

He let out a little chuckle and shook his head. "So I guess I'll come in then?"

"Yep." She managed to compose herself enough to let him pass, and as she did, his scent of leather and sage was so masculine it made her head swim. And it was so...him. "I'll just be a minute. There's sweet tea in the fridge and glasses above the toaster. Help yourself."

She practically sprinted up the stairs to her bedroom, where she threw open her closet doors and peered inside for anything that (a) fit, (b) didn't need ironing, and (c) didn't look like she had just finished doing housework. She saw a white sweater folded on a shelf and grabbed it. *I hate white. I'll probably spill something down the front with my luck.* Throwing it on the bed, she looked again. *Aha.* She reached for the gray Queen t-shirt and slipped it over her head and remembered a photo she'd seen on the cover of one of the fashion magazines in the grocery store checkout line. There was supermodel Julie Scott dressed in a T-shirt with a jacket over it, looking put together but not with a lot of fuss and effort. Madeleine added her camel blazer over the top, cuffed the sleeves, and hoped for the best.

Stopping to check her look in the mirror to throw on some big gold hoop earrings, she actually liked what she saw. *This isn't terrible at all.* Satisfied with her look, she bounced down the stairs and into the kitchen.

Luke was already sipping the sweet tea and looking at her photos on the front of the refrigerator. He gulped down his drink when he saw her. "Whoa. That's a cute look."

She did a little spin. "Thanks. Just something I threw together in no time." *Literally.* "I see you found the tea."

"Sure did. This might be some of the best sweet tea I've ever had. But don't go telling my mom I said so. Her sweet tea is her pride." The way his eyes sparkled with mischief made her smile.

"Every good Southern woman takes pride in her sweet tea. But your secret's safe with me." She moved next to him to get a glass of her own. He reached up to get the glass down for her. "Thanks." He was close, nearly leaning into her shoulder. The way her heart was fluttering, she wasn't sure she'd get through the night.

They'd been this close yesterday in the bakery, but in such a public place, it hadn't seemed quite so intimate there. But now, standing in her kitchen, just the two of them, it felt different. Electric almost.

"I put the tea back in the fridge," he said, searching her face. He brought his arm down from the upper cabinet and held the glass just above her head. She reached for the glass, but he lifted it higher. "I'll get it. Want some ice?"

Um, yes. I could use something to cool down. She came back to her senses and turned to get the pitcher. "Yes, please."

He filled her glass with ice and poured the tea. When he handed it to her, the cold radiated over her fingertips. She wanted to press the tea against her forehead to calm her currently overheating self. She could only hope that she still looked put together, not like a soufflé about to collapse in on itself. She headed into the living room, adding a little extra sway to her hips as he followed her.

"My momma taught me how to make the tea. Mine's never quite the same as hers, though." She sat on the overstuffed armchair. *Maybe not the couch for now. A little separation is good. It's still early, and we haven't even left the house yet.* "I swear, we could be making two pitchers side by side and hers would always come out better. Daddy always said it was because she was extra sweet."

Luke sat on the front edge of the sofa, his leg bobbing up and down, looking like he was ready to pounce on something. "Well, then I don't see how you could be at a disadvantage. You're about as sweet as they come, Madeleine Malone."

She felt her cheeks warm at his compliment and took a sip of tea to hide her blush. The ice-cold liquid felt nice as it went down, and she swallowed more than what her momma had taught her a lady should.

"So, are you going to fill me in on the plans for this afternoon, or do I have to guess all day?"

"Hmmm. Maybe I should keep you guessing." She tapped her finger against her lips playfully.

He put on a fake pout. "That's not nice."

"But fair is fair. You took me on a picnic at the baseball field without telling me. So, I think I deserve a day of secrets."

"As I remember, that picnic ended up being a nice evening. Don't you agree?" He grinned at her, a twinkle in his eye as he leaned in her direction, resting his elbows on his knees.

She remembered the way his hand pressed against the back of her neck when he had brought her closer to him, the cool breeze blowing strands of hair against her cheek. It had definitely been a nice evening. Perfect, she might even add. "I'd say we enjoyed ourselves, yes." She winked across the room at him.

He finished his tea with one quick swig. "Then let's get to it. I can't wait to see if Ryleigh's changed all that much since I left. I can't imagine where you're taking me on a sleepy Sunday afternoon, but since we're taking my truck, I'll need to know where to drive."

"Well, the choices were limited. But I thought maybe bowling could be fun?" She cringed. Now that she said it out loud, it sounded completely lame. True, it wasn't the most exciting thing, but Luke was right. Ryleigh wasn't exactly booming with things to do, especially on a Sunday.

He laughed. Not a little polite chuckle but a full-on belly laugh. "Bowling? You're kidding." He reached over and took her tea glass and headed to the kitchen. "I haven't been bowling since high school."

His laugh billowed with excitement, not mockery, much to Madeleine's relief. "Good. Maybe you're a little rusty, and I'll have a chance at winning. I do tend to beat Dillon most of the time."

She instantly regretted bringing up his brother. But the more time she spent with Luke, the less she wanted to worry about Dillon. *He's got to trust me. Actually, he has to trust Luke too. That's the real issue.* She wondered if the boys had talked about her. She had a feeling they had. She could only hope Dillon would come around eventually. Once he saw how happy Luke made her, surely he would understand. But that didn't make things any easier right now.

Chapter 18

Luke

The bowling alley was loud. And surprisingly busy. But it looked exactly the way Luke remembered it. And smelled the same. That mix of sweat, cheap pizza, and aerosol cleaner assaulted his nostrils the minute he held the door open for Madeleine.

Maybe I should've suggested this place for the makeover show.

Madeleine marched to the counter. "Size seven, please." She turned to him and eyeballed his cowboy boots. "Those'll have to come off."

"Yup." He shrugged. His palms rested on the counter, still wrapped in the same scratchy carpet he remembered as having been there forever.

She playfully bumped against his side with her shoulder. "That's a shame. Something about a man in cowboy boots just..." Her voice was low and quiet, and against the racket of the room, he had to lean closer to catch what she said. But he didn't miss the cute wiggle of her eyebrows.

He smiled, his mouth not far from hers. *It would be so easy to kiss her right now.* "Just what?" He leaned closer and pressed his lips to the tiny space just behind her earlobe. Just soft enough and fast enough to catch the scent of vanilla and lavender.

"Just makes me want to..." Her cheeks went pink, and she let the most adorable giggle escape her lips instead of finishing her sentence.

"Sir? What size shoe for you?" The girl working the counter set a pair of blue and red size sevens down on the counter, and Luke had never been so irritated at an interruption in his life. He really wanted to hear the end of that sentence.

He looked up to see a high school girl, curly hair dripping around her face and bubble gum smacking in her mouth. "Twelve and a half, please."

The girl nodded, grabbed shoes for Luke, and said, "That'll be thirty-six dollars. You're on lane four."

He reached for his wallet in his back pocket, handed the girl two twenty dollar bills, then took his shoes and change.

"Thanks," Madeleine said as they headed to their lane.

"I can't remember the last time I paid forty dollars for a date. Things in New York are a little different."

She sat down and kicked off her Chuck Taylors. "Are you calling me a cheap date?"

He sputtered. "Of course not." He pressed his toes against the heel of his right boot, working it off. "Well, my date, yes. Cheap no." *Was that clever, or stupid?*

With their bowling shoes on and names entered into the computer, they were ready to roll. Madeleine picked out a ball from the rack behind the lane and stepped around him as he chose his own.

He set his ball into the ball return and turned back to his date. "Ladies first." Luke pointed to the awaiting pins at the end of the late and grinned. "Good luck."

"Pssht. I don't need luck."

She held her ball in front of her with two hands and sauntered to the end of the lane. *Those jeans fit well.* He had to admit, bowling was starting to look like a fantastic idea.

The ball hit the floor of the lane and glided right down the center with a force that made Luke nervous. She didn't even turn around until the strike was complete, all pins scattered and rolling on their sides.

"Ha! Told you so," she said. She was beaming with victory when she turned to him, both arms extended and fingers pointing at him like two guns blazing.

"Watch out there. You haven't seen me bowl yet." He hoped he remembered how, but he did remember bowling wasn't exactly his forte. Not only would he embarrass himself, but he'd also lose the game, something he made a habit to avoid at all costs. Even bowling. *No gutter balls.*

As if she were reading his thoughts, she called, "Want me to put the bumpers up?"

"Very funny," he said over his shoulder as he stepped up onto the slick wood floor. The sound of pins crashing in the lane next to him only made him more nervous. *Great. Everyone around me is bowling strikes.* He could only hope to not make a total fool of himself.

He took three good strides toward the line, making sure his thumb was pointed straight ahead at the looming pins.

"Gutter ball," came a cough from behind him. It was enough to make him smile, but not enough to make his ball roll into the dreaded gutter.

He watched it roll and knock over seven pins, leaving three standing like soldiers, guarding the left side of the lane. He turned, and Madeleine was grinning at him. "Can I get you some water for that cough?"

She batted her eyes at him and folded her hands demurely in front of her. "Why, whatever do you mean?" The way she played innocent made him want to sweep her into his arms right here in front of everyone and kiss her silly. High school Luke would have, but it would have been out of cocky immaturity. He wasn't here to conquer another conquest. Madeleine wasn't just any girl. She deserved someone mature, who treated her with the respect she deserved.

"I mean that little cough," he started slowly. "It sounded serious. Maybe I need to take you home?" He stepped closer.

"I have no idea what you're talking about. I feel great." She shifted to the side and pointed to his ball coming back up the return. "I think you've got a frame to finish. I'd hate to distract you."

Too late. He smirked. "Mmm-hmm. That would be a shame."

He took his ball and to his relief, managed to take down the last three pins. She was already standing at the front of the seats, hand raised and ready for a high five.

"Nicely done."

"Thanks. I see you've recovered from your cough."

Frame after frame, she scored higher and higher. His game wasn't anything to scoff at, but he never seemed able to pull ahead. Even against a pretty girl, his competitive nature wouldn't let him ease up on trying to win, and the loss stung more than it should have for a date.

"Had enough or want to play another game?" she asked, when he'd finished his last frame. She looked cute in her T-shirt, sitting with her legs stretched in front of her and crossed at the ankles. She'd gotten hot on about the fourth frame, and her jacket sat crumpled in the seat next to her. Her shirt clung to her curves perfectly. *It's a shame she'll put that jacket back on when we go outside.*

He laughed and took a drink of his Dr. Pepper. "Up to you. This is your date to plan, remember?"

"I did have some other thoughts in mind, if you're game."

"I'm always game. You tell me where to drive, and I'll go anywhere you say."
Whoa, that sounded more serious than I meant.

"Wow. Well, I wasn't thinking of anything that special." She slid her bowling shoes off and her Chuck Taylors back on just as the crash of another bowler's strike filled the air. "What about somewhere quieter? You can tell me more about your life in New York."

He tugged his boots on. "Sure." *That would mean more talk about work. And Emily. We'll need to talk about her before she comes into town.* That wasn't exactly how he wanted this date to go.

"Are you hungry?"

He glanced at his watch. Four-thirty. Not really late enough to eat dinner. In New York, no one ate until after eight at night. But this wasn't New York. "I could eat, yeah," he lied.

"Maybe something light. There's a great new little Italian place over in Seneca. They make the best bruschetta. Mind a little bit of a drive?"

Seneca was the next closest town, only about twenty minutes away. A twenty-minute cab ride in New York was nothing to him, but that was only a few blocks away. "I think I can manage that." He scooped up both of their shoes and returned them to bubble-gum girl, who barely looked up as she took them.

"Thanks," she answered, popping her gum to punctuate her nonexistent enthusiasm.

Madeleine waited until they were out of earshot and said, "I don't think she knows she's just talked with *the* Luke Taylor, legendary hometown baseball star." She knocked her elbow against his jokingly as they walked outdoors.

The night air was a refreshing change from the stale bowling alley. "Probably because she was so taken by Madeleine Malone, bowler extraordinaire. You left her speechless."

"That must be it." She climbed into the truck, and he shut the door for her.

He hurried around and jumped into the driver's seat. "Seneca, you said?" The last time he'd been in Seneca, he'd had a different girl in the front seat. She'd thought it would be fun to swim in the lake, but Luke didn't indulge her. He was busy thinking about getting back home before Dillon and Madeleine's movie ended, so he could hopefully tell her goodnight as she left his house.

There'd be no swimming in Seneca's lake tonight, either. Texas didn't have much of a winter, but the temperatures were too cool for swimming anywhere other than a hot tub.

Madeleine shivered in the seat next to him and pulled her jacket around her.

"Cold?" he turned the temperature up.

"Some frosty air has really blown in this week, hasn't it?"

He'd been in New York for too long. "This isn't even chilly. You haven't felt cold until you've had a blast of arctic air blow between the buildings in New York this time of year."

"Well, this Texas girl isn't used to this. I'm not sure I'd make it in a New York winter."

"I'm not sure I'd make it in a Texas summer anymore." He could still remember how stifling it could be to climb into his truck on a one-hundred-and-three-degree day. It was near impossible to inhale in that kind of heat.

"I've got the perfect plan, then. Summers in New York, winters in Texas."

His heart rate leapt into a higher gear at her proposal for a future together, whether she was serious or not. "For me or you?"

"You, of course. I couldn't leave my bakery for the summer. I don't know what I'd do without it."

That sinking feeling in his stomach returned. He had to convince her to agree to the makeover. He'd already given Grey and Emily the go-ahead, never thinking Madeleine might say no. What he had originally thought would be a solution to all her financial worries, he now realized would be a devastation to her entire lifestyle. *Can I be a part of that? I'm not sure I want that attached to my name.*

He swallowed. It would be hard, uncomfortable even, but it had to be done. "Hey, so, I was wondering if you'd thought any more about the makeover show?" His voice was too bright. Too cheerful. She'd know he was hiding something. *She has to see how this is a great business decision.*

She twisted in her seat to look directly at him. "I have."

He kept his eyes on the road to avoid her gaze. "And?"

She didn't answer right away. He gripped the steering wheel tightly waiting for her to reply. If she said yes, his career would be on the trajectory he'd worked toward for years. But she'd lose the independence he didn't realize she valued so much. But if she said no, he could lose the whole project and would return to New York with egg all over his face. Egg courtesy of the town's cutest, but unaware, baker.

Madeleine could lose her bakery either way.

Luke risked a side glance to her face, trying to read her thoughts. Her eyes were closed, her lips pursed.

Finally, she shook her head and answered softly, "I'm not sure I'm ready to have the whole world watch while I tear apart what my mother built." She gently eased his hand off the steering wheel and, with fingers laced through his, rested it on his thigh. "I know how much this opportunity means to you, Luke. I'm trying to get on board, but it's not that simple."

His stomach dropped with a heavy, hard, thud of sadness. She didn't trust him, and he had to make her see how much he cared about her bakery and keeping it as nostalgically charming as ever.

He eased the truck over onto the shoulder and put it into park before twisting in his seat to look directly at her. "I would never ask you to do anything you weren't comfortable with. I agreed with Greyson to select your bakery because of you and your mother's devotion to it. Forget about my part in this project."

"But I'll have to live with the fact that I slowed down your career. I'm not okay with doing that to you, either."

"Listen," he took both of her hands in his. "I'll be fine either way. If Greyson Media believed in me enough to want me on camera for this, they'll want me for something else down the line." Despite the confidence he heard in his own voice, he wondered if that would be the case. Not likely, he feared. Emily would always be around to remind everyone how Luke's pet project had stopped before it even got off the ground.

"But–"

"No buts about it. I'll call my people tomorrow and let them know they'll have to find another town." As much as he wanted her to be comfortable, he couldn't hide his disappointment. This was a big chance, one that he'd waited a long time for. The only reason Greyson had even given him the job was because it was his own hometown. But the fact that it was his hometown made it an impossible situation.

He'd known Madeleine had the talent to bake anywhere she wanted, ever since she'd baked tarts and scones in his mom's kitchen back in high school. But she'd chosen to stay here and build a life around the family and traditions she loved. He couldn't take that away from her, even if it meant giving up this opportunity for himself. There would be others, surely.

He'd have to call Grey first thing in the morning and get ahead of the situation. Somehow, he had to paint this decisions in a positive light, one that kept Luke looking like he was in control and still useful. And he had no idea what that might look like, but it had to happen somehow.

"I'm sorry, Luke." Her voice was barely above a whisper, and she took her hands from his, tucking them underneath her thighs.

"I understand." A new thought made his already dry throat constrict even more. *Emily won't understand. She'll jump at the chance to make me look like I screwed this up, only to make herself look like the hero when she finds another town.*

The silence was loud, filling every space in the truck. Luke didn't want to end the night on this note, but it couldn't be helped. She'd made her decision, and he'd promised to stand by it. He just wished it didn't come at such an expense for them both.

Madeleine stared out the windshield, sitting perfectly still as if she were a statue frozen in regret and sadness.

Apparently, Dillon was right. He called it from the very beginning. Luke had broken her heart. Maybe not by leaving town and discarding the relationship but by pressuring her to do something she couldn't be comfortable with.

As he shifted the truck into drive and pulled back onto the road, he realized Madeleine's heart wasn't the only one breaking.

Chapter 19

Madeleine

Madeleine rolled over in her bed and switched off the alarm buzzing. Four-thirty in the morning. She'd only just fallen asleep two hours before, and the last thing she wanted to do was climb out of her warm bed and take a shower.

She couldn't get to sleep last night for anything. The day's events swirled in her mind, and her emotions ranged from anticipation and excitement to devastation and sorrow. They'd decided to go ahead to Seneca for dinner, which had been fine. They avoided any conversation about the makeover and mostly talked about different people they knew from high school and where they were now. Luke had dropped her off at her house, walked her to the door, and had even kissed her goodnight. But she sensed his preoccupation, even in the way his lips brushed against hers.

Her thoughts about last night tripped over each other, each one more confusing than the last. One minute, she'd been flirting over a bowling game and the next, practically ruining Luke's career. Not to mention, she'd likely stalled out any relationship they'd started to build.

But The Bean and Batter needed opening this morning, and she was the one to do it. It was important to her. It meant something. It meant enough to give up on any misguided daydreams of a future with Luke Taylor.

At least Dillon will be happy. She stumbled to the kitchen and flipped on the coffee pot, thankful for her evening routine of measuring out the water and coffee grounds. She was too bleary-eyed to think this morning about anything as difficult as making a pot of coffee.

It wasn't long before she'd showered, brushed her teeth, thrown on her black leggings and an oversized coral-pink sweater, plaited a quick side braid trailing over her right shoulder, and zipped up her tall black boots. She looked in the mirror and mourned the dark circles under her eyes that the concealer couldn't fully cover. *Well, this will have to do for today. It's the best I've got to give.*

The Bean and Batter was dark and quiet and cold when she walked in. It smelled good, like freshly ground coffee and caramelized sugar, but even the familiar scents of the place she loved weren't enough to lift her spirits.

We must have been slow yesterday. This place is spotless. Becca always made it a habit of cleaning when she had downtime between customers, and judging by the shine on every tabletop and counter surface, she'd had plenty of time to clean.

Madeleine picked up the bank bag, which held yesterday's receipts. It was light and thin, confirming her suspicions of too few customers. She sighed and collapsed into the chair at her desk, burying her head in her hands. *Mom, how did you make this place work so well?*

The tears came, and she watched them splash on the bank bag laying on her desk. *I can't keep this place going. If something doesn't change, I'll lose everything.* She reached over the desk, grabbed a roll of toilet paper and tore off a few squares, blew her nose, and swiped under her eyes. *So much for concealing dark circles. Just add red blotches to complete my look.*

She shook her head to clear out the sadness, then busied herself with filling the display case and grinding some coffee beans for the morning. She knew Becca would appreciate that help. A basket of apples sitting on the back counter caught her attention, and she remembered that she needed to use them up. A caramel sauce would be just the thing, knowing she could slice apples to order and add a ramekin of sauce with them. *Maybe I'll whip up a caramel apple tart if we're slow later today.*

The back door swung open, and Becca's familiar humming made Madeleine smile. It was one of those funny things about Becca she loved. After working side by side with her for three years, she never tired of hearing her assistant humming anything from show tunes to eighties rock. "Morning, Madeleine," came the singsong greeting as she tossed her jacket on the hooks behind the office door.

Madeleine knew she couldn't hide the fact that she'd been crying. Not from Becca, for sure. "Hey," she said, her voice flat.

Becca stopped in her tracks when she came around the counter, her eyes wide and her jaw slack. Slowly, she asked, "Rough night? I expected you to come in practically dancing on air, what with your date yesterday and all."

"Yeah, well, things didn't go exactly as I would have hoped." Her voice nearly gave out as she choked on her words.

Becca perched on the corner of the counter, her eyes sympathetic. "Obviously. What happened?"

Madeleine pressed the heels of her hands against her eyes, hoping that when she opened them again things would be clearer. "Becca. Can I ask you a question?"

"I think you just did, but yes."

"Very funny. But I need you to be honest with me. Please."

"Okaaayy." Her voice was low and hesitant. "But if this is a question of whether I think Luke is good for you, I can't say. I hardly know him."

"It's not about Luke." She looked at Becca, whose eyebrows were raised in what was either concern or curiosity. Or both. One thing she knew for sure, Becca would be brutally truthful. She always had a knack for cutting right to the heart of a situation and spelling it out simply. Madeleine needed that kind of answer right now. Regardless of what the answer might be, knowing it would help her relax. "Well, I mean, it is about Luke. But not if he's right for me or not."

"Well, what is it then?"

"Do you like working here? Like not the work itself, but working in this place?"

Becca crossed to the door and grabbed an apron. She tossed it over her head and wrapped the strings around her waist. "The truth?"

"I don't want anything less."

"I think it's a fine bakery, Madeleine." She hesitated, focused on tying the bow at her waist.

"But just fine?" *Interesting word choice.* It bittered the air, like too much vinegar in a pie crust. Her mother taught her a little splash with the ice water kept the crust tender, but too much would make the crust taste bitter on the tongue. Kind of like the word fine. It felt bitter and tough to swallow, especially from Becca, someone who Madeleine expected to see this little bakery in a way similar to her own view.

In true Becca fashion, she didn't want to dance around the topic and blurted, "What is this about? I guess I don't understand what you're asking."

Madeleine sighed and tied her own apron around her waist for the day. Even though she'd rather have sat to really listen to her friend's opinion, there was work to do. Enough time had already been wasted on tears and worry, and customers would be knocking on the door any minute. "Luke's company wants to do a makeover show here."

Becca's eyes lit up as she flipped on the lamps and took chairs down from atop the tables. "Like one of those TV shows where a designer comes in and redecorates everything?" She practically squealed the question aloud.

"Exactly like that, yes." She stepped past Becca and into the kitchen, grabbing the container of sugar as she went. Becca's excitement rattled the sadness loose, just a tiny bit. Which surprised her, actually.

"And there's always a cute carpenter, or host or something?"

Madeleine couldn't stop the corners of her mouth from tipping up. "Well, um," she cleared her throat. "I'd say they already have a cute host."

Becca's eyes grew wide. "Luke?"

Madeleine nodded, then grabbed a saucepan.

"What's the problem, then? Who better to take care of your bakery than the guy who has a reason to protect it?" She ducked into the walk-in fridge.

Madeleine nearly dropped the canister of sugar as the white confection poured into her pan. She'd not thought of that angle before. "That's true," she said, twisting the gas burner on and grabbing a measuring cup from the shelf. "I didn't think about his investment into this space being tied to us." *Is there really an 'us' yet, though?*

"Of *course* he will protect this place. I saw how he looked at you yesterday. He's completely hooked and wouldn't do anything to mess this up." She carried a tray of cupcakes and began lining them up in the glass case, ready to sell. As she placed the last pink-frosted one, she stood and turned. "Besides, if he does anything you don't like, I got the impression that Dillon is more than ready to take him out. I'm pretty sure he's not a fan of this new relationship."

"True. But we've talked, and I hope he can trust me to be a big girl and make my own decisions." Things seemed to be near bubbling, and not just in the caramel saucepan. Between her relationships with the Taylor boys, her bakery finances, and now this makeover, she wasn't sure what else she could handle.

Becca's phone chimed, and Madeleine glanced at the clock on the wall. Six in the morning. "Will you unlock the door for me? I can't walk away from this caramel."

"On it." The squeak of Becca's red Converses slowed as she approached the door. "Uh, Madeleine? You're gonna want to walk away from that caramel sauce. Something much sweeter is waiting outside for you."

She leaned back as far as she could, straining to see the parking lot while still stirring the caramel. The sun glinted off the truck's door as Luke swung it shut and made his way to the front door.

The sugary water started to boil in the pan, and the rising, popping bubbles mirrored Madeleine's anxiety level. *Early start today, Luke.*

The familiar turn and pull of the bakery's doorknob usually excited Madeleine, because it meant another customer had come to spend money in her little bakery. But this morning, her emotions felt like they'd been whipped in the mixing bowl too long, and she couldn't make sense of them.

"Hey, Luke," Becca chirped.

No need to be so chipper, Becca. He probably has thought about how I've ruined his entire career and is here to tell me what a selfish person I am and how he hates me for it.

"Becca." His curt response only confirmed Madeleine's theory.

Yet his boots came closer to the back of the café. *Brave.*

Past the sales counter. *Oh no.*

Near the kitchen door. *Too close.*

Into the kitchen. *That's bold.*

Madeleine took the sauce off the heat, poured in some heavy cream, and stirred like it was the most important task in the world, not stopping to look at the man standing just inside the threshold. She could only imagine the way his eyes were narrowed in anger as he watched her stir in silence.

A bit of butter went into the sauce and the stirring continued.

Still, neither said anything to the other. She was growing more and more certain of his anger at her.

The sauce finished, it needed to cool. *Now what? I'll have to get past him to get to the front of the café, and there's nothing to bake back here now.* She considered pouring the caramel into the ramekins, but there they sat, traitorously, on the counter directly beside where Luke leaned. She couldn't possibly go over that close without saying something. But why wasn't he saying anything?

"Madeleine?" Becca stuck her head into the kitchen. "You good?" The way she shifted her eyes and nodded her head toward Luke was anything but subtle.

And there he was. Tall, arms crossed, his back leaned against the door frame. She tried to keep her eyes off his face, not wanting to see his...anger?

Frustration? Disappointment? It was probably some combination of it all. But her eyes betrayed her will and naturally drifted to that perfectly scruffy chin. Then up to those beautiful, very kissable lips.

Lips that were...smiling?

Chapter 20

Luke

The way she attacked the sauce in the pan didn't improve Luke's confidence in his plan. He hadn't slept all night. After he went home, he sat in the living room and stared at the walls. He must've looked bad. When Dillon came home after a night out, he stopped and asked what was wrong. It was the first nice thing he'd said since he was at The Bean and Batter yesterday morning.

Right now, his back pocket felt full. He'd taken a big gamble on this plan, and if it didn't work, he was out of ideas. But if it did, the payoff might be big. It just might help Madeleine see things differently.

If only she'd look at him.

Becca. He caught her eye as she flitted from the espresso machine to the sink, getting ready for the customers. The look he gave her said everything: *help*.

It worked. Madeleine tried to avoid looking his way, but Becca's soft "Madeleine? You good?" drew her attention. Luke stood taller and let his smile spread.

"Morning, Luke." Her voice was anxious, hesitant. Her eyes looked puffy. Had she been crying? He had no doubt his lack of sleep last night showed on his face. He hadn't even bothered to shave before driving here.

"Madeleine, I really want to talk with you. I've got an idea."

She squished her lips over to one side. "Mmm, can I finish this sauce really quickly?" She came closer to him, and for a minute, Luke wondered if she was going to kiss him or slap him. But she did neither. She came within a foot of him, and at the last minute, ducked to the bottom shelf next to him. "Excuse me. I just need some ramekins." She sat a stack of the little round dishes on the counter, still squatting down and grabbing more.

When she stood, Luke took her by the elbow as she turned away from him. "Madeleine. Can you stop?"

She looked first at his hand, holding her elbow, then up at him. "Luke, I really need to take care of—"

"How can I help?"

She sighed. "I just need to pour this caramel into these. You could lay them out on the counter here," she added, "please?"

"Of course. But when that's finished, can we talk?" He raised his eyebrows at her and tried to look encouraging.

"Luke, I already feel terrible about how things are going down, but I can't see any other way." She was already out of his grasp and headed to get the caramel. "I'm so sorry. Really, I am."

He laid the white dishes out on the counter in a near perfect grid. "I might have a solution if you'll just give me a chance to explain."

She started ladling the rich sauce out, filling each ramekin halfway before moving to the next one. The way she bit her lower lip as she worked made Luke smile. He knew she was completely dedicated to everything about The Bean and Batter. *I can spin that to my advantage and help her.*

He reached into his back pocket and pulled out two sheets of paper, fresh off the printer and folded into thirds. The idea struck him around four-thirty this morning, and he hadn't stopped to think it through before making the purchase. "Look at these and tell me what you think." He held the pages toward her.

"What's this?" she asked as she set the saucepan down and took the papers, giving Luke a tiny lift of hope at her willingness to at least stop working and give his idea a chance.

"Just look." His heartbeat thumped in his ears. He could only hope she would go for the idea. If she didn't, there'd be no show, no hosting gig, and no second chance. Not only that, there would be no way this relationship would move forward.

He held his breath as she unfolded the pages and scanned them.

First, the airline ticket. Her name printed in bold letters on top.

She shifted one page behind the other.

Next, a picture of Greyson Media's headquarters.

He struggled to swallow the growing lump in his throat.

Finally, a list of some of New York City's best bakeries.

She shifted her weight to lean against the counter, shuffling through the pages again.

"Well?" His voice was raspy, unsure.

She didn't take her eyes off the list. "What have you done?"

Uh oh. "What do you mean? I thought it might help you if you could see some other cafés in the city to get ideas." His stomach twisted as she shook her head.

"Luke. I can't do this."

"I'm not asking you to move there, Madeleine. Just take a step forward."

"I'm not sure I'm ready for that step. It's a really big one."

He stepped toward her, tipping her chin upward with his finger. "I'll be right there beside you. I would never ask you to do anything you aren't comfortable with, but I think this trip might help you see things a little differently."

She sighed and stepped backward. "This is too big, Luke. I can't ask you to pay for this." She held the papers toward him, but he put a hand over hers and pressed them back in her direction.

"You let me worry about the expenses." *Grey will hopefully cover it all.*

She shook her head, the pages rustling as she waved them back and forth. "I've never been to New York City. I'm not sure it's really my scene."

"How will you know if you don't ever go there? Trust me, there is a place for everyone in New York. Quiet spaces, loud spaces, creative spaces, we've got it all." *She's going to love seeing it. I can't wait to show her some of my favorite spots.*

"Where will I stay?"

"Your choice. I've got plenty of space in my apartment, but if you're more comfortable in a hotel, I can arrange that too."

"But I can't get away from this place for so long."

Becca's voice chimed in from the front counter. "Oh, yes you can. I'll handle things here."

Madeleine's laughter burst forth, and Luke felt his shoulders relax, releasing the tension he'd been holding in every one of his muscles. He let a little chuckle escape but didn't dare to completely give in to the happy feeling that was rising. After all, she hadn't agreed to take the trip yet.

Madeleine leaned to her right, peering around Luke. "Becca, I don't need any help with this."

"That's what you think." came her teasing reply. "If you don't take this chance, you'll regret it forever."

Luke called over his shoulder, "Thanks for the help, Becca. I'll take all I can get right now." He shot a wink in her direction, and she smiled back at him. Turning back to Madeleine, he lowered his chin. "There. Now I think you're out of excuses. What do you say? Are we headed for the Big Apple?"

Chapter 21

Madeleine

Madeleine gripped the armrest as the plane touched down. The trip had been uneventful, yet she couldn't stop the constant barrage of nervous thoughts tumbling around in her brain.

What can I do to repay him for this ticket?

Should I have stayed in a hotel?

Maybe a makeover of the bakery wouldn't be such a bad thing after all.

Luke took hold of her hand and pried her fingers from the cool metal. "We're safely on the ground. You can relax now."

Yeah, I don't see that happening any time soon.

She had been surprised to find their seats in first class, but Luke seemed right at home, settling in right away. When she questioned him about the price of the ticket, he waved his hand and said it was nothing, that he wanted this trip to be special for her. Taking her bag and stowing it in the overhead compartment, he offered her the window seat. "You'll be able to see the Statue of Liberty when we fly into the city."

Another surprise came in the form of a driver waiting for them at baggage claim.

"Mr. Taylor, welcome home," the driver greeted them at the bottom of the escalator. "And Ms. Malone, it's nice to meet you. Can I take your bag?"

"Sure. Thank you very much." Madeleine passed her leather messenger bag to the man in a black suit then followed Luke toward the baggage carousel, already spinning with luggage riding the loop waiting to be picked up. "No baggage today?"

Luke shrugged. "Checked it this time."

Madeleine felt her cheeks warm. Someone who traveled as much as Luke probably never checked his luggage. But he hadn't said anything at the Dallas airport when she asked about checking hers.

"Mike, does Dennis have everything set at home?" The way Luke spoke, all business, was something new. He'd never been like this in Ryleigh. But here he was different. The softness was gone, replaced with short, curt questions, a more powerful stride, and a colder tone in his voice.

Thankfully, he's been the same with me. She realized this city-boy-Luke was even more appealing to her. Watching him navigate all angles of this situation made her feel safe, like he'd thought of everything and all she had to do was stay by his side. She breathed a sigh of relief.

"Yes, sir. He's got the suite ready for Ms. Malone. And the reservations are also set for tomorrow as well."

Suite? Details about this new Luke were starting to form a new picture of the star baseball-player-turned-executive. Luke wasn't a struggling, bottom-rung employee at Greyson Media. He'd made a name for himself here in the city, just like he had at home. A smile crept over her lips at the thought of his success.

Luke reached to grab her silver hardback suitcase as it crept near, and Mike stepped in. "I've got that, sir. And I believe that one is yours?" He pointed to Luke's small black rolling bag coming through the small doorway leading to the exterior of the airport where baggage handlers worked.

"Thanks, Mike. I'll grab that one and then we will be on our way."

Before Madeleine could think about anything else, Luke was back at her side, Mike rolled two bags behind him, and they were headed outside. The blast of chilly October air hit her as the doors opened, and she welcomed the car's warmth once they got inside.

"Not quite Texas weather, is it?" Luke grinned at her as he took her hands, pressing them between his own.

"Not quite." His palms were warm around hers. "I have gloves somewhere, I think."

"It will be warmer later, I'm sure."

Hmm. I'm sure it will be. But that's not the weather, really.

The car settled into a quiet hum as Mike steered onto a highway and into the city. Madeleine's heart began to jump in her chest like a rabbit as the reality of where she was began to set in. New York City. The place she'd dreamed about since she was a little girl. The Rockettes, the Empire State Building, the crowded streets and dirty subway stations, and the hustle of Times Square all called to her, and now she was within moments of finally seeing them all.

The city whisked by as she peered out the window, looking at the rows of brownstones along one street, bringing up memories of Sesame Street. Suddenly, the car plunged into darkness illuminated by an eerie orange light coming from the sides of the tunnel. She let out a quiet "oh" of surprise.

"Queens Midtown Tunnel, Ms. Malone. Nothing to worry about," Mike called from the front seat.

She turned to Luke, who was watching her intently, the corners of his lips turned up in amusement. "Yes, we're underwater if that's what you're wondering."

"Oh. I was hoping we'd take the Brooklyn Bridge over."

Luke laughed, definitely amused at Madeleine's comment. "My dear, the Brooklyn Bridge is downtown. We aren't coming in from that way. There's more than one way in and out of Manhattan."

"Thankfully," added Mike. "Otherwise, no one would ever get anywhere if we all had to use the same bridge."

Madeleine knew these men weren't making fun of her, but there was no way to stop her cheeks from growing hot. Once again, all she could muster was a quiet, "oh."

Luke scooted closer to her, his thigh resting against the side of her own, and his hand found her knee. "I'll show you the Brooklyn Bridge while you're here, I promise," he murmured into her ear.

The lump in her throat caught and she couldn't answer him, but the bubble of excitement that popped only seconds ago was growing again. Only this time, it had nothing to do with the city, but more about the man who lived here.

The ride turned to a slow, steady rhythm of changing lanes, brakes squealing, and Madeleine watching the blocks pass. The car turned, and Madeleine read Third Avenue on a street sign. It wasn't hard to realize this was a different area of town than the airport. Trees were planted along the side of the streets, and taxis flooded the roadways. No longer flying through lanes like they had in the tunnels, Mike expertly maneuvered between the delivery trucks and cabs. The constant honking of horns seemed unnecessary to Madeleine, emphasized by a quick "beep" from Mike in the front.

She leaned her forehead against the cool window and peered upward. The silver skyscrapers stretched into the stratosphere, and Madeleine was grateful the traffic slowed, giving her time to really look at her surroundings. She watched ladies in skirts and tennis shoes bustle down the sidewalk, passing men with headphones tucked into their ears and a phone lifted to switch music or make a call. Madeleine could only guess which. Bloomingdales loomed large out Luke's window, and she leaned forward to catch a glimpse of their doors as Mike inched through the traffic.

She turned back to look out her own window, and a colorful window display caught her attention, the bright circles and colorful stripes standing out among the stately buildings surrounding it.

A candy shop? How cute.

"Dylan's. It's a fun stop. If you like sweets, that is."

"Seems like somewhere I should see."

"We will add it to the list. I'll call and arrange a private tour. We did some media work for them a few months back, so I'm sure they'll be more than happy to have us."

Madeleine shifted her knees toward Luke and looked at him, his eyes sparkling with joy. "You can do that?"

"Sure I can. I know the right people." He shrugged it off like it wasn't any big deal.

That flutter in her stomach was likely from the way he seemed so comfortable here in this new place, but Madeleine tried to brush it off as a breakfast that was too light and too long ago.

The blocks ticked off, and Madeleine kept count as the numbers of the cross-streets went higher and higher. *I wish I had asked which part of the city he lived in.* She knew this was a nicer area, as many of the buildings reminded her of those on TV shows, with awnings and big glass doors.

According to every movie or show she'd watched, there were only two types of places to live in New York. The ones with a doorman and an awning, usually accompanied by ladies in fur wraps with tiny dogs wearing diamond collars, and some poor girl pretending to be a painter so she could get access to the penthouse apartment where, of course, the man of her dreams lived. But, his mother didn't approve and so the girl had walked away from the relationship last week, but realized just last night that she couldn't let something like an overbearing, fur-wrap-wearing mother keep them apart.

Or there was the other places to live, the ones with a buzzer outside that the poor guy pressed to ring his ex-girlfriend's apartment, and she likely won't let him up anyhow because she didn't realize that he had been sitting in that café with the jewelry designer of her engagement ring and not cheating on her. But he would still sneak into the building because that, conveniently, was the exact moment that someone else would leave in a rush and not notice him. Everything was bound to work out in both of these situations, but not without a little moment of drama for the couples.

Madeleine knew she was in the area with the awnings and doormen, and a tiny tickle at the corners of her cheeks tugged upward when she dared to hope Luke's home might be near.

Don't be silly. We are probably just passing through.

Just as she decided they would not be stopping, Mike slowed and turned left onto 77th St.

This was definitely a doorman and awning neighborhood.

Mike slowed in front of a building and shifted the car into park. The gold lettering, 61 East Seventy Seventh, scrawled across the black awning outside the door. "Well, looks like home is still the same as ever." Mike twisted around in his seat and smiled before jumping out to open Madeleine's door.

She stepped onto the sidewalk and inhaled her first breath of Manhattan air. Things were most definitely different here. The crispness of Ryleigh was missing, but the buzz of New York almost seemed to live in the chilly breeze that blew a lock of hair down from her topknot.

Luke was around the car and at her side, his hand resting on the small of her back while he guided her toward the stone entrance of his building. "No place like home, right?"

The nervous giggle escaped before she could stop it. "I suppose. This is definitely nothing like *my* home. that's for sure."

The doorman stood before them holding the golden door ajar, his face warm and welcoming. "Mr. Taylor, good to see you're home. Mike called and said you'd be in today. Ms. Malone, it's a pleasure to have you staying as well."

He knows my name?

Madeleine cleared her throat, surprise threatening to take her voice. "Thank you so much, Mr..."

"Dennis, ma'am. If you need anything, don't hesitate to call on Dennis. I'm your man." His smile was genuine. He reminded Madeleine of Joe at the barbeque place. Always friendly. *See? New Yorkers are just as nice as back home.*

Mike rolled the suitcases into the lobby. "Do you need help up, Luke?"

"No, I think we can manage. Thanks, though."

Dennis pressed the elevator button, and the doors split open.

Luke held his hand against the side, the other holding Madeleine's suitcase. "Step on in. Your adventure begins today, Madeleine."

Chapter 22

Luke

Luke needed to press his lips together to keep from laughing out loud at how wide Madeleine's eyes grew as she surveyed his apartment. It wasn't the most impressive apartment in the city, but it certainly wasn't anything to brush off. After all, he was on the Upper East Side, just a few blocks from Central Park. Not just anyone could get a place like this, but Luke's competitive nature helped him rise quickly enough in Greyson Media, and this was easily within reach for him now.

He rolled both suitcases over to the end of the couch and sat on its arm.

"The fireplace is nice," she nodded toward the lit fireplace, but Luke didn't need any extra heat just now.

"Dennis took care of that before we arrived." Watching Madeleine timidly step further into his living room sent a wash of warmth over his body. *She's here. In my New York apartment.* The collision of his two worlds in this moment felt surreal, but the anticipation of how it would play out excited him.

Her fingers grazed over the bottom rail of the spiral staircase leading to the small upper floor. She glanced upward, leaning into the middle of the steps to see where they led.

"Just a bedroom and a small office up there." His voice was tight in his throat, almost raspy. Maybe his nerves were more on edge than he thought they would be.

Her eyebrows ticked up when she looked his way. "A bedroom? As in one?"

The corner of his mouth tipped upward. He'd been ready for this reaction since he decided to bring her to the city. It might be fun to let her worry for a minute or two. "Yes, one."

Her eyes narrowed.

He stood and took three long strides toward her, pulling her close. Her mouth parted slightly in surprise, and the warmth of her breath on his neck only added to his fun of this much-anticipated moment. "Listen, this isn't Ryleigh anymore. Things here are different. The city is big, but the living spaces are…" he let his eyes wander over her face, making her wait a second longer before leaning to her ear and whispering, "cozier."

She pressed a hand on his chest, making his heart thrum. "I'm all for cozy. That fire, the couch, a blanket, and a movie together sounds great. But I'm sure one bedroom is not what I expected."

"Hmm. We may have a problem then." He was enjoying the way she squirmed in his arms, but he knew it was all play. She'd been snuggled up to him for the majority of their flight. They hadn't kissed since their badly-turned date night at the bowling alley, but the tension between the two of them had certainly melted away after she agreed to this trip. "Did you want to go upstairs and see what we can do about this little issue?"

As soon as his hand was off her waist, she leaned away and stepped up onto the first step. "I'd say so. Because if I need Dennis to call me a cab to the nearest hotel, we'd better get that started."

"Oh, you'd leave me here alone and go to a hotel, would you?"

She was already halfway up the spiral stairs, her hand sliding over the metal rail as she went. He grinned, knowing she was only two or three more steps away from seeing into the upstairs loft. He only needed to wait here at the bottom of the steps.

She paused, looking into the little office space for a second, took two more steps upward and peered into the bedroom beyond. Then, the moment Luke watched for finally happened. She looked back down at Luke, and her smile made him want to race up the steps two at a time and sweep her into his arms once again. *Play this cool.*

"I should've known." The relief in her voice was comical.

"You didn't think I'd ask that of you, did you?"

"You had me worried for a second, yes."

"Wow. That hurts." He placed a palm over his heart and pretended it had been pierced by a dagger. "But you'll sleep in my bed tonight. I had Dennis set up that extra bed in the office for me. You can have the bedroom all to yourself."

"Well, that's a good thing, because I would hate to have to leave this lovely space and go to a cold, empty hotel room." She took her time coming down the steps, slowly letting her toes tap on each stair, sashaying her hips with each level. The intensity in her eyes made Luke need to grasp the handrails to keep himself grounded.

"Listen," his voice was tense, filled with longing as he spoke. He cleared his throat to shake the tightness away. "As cozy as it is here, we've got things to see and do tonight. I've got some sweet plans for us. The upstairs can wait."

"Oh? What kind of plans, Luke Taylor? And did you arrange these, or did Dennis do that too?" She stood on the bottom step, making her just tall enough for her eyes to be even with his.

He chuckled. "Dennis is very helpful, but I made these plans all on my own."

"Well then, I can't wait to see what they are. Do I get to know, or are they a surprise?" Her voice held a tiny giggle of excitement.

"Oh, you'll have to wait and see. But I can tell you, we need to grab some lunch. I'm starving."

Madeleine stepped down off the stairs and tapped his nose with a finger. "Plus, you've got a whole city to show me, right?"

He grinned and slipped his arm around her waist, guiding her toward the door. "I don't think we could see the whole city. At least not in this one trip. We'll save some for next time." *Because there must be a next time.*

"So you think I'll come back here, do you?"

"Oh, I feel pretty positive you will once you've tasted what the city has to offer."

Chapter 23

Madeleine

At the next red light, Madeleine slid over in her seat closer to Luke. New York's cold was something she wasn't used to, even though she was dressed in her warmest sweater, a wool coat, hat, scarf, and gloves, all coordinated thanks to Becca's help with packing.

So, leggings look cute, but aren't any good for warmth. Thanks, Becca.

He leaned slightly away from her, leaving a cold gap between them. For a moment, Madeleine's heart sank at his rejection, until he reached over and turned the heat up a few degrees. He settled back against her side and placed his hand on her knee, offering a tiny circle of warmth there. "Cold?"

"Yep. I don't know how you live here. It's sinking all the way to my core."

"The heater will kick in soon. But until then, you're stuck with the Luke Taylor 3000Instaheat." His hip pressed against hers when he moved closer.

She feigned a sigh. "Oh, if I must, then I suppose that will have to do." The light turned green, and Madeleine looked out the window as they turned left. Already, she could see why Luke loved this city. Down every side street, activity buzzed. People ducked in and out of shops, car horns beeped, and men hailed cabs while talking into their phones. It all seemed to teem with a sense of urgency. For someone like Luke, that go-getter world fit him perfectly.

Mike glanced into his rearview mirror at Luke. "You sure you want to take this peach over to Ray's this afternoon?" Mike honked his horn as he pressed the front corner of the car into the right lane. "Seems like her first stop in the city ought to be something a little more, oh, I don't know...fancy?"

"We'll do fancy later. I've been away from the city too long, and I've got to stop in at Ray's. Some things can't wait." He smirked at his driver's reflection in the mirror, and watched the man shrug back.

Madeleine's stomach grumbled, as if protesting Luke's business stop. She hadn't eaten anything this morning in Ryleigh, because the flight was so early. Once on the plane, her nerves wouldn't let her eat. Now, with the promise of lunch on the horizon, her hunger wasn't in any mood to stop and meet this Ray person.

"Well, alright. You're the boss," Mike grumbled as he made the right turn, his bumper coming frighteningly close to the car in front of them.

A blur of streets passed, filled with busy people, shops and tiny markets, hot dog vendors, and pretzel carts. Finally, Mike eased the car around a corner. Right there, in front of Madeleine, Times Square lit up. Even in the middle of the afternoon, the lights were dizzying. People were everywhere. A gasp escaped her lips, and she smiled. "Oh wow. I had no idea we were coming here. What about Ray?"

Mike pulled the car into the driveway of a hotel, where a doorman whistled at him. He rolled the window down. "Hey, I'm just dropping off. Give me a minute, yeah?"

The doorman shook his head and turned away, clearly irritated.

"We'll be quick, Mike." Luke was already leaning across Madeleine's lap to open the door, but the hotel's valet was already opening it, his smile welcoming, even though it was full of crooked teeth.

"Hi. Don't mind Rob over there. He's from Jersey, but we don't hold that against him. Are we checking in?"

Madeleine stumbled over her thoughts, now confused. *I thought I was staying at Luke's?* But Mike took over before she could answer.

"Nah, man. Just using your driveway here. Ms. Malone's never been to the city." He was already around the car and shaking hands with the crooked-toothed man.

"Oh, hey, Mike, I didn't realize it was you. How've you been?"

Mike laughed. "Yeah, Lou, I was starting to wonder if you'd forgotten me. I'm good. You?"

Madeleine and Luke climbed out of the car while the two men held a reunion. The icy cold washed over her cheeks as a draft of wind coursed through the alleyway. "Whoa. Please tell me Ray is inside?" she asked Luke.

"Nope. He's a few blocks over. But Times Square is no joke for driving. Good thing Mike's got buddies all over town. This is as close as you'll get in a car. The rest of the way is walking." He waved a hand at Mike, who nodded a 'see ya' in his direction, then pointed toward the street. "That way."

Luke led her to the right, and she glanced up at the street sign. 46th and Broadway. And there it was. Times Square. Full of excitement, construction, tourists, and lights. It took a minute to stop scanning past everything and focus in on the things she'd only ever seen on TV. To her left, the big Coca-Cola sign. To the right, some of the biggest ads she'd ever seen. Luke slid one arm around her waist and pulled her to him. While a whisper in her ear would have been a sweet gesture right now, the noise of the area made that moment impossible. Instead, he leaned in, kissed her cheek, and said, "Welcome to the world's busiest corner."

She turned toward him, his lips still close, and wanted to kiss him. She wanted to stand here, like that photo of the nurse and soldier taken right after World War II ended, and kiss in the middle of the street. She wanted to run to the top of those big red stairs and shout Luke's name and hear him laugh as he chased her to the uppermost step. She wrapped her arms around his neck and pulled him against her own body. Even here, in this busy corner, the world belonged to just the two of them. "It's amazing," she said, closing her eyes and leaning into him, his breath on her mouth.

An elbow jammed into Madeleine's waist, knocking her slightly off-balance, and ended the magical moment with a jolt. She turned to see who had spoiled the sweet moment, and saw a family bustling away, each parent holding the hand of a child. The light had turned green, and pedestrians were swarming around them, grumbling at the couple holding up traffic.

The corner of Luke's mouth tipped up and he shook his head. "No stopping in NYC. Gotta keep moving. Especially here. The tourists can be brutal."

He laced his fingers through hers and led her across the busy crosswalk. A moment of gratitude washed over her as she allowed him to expertly maneuver them through the seemingly endless river of people, most of whom appeared just as awestruck as she felt. After a quick turn to the left and a few more steps down the block, Luke paused. A shop window brandishing T-shirts supporting the NYPD and NYFD alongside the standard I ♥ NY logos caught her eye. *I'll need to get some shirts for Dillon, Dad, and Becca.* Even though her dad and Becca were thrilled about this trip, Dillon took a little more convincing. Bringing him some cheesy souvenirs probably wouldn't help him like the situation any better, but she would try all the same.

"Ready to meet Ray?" Luke asked, bouncing on the balls of his feet, his eyebrows lifted.

Ray works in a tourist shop? "I suppose. Is he meeting us here?"

Luke laughed and tugged her into the opening next door. The aroma of baked pizza dough and garlic smelled heavenly. "Welcome to Ray's, also known as 'Famous Original Ray's Pizza.'"

Three guys worked behind a glass counter that was almost as high as her chin. Inside the case were pizzas of all varieties: margherita, barbecue chicken, meat lovers, chicken and tomato. The closest man behind the counter stepped forward, "What kind can I get 'ya?" his New York accent thick, he waved his pie server toward the pizzas and grabbed a square sheet of foil at the same time.

Madeleine pointed to the closest pizza. "Is it sold by the slice?"

"We can do whatever you want here. By the slice, by the pie, by the dozen. Which do you want?"

They all looked delicious, but one looked more interesting than the rest. "What's on this one?"

"That's our white pizza. No tomato sauce. Ricotta and mozzarella." The word mozzarella rolled off his tongue in a way that Madeleine had only ever heard in the movies. "It's delicious. You want it?"

The line of people in the cramped space moved forward, and Madeleine felt rushed. Not that the guy was rude, he just wasn't quite as slow-paced as Joe might've been back at the BBQ House. She nodded her head. "Yes, please."

He scooped up the slice, tossed it onto the square of foil, and slid it into the brick oven behind him, then turned to Luke. "And what about you?"

"I'll have a slice of meat lovers and a slice of Hawaiian, please." Luke was already fishing his wallet out of his back pocket and stepping toward the register. He turned to Madeline. "Want a drink?"

The cramped space combined with the line starting to pile up behind them caused Madeleine's temperature to rise, so she just pointed to the first thing she saw. "Water's fine."

"And two bottles of water, please," Luke said as he handed cash across the counter to the man behind the register. "Want any garlic bread or salad or anything?"

Madeleine shook her head. She just needed to get her pizza and sit somewhere. It smelled amazing in here, but there wasn't time to visit. Everyone was in a hurry around her. Over the glass counter, the pizza guy passed her slice of white pizza, placed on a white paper plate, over then handed Luke his slices.

Further back in the narrow restaurant were about a dozen tables, each less than two feet away from the next. All of them had people seated at them, but

Luke stepped ahead and sat down at one with a kid eating alone while wearing headphones.

So we just sit with anyone here? What if he thinks we're weird? Maybe he was saving those seats? She looked around for anyone who might be headed to sit with headphones kid, but no one looked like they knew him. 'Stranger Danger' alarms were ringing in her mind, but Luke seemed totally at ease.

"Have a seat," Luke said, laughing. "He doesn't mind, right?" Luke nudged the kid and nodded toward the table, as if to ask permission to sit there.

The kid barely even looked up. "Yeah, sure," he said, before taking another bite of his pizza and scooting his chair over to make more room.

Madeleine set her pizza down, settled into the chair, and watched Luke pick up his slice, fold it in half lengthwise, and open his mouth to take a bite. He noticed her staring and paused. "It's the New York way. Gotta fold it. Only tourists eat it bite by bite."

"If you say so." Feeling a little like she'd stepped through the looking glass, Madeleine folded her own slice, took a bite, and instantly decided this was the most heavenly pizza she'd ever tasted. The garlic flavor was strong, the ricotta was sweet, and the crust was perfectly crispy.

"I knew you'd love Ray's," Luke said. "Now, let's discuss the rest of this trip. Tonight, we see Times Square. There's another Ray's closer to the apartment, but I knew you'd want to see this first. So, sightseeing it is."

"Okay," she said as soon as she'd swallowed. A prickle of excitement bubbled in her belly. Or maybe it was the delicious pizza. Either way, she smiled at Luke's offer to show her the city she'd always dreamed of.

"But about tomorrow. I've got a tiny bit of bad news."

Madeleine's shoulders dropped. She took a sip of her water, hoping to hide her nervousness.

"I've got to head into the office tomorrow." Luke's mouth tipped downward, and a wrinkle between his eyebrows appeared that hadn't been there before.

"Okay. Well, that's fine. I'm sure I'll find something to do." Madeleine shrugged, not wanting to inconvenience Luke, although the idea of being left alone in this city caused her to stop breathing for a second.

"But I've also got some good news about your plans for tomorrow."

"Oh, really?" She should have known better than to assume Luke would leave her without plans while he worked all day. "Are you going to share these plans with me?"

He grinned, wiped his hands on his napkin, and took her hand in his. "That, my dear, is something you'll have to wait for."

Chapter 24

Luke

The smell of coffee was exactly what Luke needed this morning although he moved slower than his usual pace, what with the extra effort to avoid clanging mugs together or closing cabinet doors too quickly. Madeleine still slept upstairs, and he didn't want to wake her just yet.

With every creak of the historic building, Luke glanced up at the ceiling, pausing to listen for her feet padding across the bedroom. But so far, nothing. Coffee cradled in one hand and his tablet in the other, Luke tiptoed to the table. He pushed aside the plastic shopping bag filled with cheap NYC T-shirts for everyone back in Ryleigh. The way Madeleine's face lit up with she first stepped into Times Square was not something he would soon forget.

I hope that's just the start of her smiles. Today will be the frosting on the cake.

He tapped the email icon on his tablet and opened the message for at least the fourth time this week, then scrolled to his favorite line, 'I would be honored to have Ms. Malone in my kitchen this week. She sounds delightful.' Delightful didn't even come close to describing Madeleine. She was enchanting.

The pictures in his phone only reinforced these thoughts as he scrolled through last night's memories, swiping right from one moment to the next. A selfie with a NYC police officer, buying her first overpriced pretzel from a cart, pointing to Liza Minelli's caricature in Sardi's restaurant, standing in front of the Schubert Theater's stage door, and, of course, buying candy at the M&Ms megastore. She'd laughed her way all over Times Square, loving seeing all the touristy sights. The mixture of her laugh with the hustle and bustle of the city quickly became Luke's favorite sound. He couldn't wait to take her to some less touristy spots in the city, places where they could enjoy each other without shouting over the din.

But first, work. His tablet buzzed with a notification, and Luke switched back to his email. A name came across his screen that deflated any excitement he'd just had.

Emily Pierotti. She'd scheduled a meeting for ten this morning with the producers of the makeover show. That was the absolute last thing he wanted to work on today. And Emily was the absolute last person he wanted to work with. Luke wasn't officially back from vacation yet. But he'd let it slip to Greyson that he was coming back into the city for a few days, and his boss convinced him to come in for one quick meeting.

"You know, just to check in, kid. I want to hear a little more about this town while you're here."

Really, Grey? And you invited Emily? Luke leaned forward on his elbows and pressed the heels of his palms into his eyes. So much for a quick check in. This was a disaster waiting to happen.

The sink upstairs started running. *She's awake.* Luke pushed Emily, Greyson, and the meeting from his mind and headed for his coffee machine, slipping the coffee pod into the top and a mug underneath. He grabbed the half and half and splashed some into the mug just as Madeleine stepped down the first step of the spiral staircase. Her feet bare, she still wore flannel pajama pants and a T-shirt with 'Ryleigh High School Football' emblazed across the front. Her hair tumbled over her shoulders, and she tucked a lock of it behind her ear.

She is breathtaking. Minus the football allegiance, that is.

"Morning, sunshine. I've got coffee ready."

She reached the bottom step and took the mug from his hand, pausing to rest her fingers atop his. "You're amazing. Thanks."

"So...Ryleigh football? I'd think you'd prefer the baseball team."

Her mouth quirked to the side, and her eyebrows furrowed. With a gentle tug on the bottom hem of her shirt, Luke cleared up her confusion. She crossed her arms across her chest to hide the shirt, but Luke just grinned.

"I can't afford to pick teams. The coaches buy coffee from me, so I love them all equally."

He stepped closer and rested his hand on her hip. "Fine. But let's remember *this baseball* player made coffee for *you*," he said with a nod to the mug in her hand.

She let out a playful sigh and rolled her eyes dramatically. "If I must keep secrets, then I guess I will. They'll never know I like the crack of a bat best." She stepped down from the last step and headed for the table.

He followed, pushing his tablet aside as he sat. Meetings and work could wait a little longer. "Speaking of secrets, today has a good one."

She swallowed the sip of coffee and looked up. "You keep bringing this up, but can I get any sort of hint?"

He put a hand on his own knee to stop its bouncing. He'd been working on this surprise for a week, and the fact that it came together was nothing short of a small miracle. *I can't wait to see her reaction.* "Ever heard of Anna Lamb?"

"Of course. I have all her cookbooks on my desk at the bakery. Any baker knows who she is."

"You have all her cookbooks already?" He dropped his eyes in false disappointment. He knew this already, having seen them in her house last week. "Well, I guess that changes things."

She set her coffee on the table with a thump. "Oh no. Did you get me one?" The way she tried to make Luke feel better made him snicker, which was hard to hide. "I'd be happy to have more than one. I can keep this other copy at my house. It's great. Really. I love it."

"You haven't even seen it yet. How do you know you love it?" Still pretending the surprise was ruined, he shrugged his shoulders in defeat.

"I'm sorry."

He let a little grin slip. "You're sorry you own a book?"

Her lashes brushed against her cheeks as she looked down in embarrassment. "I mean, I guess I am. Since it ruined your surprise."

He reached across the table, took her hand, and gave it a squeeze. "Wait here. Might as well give it to you anyhow." He practically leapt across the tiny kitchen and reached on top of the refrigerator, where Anna Lamb's book had been waiting for this very moment. The pink ribbon around it had been Dennis's idea, and Luke was glad he took the advice, even if it was tied unevenly and looked more like sneaker shoelaces rather than an elegant bow.

With the book behind his back, he adjusted his face to a mix between disappointment and apologetic. "I'm sorry to get you a gift you already own. You can exchange it if you want."

A puff of sorrow escaped Madeleine's lips, making Luke focus on their natural pink shade. A memory of her mouth pressed onto his own flashed in his mind, and he fought against the smile twitching for release. He didn't want to spoil this ruse of mock sadness with a quick, but very sweet, memory.

He drew the book from behind him and placed it gently on the table. The bow flopped like a wet noodle across the front of it.

Madeleine smiled politely before carefully untying the pitiful decoration and immediately opened the book, looking for something specific. "Thanks so much. I really do appreciate it. Want to see my favorite recipe?"

That smile Luke fought really threatened to make an appearance now. Of course, he wanted to see her favorite recipe, Almond Ambrosia Cake. The page in her own copy had been dog-eared, had a smear of something like frosting across one corner, and several gritty bits of sugar rested in the crease of the book.

Becca's help proved useful once again, not just in getting Madeleine to take this trip, but also to help Luke with this little scheme. He'd met her one evening at the bakery while Madeleine did her weekly grocery run. Becca was quick to pull this very same cookbook down from the shelf, and when she did, the book nearly naturally fell open to this recipe. Luke remembered Becca's squeal when he told her what he'd planned to do and hoped that Madeleine's reaction would be at least that fun.

"Sure. Which one?" He hoped he sounded interested, but nonchalant.

With a swift motion, Madeleine turned to page fifty-two. Her gaze crossed the page and landed on the note Luke carefully had taped over the picture of the triple layer cake, frosted in pale orange and adorned with candied pineapples on top. Her eyebrows furrowed. "What's this?" She turned toward him, her eyes wide with curiosity.

"Open it."

"Okaaay." She seemed unsure, but Luke didn't miss the measured delight dancing across her face as she carefully lifted the tape from the page. "Why would you tape something into a book? Are you some kind of animal?"

"The pages are glossy. I tested it first. This might shock you to know, but I, too, value a good book."

She turned the envelope over and slid a finger into the flap, then lifted out a light green notecard. Anna Lamb's handwriting splashed across it in dark green ink.

Luke hadn't read the note itself, but he more or less knew what it said. He watched Madeleine read the note, excitement pulsing through his veins.

The shriek that pierced the air made him jump backward.

"Luke, are you serious?" He couldn't remember ever hearing her voice at such a high pitch.

Madeleine leapt up, and he only had a second to see her eyes sparkle with excitement before she threw her arms around his neck and pressed her entire body against his. Before he realized what was happening, he found himself falling over the back of his couch, his legs tumbling into the air. Madeleine's hips pressed against his thighs and she tumbled along with him, the two of them now a jumble of knees, arms, and elbows. Her hair swept across his face, and the clean scent of lavender filled the air.

His hips and legs were still on the couch, but his head and arms were teetering very near to the white shag carpet. He'd managed to get one hand against the floor to stop from crashing totally against the ground, but his other arm was busy around Madeleine's waist, trying to keep her from falling completely onto the ground.

Madeleine was still on the couch, sprawled on her belly, peering down at him and cracking up. "I am—" Between peals of laughter, she tried to force out more words. I am ...so sorry," she finally squeaked out.

He untangled his legs from hers, his bottom half landing on the floor with a thud, which only made Madeleine laugh more. "Are you okay?" he asked through his own raucous chuckles, resting his weight on his hands and reclining backward.

She rolled over onto her side and rested her head on her hand, her elbow sinking into the couch cushions. "I'm okay. Better than okay, actually. Right now, I could fly."

Luke laughed again. "I think you just tried, hon, and I wasn't prepared for takeoff." He ran a hand through his hair, hoping to try to put himself together after their tumble. "So, good surprise?"

Her eyes became glassy with happy tears brimming at the edge. She nodded. "The best."

Chapter 25

Madeleine

M adeleine's heart bounced around in her chest with excitement. *If I make it through today without looking like a total fangirl, it will be a miracle.*

Mike pulled the car up to the bakery's door and slowed to a stop. The bright yellow awning beckoned Madeleine inside, and it seemed to take Mike an eternity to come around and open her door so she could let some of her bottled-up-inside-the-car happiness burst onto the sidewalk like sprinkles on a cake.

"You sure you want to go in?" Luke didn't need to ask. The way he grinned as he came to Madeleine's side indicated he knew what a big deal this surprise was.

"I couldn't even pretend to play this cool right now. Anna Lamb's bakery is literally right in front of me, and—"

"And she's been waiting for your arrival all week," came a voice from somewhere above. "Hang tight. I'll be right down."

Luke pointed up to a second-story window, where Anna Lamb was waving down at the couple. "Hey, Anna."

Madeleine's brain emptied of all coherent thoughts, other than *whoa. Wow. Oh wow. Wow wow wow.* Her whole body buzzed, like the sidewalk was some sort of electric generator sending waves of energy up through the soles of her shoes.

The window slid shut after Anna waved back then disappeared inside, and Madeleine realized she had just missed her first impression opportunity. Well, she hadn't missed it, she just used it up by standing with her mouth hanging open and squinting up, looking like a complete idiot. *Do better, Madeleine.*

Her brain finally switching off the chorus of wows, she looked at Luke, her stunned awe turning to worry about making a better impression. "Do I look okay?" She smiled widely. "There's not lipstick on my teeth or anything, is there?" *I wish I didn't have this heavy coat on. It's probably wrinkling my blouse.*

A low chuckle rumbled in his throat, causing Madeleine to watch his Adam's apple bob up and down. She wished she had a minute to sneak a kiss in that sweet place, thinking his embrace might calm her nerves. But before she could even finish the quick fantasy, she heard the click of the bakery's door opening.

Anna Lamb was as beautiful in person as she was in her cookbook photographs. Her auburn hair, tied in a ponytail, shone in the sun as she stepped out from under the awning. Her green eyes sparkled, and she extended her hand to Madeleine. "I'm so happy to meet you. Luke's told me all about The Bean and Batter. It sounds cute."

Madeleine shook her idol's hand and found herself speechless. *Luke told her about my bakery?* She shot a quick glance toward him and saw him smirking back at her, along with a tiny shrug of his shoulders as if to say 'guilty.'

"It's very nice to meet you, Mrs. Lamb." *There. That didn't sound too fangirlish. Normal, even.* She hoped she could keep this up all day.

Anna laughed, "Oh please. Call me Anna. Mrs. Lamb is my mother-in-law. She's great, but I think I'll let her keep that name and title."

The celebrity's warm smile eased Madeleine's jumpy stomach, and she exhaled a soft breath. "Thank you." She couldn't think what she should say next.

The awkward silence hung in the air for only a few seconds before Luke came to her rescue. "Well, I'm sure Anna's got lots to get started on, and I know Madeleine is itching to get her hands in some dough. Thanks to this trip to the city, it's been a long minute since she's baked anything." He swept his arm around her waist and pulled her into his side.

Anna looked at Madeleine. "You ready? I've got a new recipe for..." She looked at Luke, then to Madeleine and grinned. "Well, it's a secret. Luke told me you have a real talent for baking, so I've been waiting for you to get here and help me with it."

The idea of working on a new recipe with Anna caused the wow chorus to start their second rendition, but this time it came mixed with sprinkles of insecurity. The way Luke squeezed Madeleine around the waist was the confidence booster she needed. His hand slid down to take hers.

"And, that's my cue to head to the office." He lifted her hand to his mouth and pressed his lips to her knuckles. "Mike can pick you up whenever you're ready. Have a great day."

The warmth of his kiss spread up her arm and wiggled its way into her heart. He had made this entire day possible. He did this just for her. This was bigger than roses on Valentine's Day or a nice sweater at Christmas. No one had ever done something so enormously thoughtful for her, and she wasn't sure how she could ever repay him. It would take a lifetime.

Anna's voice interrupted any thoughts Madeleine entertained about that lifetime with Luke. "Let me show you around. I've also got some zucchini chocolate muffins about to come out of the oven. I added cinnamon, and I want your opinion."

With a whispered "Thank you sooo much" to Luke, Madeleine stepped under the awning and through the doorway into Anna Lamb's bakery. The scents of vanilla, sugar, and baking chocolate filled her nostrils immediately, and she inhaled the smells of home. Any hint of nerves or fear melted away with the familiarity.

"This is it. Since it's my test kitchen, it's not much to look at, but it's mine and I love it." The famous baker stepped behind the granite prep counter and lovingly stroked its smooth, glassy surface. Madeleine knew exactly how she felt. Having a place to be free to bake, experiment, taste, and mix was freedom. And if it was your own, well, that took things to a whole different level.

Madeleine looked at the exposed brick walls, the white metal shelving stacked with mixing bowls and measuring cups, and the grid of six ovens in two rows, one on top of the other, and her heart thrummed in her chest. Today would be a day like no other.

Anna slid a muffin from a baking tin and passed it to Madeleine. The cocoa brown stood out from the white ceramic plate, and the perfectly rounded top made her mouth water. "Fresh from the oven. Give it a try."

Madeleine broke a bite off and popped it into her mouth. She loved a warm muffin, and particularly enjoyed the chocolate chips, still creamy and smooth, melting against her tongue. *Oh, this is divine.*

"How's the cinnamon?"

Madeleine swallowed, but reached for another bite. One simply wasn't enough. Not to give Anna Lamb her opinion, at least. She'd better be sure of what she was about to say. Carefully phrasing her thoughts, she said, "Actually, I'd add more. It's a little too subtle for me."

Anna placed a muffin of her own onto a plate and took a bite. She chewed thoughtfully. "I think you're right."

A tingle of joy pulsed down Madeleine's spine. *I can't believe she agrees with my suggestion. This cannot be real. What life is this?*

Anna scuttled over to a notebook laying at the other end of the counter and brought it closer. After making a note on one of the pages, she looked up. "This is how I keep myself on track. It's my lifeline." She held the small journal up, its corners ragged and the edges covered in a rainbow of sticky notes.

A flash of a memory jumped into Madeleine's mind. Her mother always kept her recipes like this, some torn from magazines and tucked into a notebook, some handwritten, most with splashes of vanilla on the pages, and the edges of the book seemed to have more colored markers stuck to it than should be possible. A pang of loss struck Madeleine in her chest, taking her by surprise. Standing in a kitchen with another woman who loved to bake as much as she did caused the healing tear in her heart to feel opened once again.

Anna closed the journal and looked up with a smile that shifted quickly. "You okay?"

Madeleine squeezed her eyes shut for a millisecond, then blinked a few quick blinks. "Yep. Totally good. Just thinking about how special having my own bakery really is."

"I know exactly what you mean." Anna nodded and looked around the room at her space. "All this stainless steel is cozier than any bed with freshly washed linens, if that makes any sense at all."

It made perfect sense. Madeleine shook the wistful thoughts away and turned to her idol. "I guess we should get to baking, huh?"

Madeleine rolled her shoulders back, stretching her muscles after kneading the French bread dough and shaping it into a ball to rise. A day in the kitchen was sweeter than anything else. And working alongside Anna for the day would definitely go in the record books as her best day ever.

"Luke said you had a good eye for dough, and he wasn't kidding." Anna scribbled one more note into the pages of her book, closed the cover, and motioned for Madeleine to follow. She led her through another doorway, this time into a small office. The bright yellow couch pressed against the wall with wide, rosy stripes made a bold statement. Anna picked up a few books from her white desk and sat on the couch, tucking one leg underneath her. "Have a seat," she said, indicating the open space next to her.

Madeleine did as she was told, but couldn't stop eyeing the beautiful office. The pops of gold and bright pink made the room friendly and welcoming, and she could almost feel a sweet inspiration coursing through her veins as she absorbed the colors and beauty. *My space looks dull compared to this.* She looked up at the ceiling and even it was stunning, with tin tiles whitewashed and sparkling. *It's no wonder she has such amazing recipes. Anyone could work here and be brilliant.*

From the corner of her eye, Madeleine caught Anna watching her, a knowing smile playing on her lips.

Madeleine's cheeks felt warm, and she wished she could hide her embarrassment. "What a lovely space. I wish I had somewhere like this to work."

Anna ticked her head to the side. "Having your own inspiring space is so important. It took me some time to get this just right, but I love it. Do you have an office in your bakery?"

"I do. But it's nothing like this." She remembered the stacks of take-away boxes, the basket of flour-coated aprons and towels waiting to be washed, the generic tan tile with its chips and cracks, and she again felt her skin warm. It wasn't like Anna could see her thoughts, but even thinking about such a drab space while sitting in this beautiful one was embarrassing. Anna's desk didn't have piles of unpaid bills on the corner like hers did. *What would I give to have that burden taken away? Maybe the show would bring in enough customers that I could pay off a few bills?*

"These are some of my favorite design books." Anna pulled a book from her bookshelf behind her desk. She flipped to one of the pages, its corner dog-eared. "The idea for this office came from this photo."

Madeleine saw a living room decorated in pinks and a dark teal color, still bright but cozy. "It's perfect," she murmured to herself.

"I thought so, too. But I changed the teal to yellow, since that's my signature color. And here we are." She waved a hand through the air to indicate her completed office. "Sometimes, seeing someone else's vision come together can help me realize my own vision is possible too. Don't you think?"

Unsure what she meant, Madeleine pressed her lips together. "Hmm?"

"Luke mentioned that your bakery, while quaint, might be due for an update. I find that taking an old recipe and giving it new life works on more than just baking. Maybe you can find some design ideas in these books." She passed the stack of books to Madeleine. "Here, keep them."

She stood and moved to the doorway. "I'd say our pie crust dough is chilled by now. Time to make something beautiful out of that old recipe."

Madeleine swallowed the lump forming in her throat and sat for a moment, staring at the picture in the book again. How did she get here? Sitting in Anna Lamb's office, the smell of cinnamon and vanilla swirling around her, and a gorgeous man coming back to pick her up in a few hours to whisk her to dinner in New York City? She sat in complete disbelief, as if the bubble of a dream would burst with a quick pop. But, here she was. No dreams, no bubble. Just a sweet reality filled with possibilities.

Chapter 26

Luke tugged open the door to Henry Greyson's office, the cool metal handle all too familiar.

"Luke Taylor." The older gentleman smiled and stood behind his desk. "Emily was surprised to hear you were back in the city. She didn't think you'd leave that ragtag Texas town for at least another two weeks."

The mention of Emily's name made Luke wince inwardly, but he brushed it from his mind. "Well, I had a good reason for a quick trip back here." A flash of Madeleine's eyes jumped into his thoughts, bringing a smile to his face.

"Yes, I saw the bill for your airline tickets. That's plural, Luke. Who's the guest?" Greyson motioned to the chair opposite his desk indicating Luke should sit. "I have a guess, now that I see that smile on your face. What's her name, and have you prepared her to meet Emily?"

A groan bubbled up in Luke's throat, which had suddenly gone very dry. He put his leather backpack on the ground next to him and pulled out a bottle of water. Taking a big gulp, he eyed the man who could make or break his career with one decision. "Her name is Madeleine. A friend since high school."

"Mmm-hmm." Greyson smirked. "And you brought her here because...?" His eyebrows shifted upward in a questioning angle.

"Because she's the owner of the business you're looking for with this makeover idea Emily's baked up." He smiled at his use of the word 'baked'. It was almost as if Madeleine infiltrated his every thought, every breath. Even here, in the offices of Greyson Media, a place that should be absent of her presence, she stayed with him.

Greyson leaned forward in his chair, steepling his fingers as he did. "I think Emily's got a good idea, Luke. I know the two of you have a history together, but you'll need to set that aside and make this project work."

Luke sighed. He knew this already. With a shrug and a false smile on his lips, he answered, "I know, Grey. It won't be an issue."

"Good. Then what's the problem I'm sensing?"

Luke sat up straighter in his chair, bracing himself for what he was about to try to persuade his boss to see. "I'm not so sure the town of Ryleigh is ready for a makeover."

"I don't need to remind you how much bad press we've had this past year. We need something positive on the records, and it needs to be a success."

"I know, but–"

"No buts, Luke. This company needs a win."

The door swung open, and a voice came into the room. "What's this about butts?" Emily Pierotti tossed a long, blonde ponytail over her shoulder as she looked directly at Luke. "Luke's isn't too bad if you ask me."

"No one asked, Emily." Luke rolled his eyes. "I'd say I'm happy to see you, but, I'm not."

She made a mock pout with her lips. Luke noticed they were fuller than the last time he'd been in town. *Been adding filler again, I see.* "Ouch, babe. Why'd you have to be so mean?"

"Me? Mean? That's rich, coming from you, Emily," Luke spat back.

Greyson stood. "Okay, that's enough. Luke, put the proverbial knife down. Emily, stop being so childish. I'm not here to parent you two."

Emily sat in the vacant chair next to Luke, this time the pout on her face wasn't playful.

"Luke was just telling me about Ryleigh. Says there might be some resistance there."

Emily twisted in her seat. "Oh?" She turned to Luke. "I don't need to remind you how important this is. Not to mention, your opportunity to be on camera."

Thanks for that reminder. As if I've forgotten what's on the table.

"I think we all know how much weight this makeover holds, Emily. For everyone." Greyson gave her a pointed look, making her shift down in her seat slightly. He turned to Luke. "You were saying?"

"This bakery Emily targeted for the makeover would make a great show. It's got some nice history. Opened by a sweet lady who we lost a few years ago.

Her daughter is the owner now. She's sort of a hometown treasure." He couldn't suppress the smile creeping into the corners of his mouth as he thought of how many people loved Madeleine. "And a very talented baker. Her place is one of the busiest ones in town."

"Sounds great. If the town loves her and the bakery already, we can have them get behind the makeover easily." Luke's boss folded his hands on his desk as if the matter were settled.

"Grey, did you tell Luke about the addendum to the plans?"

Luke looked at his boss, who snapped his fingers in the air. "Thanks for the reminder. I was waiting for you to get here before we told him. You want to do the honors? It's your idea."

"Sure." The deviant smile on Emily's face caused Luke concern. "I pitched this to Henry and he took it to the Board, and they think it's brilliant. Rather than just do a show that spotlights a small town business then leaves, what if we bought the businesses we refurbish?"

Luke squinted. "Why would we do that? We aren't in the real estate market."

Grey slapped his palm on his desktop. "Exactly. This is a natural segway for expansion. The investors will love it. Diversify the assets."

Luke swallowed, trying to process what this would mean for Madeleine. "You're telling me that, once this makeover is done, Greyson Media will own The Bean and Batter?"

"Yes. Isn't it genius?" Grey's chest puffed up in delight.

Luke couldn't understand why a media company would want to own a random little Texas bakery, and it didn't sit right with him. He shrugged and looked at his boss. "Doesn't make sense to me."

Grey looked puzzled. "Of course it does. We own the bakery, we control the image. Keep it close to our chest. Then we build up other little businesses in town and create our own travel destination. People will flock to all the little towns we breathe life back into, and all those tourism dollars equal financial gain." He slapped his fingertips on his desk. "Easy."

"Sure, but why own these businesses? Isn't the publicity enough?" Luke pressed. He could already imagine Madeleine's response to losing her bakery to big business. If she wasn't willing to change the floors, she definitely wouldn't want to sign over her mother's legacy.

Emily looked up from her computer and shifted her body toward him. "And who's to say after we leave, these business owners revert back to their old, run down ways? We can't have all these tourists showing up to see our beautifully renovated spaces expecting diamonds and arriving to find dust. Control the assets, control the image. Simple"

Luke swallowed, trying to keep his composure.

"Emily, go ahead and email the addendum to the contract to Luke so he can have this bakery owner sign it before the makeover starts." Grey nodded as if the conversation were finished.

Emily started typing an email on her laptop, now balanced on her knees. "Cute name, The Bean and Batter. We can work with that." She typed the name into the search box and waited for the results to populate. The familiar green-striped awning showed up, along with pictures of the inside. The teacups hanging on the wall, the worn oak service counter. The splash of pastel aprons hanging on the hook in the corner of one photo took Luke right back to apple-brie scones, soft brushes of fingers kneading dough, and his chest filled with excitement.

Beside him, Emily's sigh brought him back to the office. "Good grief. This place is totally awful. So outdated." She turned to Luke, who tried to mask his offense at Emily's blunt comment. "It's perfect." She smiled, reminding him of the Cheshire cat, before turning her computer around to show their boss.

"I can see the opening shots lining up here." She pointed to the front door. "And then I think this wall would look like a great 'confessional' space before we start demolition. I can just see Luke standing there doing the interviews." She shot a sly grin in his direction.

Greyson looked at the screen and nodded. "It's exactly what we need."

Luke didn't know how to react. On the one hand, he was excited. This was the break he'd been waiting for, and the fact that it was his hometown made the project sit solidly in his lap. But he still hadn't convinced Madeleine. The history, her mother's legacy, it was all at stake. Who did he think he was, making the decision to turn all that upside down and assume she would stand aside happily while he did? This trip was meant to convince her to allow the makeover. But a buyout? There's no way she'd agree to that.

Emily interrupted his worry with a laugh. "Oh, please tell me this is still there?" She was pointing to her screen, now angled toward Luke, a wide smirk pasted across her face. Peals of laughter filled the small office space. On the screen, was a wall of photos, all displaying the history of Ryleigh. There, in the far, right corner, was a framed newspaper clipping.

Luke's high-school-self beamed back at him, a homecoming crown balanced crookedly on his head and his arm slipped around a beautiful blonde, her tiara shining under the stadium lights. He stood next to his best friend, Jake

Matthews, whose hand rested squarely on Kristy's hip, the four of them all in the middle of laughing at something to the right of the camera. A pang of wistful aching for a simpler time struck him in the chest, and for a moment, he wanted to be that carefree kid loved by everyone in town.

But he realized, sitting here with people who wanted to turn his town into a reality television show, that he only wanted one person to love him. And right now, taking away her most prized possession stood in the way of his own success.

Chapter 27

Madeleine

The day spent in Anna's bakery came to a close faster than Madeleine liked. Getting her hands in some dough, rolling sugar onto the outside of cookies before they were baked, was the best kind of therapy for her. Being in New York made her insides tingle with excitement, but doing what she loved kept her grounded.

"Thanks again, Anna, for having me." She cradled the design books against her chest. "It was really a great day."

Anna waved a hand through the air. "It was nothing. You are welcome here anytime, especially with that palate."

Madeleine wanted to reach out and hug her new friend, but also remembered this woman was an international baking celebrity. She wasn't sure what the protocol was for hugging famous bakers.

The question was answered when Luke pulled open the front door of the bakery. The sight of his molasses-brown eyes running over her figure as he came into the room made her almost drop the books. *The books.*

She turned to Anna. "I can return these to you next week. Should I mail them here, or—" She trailed off, unsure what her other options might be.

Anna outstretched her arms and wrapped them around Madeleine. "Oh, my sweet new friend. You keep those as long as you'd like." She leaned back, her hands still holding Madeleine's elbows. She shot a glance toward Luke. "Besides, I'm sure you'll be seeing me again."

Luke cleared his throat from behind her, but didn't elaborate more.

Uncertain of what secret conversation swirled around her, Madeleine said the only thing she could think of, "I hope so. I really do appreciate your time today."

"Of course." Anna gave Madeleine's elbows a little squeeze, then stepped backward and tucked her hands in her pockets.

"I guess we'd better get moving." Luke stepped closer behind her, and put a hand on her shoulder. The tingle of his touch made her head swirl. She hadn't realized how much she missed him. They'd been together almost every day for the last three weeks, and time suddenly seemed very long without his presence. "Let me carry those books for you. Mike's parked outside."

Madeleine smiled and waved at Anna as she left, fangirl emotions returning all over again.

"So, good day?" Luke asked as he slid into the seat and took her hand.

"The best." She tipped her chin to the side, finally asking the question she'd been wondering all afternoon. "How did you work that out?"

He chuckled, and his eyes lit up with joy.

Luke leaned forward and brushed his lips lightly against the soft place just behind her ear that he always seemed to find so easily. "My dear girl, some secrets are mine to keep. At least for now."

She hoped for a moment that his lips would linger, wandering their way down her jawline, then might cover her mouth with his own, and her heart thrummed at the possibility.

But he didn't. When he pulled back from her, he didn't look at her. Instead, he turned to face the window, watching the pedestrians walking home after a day of work.

She gave his hand a squeeze. "So far, your secrets have worked out well for me, so I won't complain."

He sat back in his seat, a quiet concern flitting across his eyes for a split second, followed by a heavy sigh.

Something didn't go well today She wanted to ask him about his time at the office, because he was clearly bothered by something.

Before she could ask, he shifted his gaze back to her, drinking in her curves. "So, what should we do tonight? A show? Dinner?"

"I thought this was your city? You tell me."

"I do know this great little Italian place if you're hungry."

The idea of garlic bread and delicious marinara sauce made her stomach rumble. Loudly. She placed a hand over her middle and felt a warmth cross her cheeks.

Luke placed his hand over hers and raised his eyebrows. "I'll take that as a yes." He leaned toward the front seat. "Trattoria Dopo Teatro. 44th and 6th."

Mike gave a wave toward the backseat and turned the car down the next block. "Theatre district, Luke. You sure?"

"For their gnocchi, I'm sure."

ele

The restaurant was dim, with tealight candles on every table. The walls, covered with murals of Italy, struck Madeleine as a little cheesy, but somehow, they worked. Luke passed a slice of garlic bread to her, and she took a bite.

"How was the office today?" she asked after swallowing.

That same darkness she'd seen earlier in the car flashed across his eyes. "Fine."

"I'm not inclined to believe that." A worrisome edge began to creep into her mind, and for the first time since she'd been with Luke, she sensed something was off.

"Why?" He took a bite of bread.

"I don't know. You've just been quiet." She watched him chew thoughtfully, while he straightened all of the flatware on the table to be perfectly parallel to each other.

Finally, he responded. "They still want to carry through with the makeover. They think The Bean and Batter is the perfect place to start." His eyes dropped to his lap, suddenly very interested in his napkin.

Madeleine set down her garlic bread. She wasn't very hungry anymore. She nodded her head slowly, studying the ridges along the rim of her bread plate. "Luke, I—"

Just then, a server appeared with plates balanced on his arm like an expert. "Who had the gnocchi?"

Luke lifted his hand in the air, and the server set his plate on the table.

"And I assume, then, that the lasagna is yours," he said, before placing the dish before Madeleine. "Everything look okay?"

They both nodded, and the server walked away.

Madeleine started again. "I know how important this makeover is to you. But I'm just not sure I can get on board. You're asking me to change all the memories I've built up with my mom in that place."

"The memories will stay. It's the wall color that will change."

She sighed. "True. But I'm not sure I'm ready." She thought about the stack of design books in the backseat of Mike's car. That, combined with the comfort of home she felt sitting in Anna's beautiful office earlier, offered a new perspective on the makeover at least. But she couldn't convince herself to let go just yet.

Luke stabbed a gnocchi with his fork. "I'm asking you to trust me. I know what the bakery means to you and our town. But just think of it. This kind of exposure could bring customers from all over Texas."

Madeleine chewed her lasagna. She had thought about that, but it was secondary to her focus on losing her mother's touches in the bakery. *It could mean more money. Maybe I could pay off the credit card finally.* Anna's advice from earlier came to mind. Having a beautiful space to work was appealing, and taking help from others didn't mean giving everything up. Anna might be right on that.

Still not seeing any better solution, she swallowed, then took a drink of her water, buying herself some time to think of what to say.

Luke didn't give her a chance to respond. "You don't have to agree to the whole thing right now." He reached across the table and took her hand in his. "But tomorrow, I have some plans to help you see how amazing The Bean and Batter could be."

The squeeze he gave her hand did not settle the fluttering nerves in her stomach, but it was nice to feel his hand around hers. She smiled at him, her gaze lingering a moment too long on his lips, and she was suddenly overcome with a need to pull him to her, to be wrapped in his arms, to find his comforting embrace to reassure her that remodeling the bakery would lead to positive changes.

She set down her fork, then cleared her throat. "Can we take this to go?"

He pulled his hand away, a look of concern replacing his smile. "Everything okay?"

She placed both palms flat on the table and leaned forward. "It's great. I just think we need to get back to your place, light a fire in that fireplace, and talk this over in a more...comfortable spot." She let her chin dip and her eyebrows raise, giving him a flirtatious look. "You've got some things I want to take a closer look at." She paused for emphasis, enjoying the smile on Luke's face. "Maybe a stack of contracts? I'd like to read them at least."

"Ah. I see." He shook his head at her and rolled his eyes playfully before searching the restaurant for their server. With a quick flick of Luke's hand in the air, she appeared. "I think we will take this to go."

Chapter 28

Luke

Luke shuffled through the pages spread across his kitchen table, searching for one in particular. A creak in the rooms above him made him pause and listen, keeping his movement to a minimum. Madeleine hadn't come downstairs yet this morning, and he needed to read over this paperwork before she woke. For at least the thousandth time, he scoured every word.

Last night gave Luke hope that Madeleine might come around on the makeover. Sitting on the floor in front of the couch, her legs stretched out in front of her and books strewn around them both, the excitement was palpable. They'd spent hours flipping through Anna's books, brainstorming about new ideas for the design, and Luke enjoyed watching Madeleine's smile light up when she thought of a new recipe she could make for their grand reveal.

Of course, there'd been more than just looking through books and dreaming of floral wallpapers and polka-dotted shelf-liners. Her beauty, softly lit from the glow of the fireplace, made his heart squeeze. In that closeness, he'd have been remiss to leave her unkissed. He certainly was not going to do that.

Once she retreated to her bedroom and he finally settled into his makeshift bed in the office, he'd spent at least another hour staring at the ceiling, listening for any movement from his bedroom and wondering if Madeleine had fallen asleep yet. Or wondering if she was also too keyed up about everything that she was also staring at the ceiling.

This morning kicked off with another read through of the buyout contracts Emily emailed over. He'd been through them so many times, he'd nearly memorized whole sections. *If there is any way to keep Greyson Media from buying out the bakery, I've got to find that. A makeover is one thing. A takeover, totally different.*

Seeing Emily's zeal yesterday for this project lit a fire under Luke. He needed to find a way to make this work, both for Greyson Media and Madeleine. And it didn't help that this deal held his own career in the balance. If there were a way to save her bakery and his career at the same time, he had to find it.

A shuffling noise upstairs startled Luke into motion, stacking the pages neatly into a file folder and tucking it under his laptop, where they'd been since last night. He still wanted a crack at talking Grey out of the buyout, so keeping these contracts separate from the ones he and Madeleine looked over last night made sense. No need to worry her about something he could probably prevent, right?

He brewed a cup of coffee and started warming up a pan. He'd mixed the pancake batter earlier, because a quick online search told him letting it rest before pouring it out it would make his pancakes better.

By the time Madeleine made it downstairs, he was flipping the silver dollars in the pan. "Perfect timing. Hungry?" he called over his shoulder.

Her arms slid around his waist from behind, and she rested her head against his back, just between his shoulder blades. His heart rate sped up, and it wasn't from that second cup of coffee.

"You're still warm from the bed." He scooped the pancakes onto a plate and turned to face her, still locked in her embrace. "I'm not sure these pancakes are worth letting go for. I think you might have to stay here a minute." He leaned down and nuzzled into her hair, letting her scent of lavender and vanilla wrap around him.

"I'm not sure I'm ready to let go, either. But those pancakes look pretty tempting." Her voice was still sleepy and soft.

He leaned back and brought his fist to his chest, like a sword pierced him in the heart. "Ouch. Once again, I've lost out to baked goods," he teased. "But these aren't Anna's work, just her recipe. I make no promises on my execution."

She peeked around his arms, still enveloping her. "I'm sure they're delicious. And do I smell coffee?"

Luke let her go. "Yes ma'am. Freshly brewed." He opened the refrigerator and grabbed the half and half. "Just the way you like it," he said, adding a splash of the creamy liquid into her mug.

She murmured her thanks as she took the mug, but not before giving him a quick peck on his cheek, her breath minty and warm. Blowing the hot liquid, she kept her eyes locked onto his. "Thanks for yesterday, Luke. Meeting Anna was a dream come true."

He shrugged. "It was nothing. We worked on an event together earlier this year."

"Don't downplay what you did. It was a big deal to me." She shook her head as she spoke. "I really do appreciate everything. This trip, yesterday, all of it."

A pang of guilt racketed around his chest. He would need to tell her about the buyout before she agreed to the makeover. But not this morning. Things were finally headed in the right direction. He needed a little more time. Today's plans would hopefully be the catalyst he needed to get her to see how much the makeover would help her.

The buyout would be the answer she'd been wanting but didn't know she needed. The right moment to tell her everything would come up. Soon, he told himself. Instead of speaking up and spilling the whole truth now, he pushed aside that little whisper of deceit and grabbed the plate of pancakes.

She made quick work of them, a smile on her face the whole time. Whether they were any good or not, she was certainly making a show of enjoying her breakfast. Soon enough, she pushed her plate away and sat back in her seat. A handful of bites were left, and Luke picked up her fork to finish the rest.

The pancakes hit his tongue like sawdust. He chewed. He took a sip of coffee. He continued to work the bite around in his mouth, but there was no hope.

Madeleine pasted a smirk across her lips while she watched him struggle with his own cooking.

Finally, with the help of another swig of coffee, he swallowed.

Madeleine leaned forward. "Finished?" Her tone was deadpan, but the glint in her eyes told him she'd had the same issues with his breakfast.

"How did you eat those? They're awful."

She exploded into bursts of laughter that were so loud Luke wondered if Dennis could hear them all the way downstairs in the lobby.

He shook his head and got up to get a glass of water. He thought again and grabbed a second glass. She could probably use one after eating those monstrosities.

Her arms were crossed around her middle, holding herself as she let out another loud, raucous belly laugh. "It's just—" She could hardly speak, she was howling so much. "...one of those things," She wiped a tear from her eye "...you do for love."

Love? The heavy pancakes in his stomach instantly melted into bubbles, fizzing around and tickling his insides. His chest went hollow, as if the only thing it held was a giant, pounding drum that resounded against his ribs with such intensity he wondered how he wasn't rattling the building.

Love. He liked hearing her say it. *Do I say it back?* He wasn't sure. Or maybe he was sure. Right now, everything had flipped on its side and then rotated again, and he was forced to withstand the waves of excitement and confusion and surprise that crashed into him from all sides.

She was still giggling, and it felt like using the word love was something more serious. Heavier. And this wasn't that moment.

"Well, thank you for humoring me." He feigned a pout.

"Oh, there's plenty of humor in this situation."

She didn't bring up the word. Maybe it was an accident. The bubbling in his belly slowed, but a dull ache of disappointment replaced it.

He scraped the rest of the pancakes, along with the leftover batter down the sink, flipped on the garbage disposal, and loaded the dishes into the dishwasher. *Definitely won't be making any more of these bricks.*

By the time he sat back at the table, she had settled down. "I do appreciate the effort, though." She patted his knee. "At least the coffee's good."

"I'm good for something."

She leaned closer to him, the scent of coffee and sweetness filling his nostrils as she did. "Is that so?" Her voice was low and soft, and her breath landed on his neck. The warmth of her hand resting on his knee radiated up his leg.

He tipped his chin down, stopping his lips only centimeters away from hers. "Well, I'd like to think I am."

She was so close, he could inhale her exhales. "Oh, you're definitely good. Maybe not at pancakes, but I think I could find a nice use for you right about now." She had moved her body close to his, her hands squarely on his shoulders. The way she twisted her fingers in his T-shirt to pull him toward her drove him crazy.

Her whispers against his lips sent a shiver around his neck and down his back. He wanted to take her by the waist, pull her into his lap, and kiss her for the rest of the day. "Really? And what use might that be?" He let his lips brush against hers, the touch so light, he barely felt it himself.

He felt, rather than saw, her mouth curl into a smile. His fingers threaded their way into her long, messy tresses with one hand, while he wrapped his other hand around her side. She was fully in his embrace now, and leaned into him as she let out the tiniest of sighs.

He needed to kiss her. Now. But making her wait proved to be a fun game. He turned his face to the side slightly. "What was that? I didn't hear your answer."

Her fingers continued to knead his shoulders. "Um. What was the question?" Her breath landed on his jawline.

He leaned away, just far enough from her mouth that she couldn't quite kiss him, and whispered again, "You said you had a nice use for me."

Her eyes were closed and her breathing rapid. She stretched upward and found his jawline anyhow. The sweet kiss she planted there was small. Light. Barely even a kiss, but that was all he needed.

He couldn't wait any longer.

Hungrily, he covered her mouth with his own, feeling her press into him as he did. She fit perfectly into his embrace, but he wanted more. With one swift motion, he lifted her from her chair and pulled her onto his lap, both her legs on one side of his own. She trailed a finger up the center of his chest and wrapped her hand around the back of his neck, letting her fingers swirl in tiny circles at the base of his hairline.

Her mouth landed on his again, making his head swim. He was sure his heart was trying to make an escape from his chest, and he knew she had to feel it thrumming in his lips as she closed around them with her own.

He trailed a slow line of kisses to the side of her mouth, down around her chin, until he found his favorite place just below her earlobe. Her sweet scent only encouraged him to keep kissing. Down. Further down, onto her neck.

She tilted her head back, giving him access to the small indention between her collarbones, and he nuzzled into her, landing his lips in the softest patch they could find.

Careful, Luke. You can't get too carried away. But every cell in his body screamed for more. He pulled her closer, her frame melting against his in a way that felt perfect.

His guard fell like a line of dominos knocking one reasonable protest down after the other.

She's too sweet.

She kissed his chin. Domino down.

We have a busy day.

Her fingers trailed down his back. Domino down.

We don't live in the same town.

A tiny sigh came from somewhere in her throat. Domino down.

We aren't even officially together.

Domino down. Down. Down.

A soft buzzing sound came slowly into Luke's consciousness. He pushed it from his mind, his only focus on the woman he held, who let a tender exhale escape as he kissed again.

And the buzzing continued.

"Luke, is that your phone?" She asked, breathlessly. She was still so close, her fingers now fully entwined in his hair.

"Hmm?"

"Your phone." Her voice, not as breathless now, pierced the dream he was in.

He opened his eyes, and she was leaning away from him, her eyes open and looking at him. "What?" The buzz. Again.

This better be important. He reached behind her and glanced at the screen on his phone. The name made his stomach lurch.

Emily Pierotti.

Chapter 29

Madeleine

T he way Luke's face fell when he looked at his phone made Madeleine's heart fall even faster. Not to mention her heart rate. She scooted back into her own chair and watched him answer the call.

"Emily." He spoke with a flat tone, uninterested.

Whoever Emily is, her timing stinks. Madeleine folded one leg underneath her other and sat back in her chair. Her brain was still foggy from their impromptu make out session. She lifted her coffee to take a sip and realized her lips were throbbing and even a little tender. The early morning scruffiness of Luke's chin must have rubbed a little more forcefully than she thought.

"We can't meet today. I've already got plans." He started shuffling through a file folder filled with papers, all with Greyson Media emblazoned across the top.

She watched as he turned to one page in particular, stopping to skim a finger down the center of it, searching for something.

"Nope on dinner, either. We fly out late tonight." He threw an apologetic look toward Madeleine, but the remorse was quickly replaced by something else. Irritation? No. She couldn't quite identify his thoughts as he spoke to Emily.

"Listen, Emily, I'm working through some final details. I'll have everything buttoned up before we need to bring film crews into Ryleigh."

They're already scheduling film crews? She stood and dumped her now-cold-coffee into the sink and rinsed the mug. She didn't want Luke to feel like she was invading his space. Well, his business space anyhow.

"Fine. I'll call you later." He hung up without even saying goodbye. He stood and crossed to her, his empty mug in his hands. She tried to read the look on his face, but she couldn't quite figure it out. One thing was clear, that phone call definitely shifted his mood.

She held out her hand for the mug before he had to reach around her. Their fingers brushed against each other, and a spark of electricity ran up her arm.

"Sorry about that," he said. "Worst timing ever."

"To say the least." She hated the warmth she felt spreading across her cheeks. She wasn't embarrassed about what they'd been doing, but the fact that they were interrupted gave her a minute to cool down and think more reasonably. "Who was that?"

"One of the people I work with. She's the producer for the show and wanted to meet with you to answer any questions you might have about the makeover." He glanced at the stack of papers across the table. "Without your official 'yes' on paper, we can't move forward on anything else."

An understanding dawned on Madeleine. "And that's the 'buttoning up' you're working on?"

He pressed his lips into a thin line and shrugged, but he said nothing.

"I see."

"Madeleine, I don't want to pressure you into anything you're not ready to do." He hesitated then rested his hand on her hip. "But I really think this could take your business to a new level. I don't think your mother would want you to stay stagnant just to honor her design. She'd want you to thrive. This is your chance."

It was true. Madeleine did love so many things she saw in Anna's books last night. While she held on to so many things in the bakery that brought her mother joy, there were also just as many that frustrated her as well. The sink that seemed to always clog, for one. Or the cracking tile floors that she worried would soon become a tripping hazard. Having a longer counter to prep foods would make her morning bakes so much easier. The idea of gaining a whole new customer base appealed to her as well. More customers meant more sales, bigger income, and less stress.

She took a deep breath. "Will you be there the whole time?"

"Every second. I'll bring in an air mattress if I have to and sleep in your office so nothing happens without my oversight."

"You're sure I'll have some input on what stays and what goes?"

He nodded. "To a point, yes. The show will need a big reveal at the end, so you can't know too many details, but I will make sure you have a chance to add your opinion."

I need a minute to think and be sure I'm was making the right decision. She wished she could get her hands into some dough and knead out her thoughts. But that wasn't really possible today. Luke already told her he'd planned a big day. "Can I have just a few minutes alone to think about things?"

"Of course. I'll go shower. Unless you want to think in the shower?"

"No. You go ahead. I want another cup of coffee."

"I'll be quick." Luke turned and sprinted up the steps, taking them two at a time.

She wandered to the table and sat, reflecting on the past two days. They had been like a magical fairy tale. Whisked away to a big city, tours of all the famous landmarks, moonlight strolls in tiny streets, a day with her baking idol. It was too good to be true. But it all happened for her because this potential show opened those doors.

Can I really do this? Would Mom want me to embrace this chance? No sooner than she asked the question, she knew the answer. Her mother would absolutely be on board with this, and she would have been digging a pen out of her purse to sign those contracts days ago. Madeleine could almost hear her mother's prompting: if it meant more success for Madeleine, who cared about some outdated wallpaper and old tables?

Something in Madeleine's spirit stirred. She knew signing that contract was the right decision.

She shifted a few of Luke's pages to the side before setting her mug down, not wanting to leave a coffee ring on them. Most of them had spreadsheets of numbers on them, a few had names of contractors, but one stood out more than the rest. The bulleted list wasn't long, but the name of her bakery started each bullet point.

She pulled the page from the top of the stack and read over each bullet point. The more she read, the more her eyes grew misty. The detailed lists of modifications to her bakery were more than she expected. Everything from tearing down walls to a new color scheme was there in black and white. And at the bottom, in plain black ink, sat the signature line.

She heard the shower shut off and knew it would only be a few minutes before Luke would appear, smelling of mint toothpaste and aftershave.

Without another second's hesitation, she grabbed Luke's pen, signed her name to the contract, and nodded once in satisfaction.

That's done. A weight fell away and was replaced with a vibrating excitement. Now that the decision was made and the contract signed, the idea of a fresh start had room to rise. She stacked the papers neatly, leaving the signed page on top where Luke would see it.

Luke's footsteps coming down the stairs brought her back to the present. "Your turn." His hair was still damp, and he was tugging his shirt down over his stomach.

Madeline didn't miss the cut of his abs as the red cotton covered them. "Thanks. I won't be long."

"No rush. Our schedule is flexible today."

She paused halfway up the steps and turned around. "I moved some of those contracts around. Hope I didn't mess them up. You might check them over."

A flash of frustration crossed his face, and Madeleine had to bite her cheek to hide her delight, knowing the surprise that was coming.

And the surprise paid off. He looked down, then back at her, his mouth slowly shifting into a wide smile. Wordlessly, he picked up the signed contract and held it toward her, pointing first to her signature, then to her, and back to her curly script on the page. "You..."

She nodded. Despite her best efforts, a tiny, gleeful sound slipped out.

He put the contract down and ran both hands through his hair. Joy danced in his eyes, and Madeleine's heartbeat sped up because of it. "I..." He laughed. "You just..."

"You better figure out how to make more coherent sentences, sir, before they put you in front of that camera. You promised me you'd be there the whole time and I can't have you getting replaced now."

He let out a whoop and crossed to the stairs in one stride. Skipping two stairs at a time, he climbed to her in a flash. She barely had time to react before his arms pulled her to him and he pressed his lips to hers.

This kiss wasn't like their earlier make-out session. This was fast and passionate. Celebratory. He laughed as he moved his mouth across hers, and the vibrations of his chuckle tickled her lips. She hadn't ever been kissed like this, and it made her tingle all the way to her fingertips. She'd be more than content to stay right here on these stairs and do this for the rest of the day.

But Luke had other ideas. "This changes what we're doing today, you know," he said, his lips brushing against hers as he spoke. "I'll have to call Mike and tell it's 'Operation Sweet Tooth' time."

"What on earth are you talking about?" Still lightheaded from excitement, she clung to his biceps as she leaned back to see his face.

He shook his head. "Can't tell you anything except Mike and I've been saving these plans for the day you decided to let this makeover happen."

Very sly, Luke Taylor. And very confident.

"You'd better get into that shower before we lose any more time." He lifted her hand above her head and gave her a little spin as if the steps were their personal dance floor.

"Gonna tell me what we're doing?" She headed up two steps while he stepped down and moved back to the kitchen table.

"Nope, but I can say you'll have a sweet tour guide." He winked at her before picking up the contracts.

Madeleine heard him shuffling through the pages as she made her way upstairs.

"Hey, Madeleine?" He called after her. "Hold on. You didn't..."

She leaned over the rails and flashed him a flirty smirk. "I didn't what?"

He looked up at her, and she thought she saw that same look he had after talking on the phone flash across his face again. "Um, never mind. We can look at this later."

She showered, dressed, threw her hair in a ponytail, and applied a coat of mascara in record time.

After tugging on her tall, brown boots, she checked her reflection in the mirror and smiled at the way the rarely-worn heels made her legs look nicely curvy. One swipe of lip gloss was the final touch before making her way downstairs, where Luke sat checking his email.

He closed the lid of his laptop before letting his gaze slide over her, starting at her toes and working its way up, settling on her eyes.

A wave of heat washed over her at the same pace as Luke's trailing view. She tucked a stray lock of hair behind her ear before looking back at the steps. *Now would be the worst time to fall.* She gripped the handrail a little tighter for the rest of her descent, knowing Luke still watched her.

"You look cute." He seemed to drink her in from his place at the table.

She tipped her foot onto the floor, finally reaching the bottom of the stairs. "What, this sweater?" She fiddled with the hem of her favorite oatmeal cable knit and did a quick turn.

Her foot didn't want to turn with her. As a matter of fact, the ball of her foot stayed planted, but her ankle was more than cooperative, spinning at its own rate. She tried to grab the handrail of the steps as she whirled around uncontrollably, but it slipped from her fingertips. *Oh, sugar. Please let me stay on my own two feet.* She planted her other foot firmly, but images of Bambi learning to ice skate were now at the forefront of her brain, and she knew she had just completed her supermodel spin with the same grace and poise as the baby deer.

Luke was already out of his seat before she came to a stop. "Whoa," he said as he caught her post-spin, but he was also laughing as he stopped her.

The strength in his hands gripping her waist was reassuring. She joined his laughter and rolled her eyes. "It's these boots. Dillon always says I can't be trusted in anything except my bare feet."

"Apparently, he's not wrong." His voice still held the rumblings of a chuckle. "Think you can make it all day in those or do you need a minute to change?"

"Will we be walking, or is Mike driving?"

"A little of both." He was still close to her, his hands still firmly grasping her waist. "But I think I can keep a pretty good hold on you if you need."

Playfully, she flipped her ponytail like she was in high school again. "Oh, I suppose if I *must*. I mean, who am I to deny you such chivalry?" She winked.

He stepped back and made a swift bow, sweeping his arm grandly in front of him as he did. "Why thank you, madam. It's so kind of you to think of me."

When he stood, she met his smile with one of her own, then took his outstretched hand in hers.

"Mike is waiting downstairs."

"But you haven't even told me what we're doing today.""Yes, I did." He led her to the door of his apartment and held it open for her.

They stepped into the elevator. "No, you didn't."

"I did say you'd have a sweet tour guide for the day." He held his arms wide, presenting himself as the promised guide.

She gave him a sidelong glance as the elevator doors closed. "And what will we be touring?" She drew out her sentence slowly as something like suspicion and excitement mixed around her insides.

"Bakeries. I want you to see the best the city has to offer. Think of it as research. A day of makeover inspiration." He smiled at her, his eyes wide with delight at his plans.

Chapter 30

Luke

"The Frosted Cupcake," Mike announced from the driver's seat as he put the car into park.

Madeleine looked at Luke with question in her eyes. His heart sped up, knowing the surprises he'd planned. He hoped his hours of internet searching would pay off by the end of the day, and her delight would be all that remained. Well, that and maybe a satiated sweet tooth.

"Our first stop. Today is all about bakeries. It's a crash course tour of New York City's finest little shops and cafés. Your only job is to look around, tell me what you like and what you don't."

"No taste testing?" She tipped her head to the side and scrunched her nose.

"Well, I think it would be rude to just walk around and not buy something, don't you?"

Her eyebrows shot up. "I absolutely do."

Her perked up grin gave him hope for success. "Order whatever you like. Greyson Media's picking up the bill."

The windows outside The Frosted Cupcake practically screamed sugar. Painted with a bright purple trim, their displays were filled with cake stands laden with colorful mini-cakes, all frosted in rainbow colors.

Madeleine's eyes grew wide as she stepped through the doors, and Luke watched her inhale the sugary scent wafting around them.

The lavender-striped walls reminded Luke of a circus tent, and the fantastic atmosphere felt like a party.

Madeleine stepped to the counter, where a twenty-something-woman wearing two space buns high on the crown of her head perkily greeted her. "Hi there. Welcome to The Frosted Cupcake. What sweets can we tempt you with?" She was tiny and moved with graceful sweeps of her hands as she spoke, only adding to the circus feeling of the room. Luke half-expected her to jump onto a tightrope above him at any moment.

Madeleine placed a finger to her lips as she perused the glass display counter. She glanced at Luke and smiled. "So much to choose from," she murmured before turning back to the girl. "What's your most popular?"

"The lavender honeybee." She pointed to a cupcake in the center of the top row. Frosted in a paler purple than the walls and topped with a honeycomb crisp, it looked like a toothache waiting to happen. "It's lavender-vanilla cake, with a honey custard filling, frosted with lavender buttercream. It's our signature treat." She bounced on her heels as she finished the last sentence, and Luke looked up, checking for any trapeze swings that might be about to descend.

"Then I think we should try that one." Madeleine turned back to Luke for his approval, and he nodded his head.

"Whatever you like sounds great to me." *I have no idea what a lavender buttercream is. She's the expert.*

The cupcake plated and the bill paid, Madeleine moved toward the nearest little round table with marble tabletops and iron legs. The heavy lilac-colored iron chair screeched against the floor when Luke pulled it out for her.

She used her fork to slice the sweet treat in half, revealing the golden custard now oozing out from the middle.

A rush of warmth spread across Luke's chest when he saw the corner of her mouth tip up in a smile at the sight of the delicious confection. *Maybe planning a makeover together can be successful after all.*

"Want the first bite?" she asked, holding the loaded fork in his direction.

"All yours." He wanted to watch those perfect lips take in that sweet bite. He wasn't disappointed.

Neither was she.

She looked up at the gilded tile ceiling and a tiny moan of delight came from her throat, exposing that soft space between her collarbones that was so kissable.

She swallowed, already cutting her next bite. "That is unreal." She pushed the plate toward him but kept the fork. "You need to try some."

He motioned to the fork, already back in her mouth. "Can I borrow that?"

She blushed and handed it over as she chewed the next bite.

He sliced a bit of cake, and she interrupted him as he lifted the fork. "Be sure you get a bit of the custard with it."

He laughed. "You're the boss." He dove back into the middle of the cupcake and ate. Now he knew why she reacted with such passion. It was good. Not just good, it was amazingly sweet, but not toothache sweet. Just fill-your-mouth-and-wish-for-more level of delicious.

The way she smiled at him, watching him enjoy this bite, made him a little self-conscious. She expected a big reaction, and her delight in seeing him excited over baked goods was adorable. "Heavenly, isn't it?"

He nodded and passed the fork back to her. "Incredible." He looked around the small bakery, noticing the white picture frames holding images of bakery ingredients, and reached for his notebook, resting under her plate. "Okay, down to business. What do you like about this place? The food notwithstanding."

She looked around the room slowly, taking in details of the space before speaking. "Honestly, the food is about it. This isn't my vibe. Too 'Alice in Wonderland' for me."

"Okay. That's fair," he said as he scribbled some notes onto the page and snapped a few photos with his phone.

"It's cute, but not warm, you know?"

He had to agree. The cold of the marble tabletops, the stark contrast of the white on purple, the impersonal photos, it just didn't feel like Madeleine. She was warmth, kindness. And love. Again, the word came into his mind before he could stop it. *Could she love me?* Yesterday's meeting with Grey when he passed over the pages to finalize their ownership of the Bean and Batter flashed in his memories. *Not if I let Greyson Media buy her bakery.*

"Luke? You okay?" She interrupted his thoughts.

"Hmm?" He blinked at her. "Yeah, I'm good. Just thinking about the makeover.

Her smile brightened, but guilt seeped into his thoughts. *She didn't see the buyout addendum.* Luke had kept it tucked under his laptop, covered in his scrawling notes and highlighted sentences. He'd been searching through it, hoping to find some way to rework the deal with Grey. Now that she'd agreed to the makeover, Emily could finalize the filming schedule, but Luke needed more time to talk Grey out of the buyout plan.

Madeleine looked wistfully at the last few bites of cupcake left on the plate. "I wish I could finish that, but I'm afraid I'll be too full for whatever the next place has."

"Are you kidding me?" he asked as they stood and he guided her toward the door, his hand lightly pressing the small of her back. "You can make that at home. Call Anna, I'm sure she can help."

She glanced sidelong at him, which was followed by an eye roll. "Oh, call Anna," she said, her voice high and mocking. "She'll help," she teased. "Like we're best friends now, and she's got time to develop recipes with some small-town mega-fan."

Luke wiggled his eyebrows. "Well, about that." He stopped in his tracks, letting his hand slide over to her elbow and down to her fingertips, which he wove through his own. "I have a feeling you might be seeing more of her. You just never know what the future holds..." He let his voice trail off. He'd baited her now and hoped she'd bite.

Her chin dropped and her whole face squished together, like she'd tasted lemons. "Luke." She dragged his name out slowly, like she'd asked a suspicious question. "What do you mean?"

"Oh. Sorry." He feigned confusion. "What were we just saying? Hey, look. Mike's here." He motioned toward the car pulling up to the curb before pulling her toward it.

Like a stubborn mule, her feet didn't follow. "Oh, no," she laughed. "You've already started this. Now finish it."

He feigned regret. "No. I can't. I might be in trouble with Greyson Media."

"Oh? Gosh, that's too bad." She had already pulled him back to where she stood, still holding his hand, while her other fingers rested on his shoulder. "I'd hate to see you in trouble."

That mock pout on her lips made him want to kiss her right there on the sidewalk, and the way she let her fingers trail along his collarbone made his breath hitch. "You're awfully cute when you're persuasive."

"I know." She winked at him and moved one step closer.

"And how am I supposed to resist that?" He could smell the lavender on her breath as he tipped his forehead toward hers.

She giggled, which nearly made him crazy. "You're not," she said, letting her fingers drum on the middle of his chest as if she were impatient. "So don't keep a girl waiting. Spill your secrets, sir."

A car horn blasted from the street, taking Luke's attention. The delivery truck driver behind Mike's car had his window rolled down and was flailing his arm at them. "Hey, move it, man. You can't just stop wherever," he yelled at Mike, his New York accent thick.

Mike stood and held the backseat door open for them, shrugging as he did so. "Luke, I'm sorry. Either you two have to get in, or I've got to circle the block."

"We'll get in," Luke said matter-of-factly

"Circle the block," Madeleine said at the same time.

Mike just stared at them both, unsure of what he should do.

"Let's g-o-o-o," the truck driver barked.

Luke huffed at the man and waved his free hand toward Mike's car, as if to say 'Okay, we're getting in' before pulling Madeleine toward the awaiting door.

As he watched her climb into the car, a mix of emotions swirled into his brain, now that it wasn't fogged up with Madeleine's sweetness. *She's not going to give up. How can I tell her about the buyout now? I've kept this from her too long.*

She held her hand toward him. "Luke? Get in. I think we have some unfinished business to discuss.

His stomach lurched into his throat. *She has no idea.*

Chapter 39

Madeleine

The late-night flight home was uneventful so far. Well, as uneventful as a first-class seat, complete with any amenity Madeleine could ask for, not to mention Luke's chest to lean against as she closed her eyes for takeoff. He managed to slip his arm behind her and pull her closer to him once she got settled, and it gave her sense of contentment.

Today had been a whirlwind of emotions, starting with their cute kisses over coffee, then the relief of finally deciding to let the makeover happen, and ending up with a tasting tour of some of the city's cutest bakeries. A box of delicious treats, something from each one of the six places Luke took her, rested under the seat in front of her. Her dad would want to taste some, and Dillon and Becca would eat the rest. But right now, all Madeleine wanted to do was relax. It might be the sugar crash, but sitting here, resting her head on Luke's chest, listening to his breath flowing in and out, had to be the most perfect place on earth. The cabin lights were darkened, and most passengers had, by now, settled into a restful sleep.

He leaned down and nuzzled his face into her hair, now pulled down and cascading around her shoulders. "Tired?" he asked.

"A little. You?"

"Not much. I've got some work to do. Will my computer bother you?"

She could hardly hold her eyes open. "Nope," she said, unable to mutter anything else.

"Get some sleep. I'll wake you when they bring food." He stroked her hair from her forehead and leaned over to kiss it. Her breathing slowed, and her eyelids felt heavy.

Luke lowered his tray and placed his laptop onto it. He dimmed the screen, then clicked on his email icon.

Madeleine's eyes were almost closed, until she saw her name in the email he was reading. She recalled the pages from earlier detailing the makeover, and her stomach fluttered. Without moving, and hoping Luke thought she had fallen asleep, she read the message. It was short, but one sentence was all she needed to read. "We'd like to be there next Tuesday to start filming, and start demolition by Wednesday."

Hoping she might sneak a peek at the makeover plans, she stayed still. *As long as he thinks I'm asleep, I can lay here.* But suddenly her body felt too rigid, too stiff. Not like a relaxed, sleeping person, but more like a mannequin in the window of Macy's on 34th. And her breathing. It was not natural. Suddenly she couldn't remember what breathing was supposed to be like. Slow? Long and deep? Was she inhaling too deeply?

Luke clicked reply. Madeleine saw that he was answering Emily. Once again, that name floated in between them.

He typed a quick response. "We should be ready. I haven't had a chance to go over the addendum with Madeleine. There's still that major detail to work on. Luke." He hit send with a click that, to Madeleine, sounded like a door slamming shut on so many hopes and dreams for the future of her bakery.

What major detail? She had to find out what details he knew but hadn't shared.

She took a deep breath and sat up, smoothing down her hair as she did.

Luke twisted in his seat in surprise, while stroking little circles on her back just below her neck. "Thought you'd gone to sleep."

"I tried. But something is bothering me."

"Is it the light from my computer? I'm sorry. I can work later." He closed his laptop and pushed his tray away from him.

"No. It's not that." She tucked her hair behind her ear and looked at him. Here, in the darkened airplane, he looked so perfect. So relaxed. But she had to get some answers.

"Luke." She took a deep breath, steeling her nerves. "I just saw what you wrote in that email."

His jaw clenched and he looked up, studying the air vents above his head. The tiny nod was enough of an answer to make Madeleine wish she hadn't asked.

"What details still need to be discussed?" Her voice shot into a quiet screech.

He answered, but still wouldn't turn to look at her. "When I went in to the office yesterday, while you were with Anna, there was a meeting."

"A meeting? With who?"

"My boss, Henry Greyson. And he's excited about this idea. Then Emily came in, and she was pushing for progress, too, and—"

Luke's whole body had tensed, and she leaned away from him. "I think you need to tell me about Emily." *Because you're definitely not telling me something, here.*

Luke cleared his throat, then looked straight into Madeleine's eyes. He paused there for only a second, then looked away. She watched the muscles in his jaw clench and unclench, tighten then relax. Finally, he spoke. "Emily is someone I work with. But that's not what I'm trying to tell you about."

"But when you say her name, you make a face. I can't tell what you're keeping from me." prompted Madeleine.

He sighed. "She's an ex." He ran his fingers through his hair and let out a thin breath.

"I see." Her voice was calm, but her insides were not. She paused, then asked, "And how serious were you two?" Inwardly, Madeleine couldn't shake this new worry that Emily might still have a hold on Luke. After all, she lived in New York, and they worked together. Madeleine couldn't compete with that kind of big-city-glamour-girl.

"I wanted it to be more serious. She couldn't do that."

Fantastic. He's still pining over this ex-girlfriend and probably hopes this project will bring them back together.

"And she's tied to this makeover show?"

Luke finally looked at her. "She's the project lead. The show's producer."

Now it was Madeleine's turn to nod silently, processing what he'd just said. Her throat was tight, and her day of sweet snacking was now regrettable. She rubbed the back of her neck with her hand, hoping to massage some of the tension away. Luke's hand slid upward and covered hers.

"I'm sorry I didn't tell you about her earlier."

Madeleine pulled her hand out from under his and placed it in her lap. She bit her lip, dreading the question she knew needed asking. "Usually producers are on-site. Should we be expecting Emily in Ryleigh anytime soon?"

Luke pursed his lips and nodded.

"When?" she asked, even though his email already gave her the answer.

"Next Sunday night."

"Luke, it's Saturday now. You haven't given me enough time to get everything in the bakery ready."

Luke pulled his arm out from behind her, slid his laptop under the seat in front of him, closed his tray table, and twisted to face her. The way he took both hands in hers was not comforting. "There's something else we need to talk about."

"Okay."

"Please know that I've already been working to keep this from happening."

A knot was beginning to form in Madeleine's stomach, and she worried that she might be sick. "Stop what, Luke? You're making me nervous."

"I promise I'm not through fighting this. I'll hire lawyers on your behalf if I have to." He squeezed her hands so tightly as he spoke, only adding to her increasing anxiety.

"Lawyers? What are you talking about?"

He took a deep breath. His thumb swiped back and forth across the back of her hand, like a pendulum on a clock, ticking away the seconds, until he spoke. "There's a addendum page of the contract that says once you agree to this makeover, Greyson Media will own The Bean and Batter."

"They will what?" She screeched. So much for being quiet on the evening flight. The formerly sleeping lady across the aisle peered over at them through one lifted eyelid. "What do you mean?" Madeleine's throat was completely dry, and she pressed against her seatback in an attempt to stop her trembling.

"Madeleine, please. The paperwork wasn't with the contracts you signed this morning. But it isn't final. I can fix this." His words were pleading but coming at her at a rapid pace.

She jerked her hands away from his. "But, Luke, you've missed the point. You shouldn't have ever let it get this far. You swept me off to New York, enchanted me with adorable bakeries, and made me believe that I would actually have a say in how this story would end. And I was happy to agree to it all."

"I know, but I really think—"

A flight attendant walked toward the two of them, likely hoping to quiet them down. "Is there anything I can get the two of you?"

"Yes. A glass of water, please." Madeleine replied.

Luke barely glanced at the woman but shook his head. He lowered his voice to a whisper. "First off, I am sorry. Truly, truly sorry."

The softness around his eyes told Madeleine he meant what he said, but the squeezing around her heart made it difficult to do anything except stay angry. She remained silent, arms crossed over her chest, and still trying to control her shaking.

Luke pressed his hand against her wrist, but she twisted away from his touch. "Please don't do this. I can fix it."

"Stop saying that. My mother's bakery is the one connection I have left to her. You can't fix this, Luke. The damage is done." She swiped angrily at the tear running down her cheek.

The flight attendant returned with a glass of water. "Miss? Can I get you anything else?" She paused for an extra second before handing the water to Madeleine. "A fresh cloth for your face, perhaps?"

"Thank you, but I'm fine."

The attendant stood taller. "If you need help, I'm just a push of a button away." She gave Luke a pointed glance before stepping toward the galley.

Madeleine couldn't look at Luke, not that she wanted to anyhow. Her whole world seemed to be spinning out of control. First, she lost her mother. Then, her bakery's financial state went sour. Just when she thought her heart was beginning to heal, Luke swept in and sprinkled sugar across all her worries. She had even decided she could convince Dillon to like this situation, once he saw how happy she was with Luke.

But now, things were no longer sugary sweet. Her perfect Muffin Man no longer looked like that gorgeous picture placed next to the recipe in cookbooks.

Madeleine knew there was no way to rescue this ruined bake.

Chapter 32

Luke's phone sat on the console of his pickup as he drove home after dropping Madeleine at home. The flight had ended with the two of them seated next to each other but worlds apart. *She has every right to be angry with me. I should have been honest from the start. About the show, about my dreams to finally get on camera, about the makeover, the buyout, Emily. All of it.*

She'd been silent on the drive from Dallas to Ryleigh, and he knew she needed to be left alone. But the heartbreak he saw on her face was nearly unbearable to watch.

He eased his truck into his brother's driveway, shifted it into park, and rested his head on the steering wheel. What should have been a whirlwind trip for two filled with fun and delight turned into a major breakdown. He didn't think any of this was fixable. And now, with Emily lining up crews to arrive in just a few days, he wasn't sure what to do. He'd thrown this pitch out, and it was definitely a swing and a miss.

His phone buzzed, and he snatched it from the console. Madeleine's name flashed on his screen, and a glimmer of hope made him perk up. "Hey. You okay?"

She was crying. He wasn't surprised at the sniffling coming through the phone. She'd managed to keep her tears in check for long enough as they drove, but he figured arriving home gave her the chance to let all her emotions out.

"I am not okay, no."

"I know. Madeleine, I am so sorry. I promise I'm going to figure this out. I won't let Greyson Media take your bakery from you."

She said nothing in reply but soft sobs.

He waited, his guilt making his stomach twist into knots. It took every bit of self-control he had not to throw his truck into reverse and drive straight to her house and hold her while she cried. *She probably wouldn't even let me through the door.*

Finally, she took a deep breath. "It's not Greyson Media I'm worried about."

A chord of confusion made him pause. "Uhh, what?"

She sniffled again, then inhaled a shaky breath. "I was just going through the mail, and I have a note from the..." Her voice was growing into a big wail with each syllable.

"From the what?" He couldn't figure out what her last word had been, she'd been crying so hard.

"The bank," she managed to say. "They say I have ninety days before fore-closure."

His arms were suddenly heavy, and his head ached. "Oh, babe. I'm so sorry." He seemed to be saying that a lot lately. But this time, it wasn't an apology for his stupidity. It was empathy, because these last few weeks had shown him exactly how much the bakery meant to Madeleine. He started his truck up and headed back down the driveway without thinking.

"I'll be right over. Can I bring you anything?"

She hiccupped a little sob. "Yes. Bring me those contracts. I think giving Greyson Media might be my only way to keep Mom's bakery open."

***

Monday morning arrived faster than he expected. Today was the day his two worlds would collide with Emily Pierotti's arrival in Ryleigh, Texas.

His calendar app buzzed, with the reminder of a meeting with Ryleigh's mayor, James Carter. *Hurry up, Emily.* She needed to attend this meeting as well.

"Em. Mayor meeting in ten. Are you close?" He hit send on his text, only to get a text from Emily at the same time.

"I'm at the mayor's office. Where are you?"

Luke turned the ignition key on his truck and headed for Main street. Ryleigh's City Hall was, naturally, right in the center of town on Main Street.

But that wasn't in the forefront of Luke's mind. The Bean and Batter was only two blocks off of Main. Only two blocks over, Madeleine would be mixing up some batter or brewing a latte, and he would be sitting in a meeting discussing how Greyson Media would be taking over the town. He fought the urge to turn left instead of right as he reached the crossroads. He wanted nothing more than to walk into The Bean and Batter, wrap his arms around Madeleine, and tell her everything would be okay.

But he didn't know that for sure. And until he met with Emily, he couldn't guarantee anything.

Emily stood outside the doors to City Hall, the pointed toe of her stiletto heel tapping the pavement as Luke walked toward her. Despite her impatient tapping, he watched a smile creep across her lips and her eyes drink him in, head to toe. "Well, Mr. Taylor. You wear country bumpkin well." She pointed to his jeans and cowboy boots. "I think I might even prefer this 'down home country boy' look to the city slicker I knew." She let her finger wander under his chin as she spoke.

Luke jerked away from her. "Stop. We're not dating anymore. This is strictly business. Got it?"

She flipped her hand toward her face and fanned it. "Why fiddle-dee-dee," she said, using a ridiculously exaggerated Southern accent. "You're awfully serious today, Mr. Taylor. I only wanted to say hello." Her bottom lip stuck out in a pout, and she furrowed her eyebrows at him.

"You don't know small town life like I do. The rumor mill here runs faster than the six train, and the last thing I need is for some old biddy to see us being more friendly than business standing here on Main Street."

An eye roll was all she gave him before turning toward the door, which Luke reached to hold open for her.

Mayor Carter sat at his desk poring over some documents with the Greyson Media logo splashed across the top. "Luke Taylor, it is good to have you in my office. I was just going over the final details for the reality series."

He stood and reached a hand out to shake Luke's.

"I see that. And I'd like to introduce Emily Pierotti. She'll be heading up this project."

Mayor Carter took her hand and shook it. "We're glad to have you, Mrs. Pierotti."

"Uh, it's Ms. Pierotti, thank you," she answered.

"Ah. My apologies. Of course, once word gets around that there's a new single lady in town, I'm afraid the mama's league will be clamoring to introduce you to their sons." He ran a hand across his round belly as he laughed good-naturedly.

Emily gave Luke a sidelong glance, and he shrugged back at her as if to say, 'I told you so.'

"I'm sure I can handle the moms of Ryleigh. I'm more concerned about how we are going to revitalize the town with this show."

Clever, Emily. Always turning the conversation your direction.

Mayor Carter motioned to the two chairs opposite his desk and sat. "Yes, well, I do have to say that when Luke stopped by a few weeks ago, I was surprised to see he'd come home. But I listened to his idea and couldn't be more excited."

Pointing to the stack of pages cluttering the desk, Emily answered, "I see you've received all the specs that we will need. Did you have any questions on the filming schedule?"

He shuffled through the papers and pulled out the schedule. "Nope, no. It all looks pretty clear here. You seem to have thought of everything." He looked up at her, then shifted his focus to Luke. "But I am a little worried about the makeover. You know how Mrs. Malone poured her heart and soul into that bakery. Are you sure Madeleine is ready for that much change?"

The lump that seemed to have taken up permanent residence in Luke's throat ever since his flight home swelled. He scratched at his neck, hoping to free up his voice, but it was no use. Emily would have already picked up on his hesitation. She'd known him too long not to notice.

She pulled some documents from her bag and held them toward the mayor. "Luke has already assured me she is excited for the project. Thrilled, even. Wouldn't you agree, Luke?" She glanced his way, her eyes wide and expecting a solid confirmation of what she'd just promised Mayor Carter.

He managed to muster an "Mm-hmm" along with a nod. He felt sick to his stomach. The office was too small and getting warmer by the second.

"All we need now is your signature here for a photo release, Mr. Mayor."

Luke watched as the mayor signed the pages, focusing on the scritch-scratch of the pen against the paper and willing it to move faster. He could feel Emily's watchful eyes on him, and for a moment, he was grateful for their history. Three years together meant she would have seen his panic rising. She might not understand what caused it, but her next comment was all he wanted to hear.

"Well, Mayor Carter, everything seems to be in order." She was already on her feet now, sliding the papers into her bag then holding her hand out to shake the mayor's. "Luke and I have quite a bit of work ahead of us." She took Luke's elbow, making it look as if he were escorting her out of the room. "We will be in touch soon."

And just like that, Emily had maneuvered through Luke's tension like an expert.

No. Not like an expert. Like a girlfriend. Like someone who could read even the tiniest bits of his body language and knew how to respond.

The cool Texas air swiped across Luke's face, and he took a deep breath. Emily didn't let go of his arm. Crossing to his truck with Emily right beside him, he muttered, "We need to talk."

"Yeah, we do."

Once he stood next to his truck, leaning on the tailgate, he wasn't really sure where to start.

Emily handled that for him. "What is going on with you? I assume there's a problem, or you wouldn't have flipped out back there."

The lump in his throat continued to plague him. He couldn't seem to find his voice.

The familiar sensation of her palm resting against his chest eased his breathing. Slowed his thinking. Relaxed his shoulders. He drew closer to her, inhaling the scent of her floral perfume. Jasmine mixed with roses. *She's still wearing the same one I chose for her.*

"Em, I'm not sure I can do this."

"Do what?" She tipped her chin up to look at him, but he saw her eyes flicker to his lips.

"This buyout. It feels wrong." He focused on Emily's green eyes to slow his rising worry.

She nodded, her eyes laced with judgment. "Oh. I see. So the mayor wasn't wrong in his concerns."

He shook his head.

"Well, I'm sure that with the proper motivation...and by that I mean, you." She paused and ran her fingers down the center of his chest, stopping just above his belly button, "Madeleine can be convinced to get on board."

The sound of tires crunching across pavement drew Luke's attention. He squinted into the sun, and, to his horror, watched a red pickup truck headed in their direction, slowing as it approached. *Oh no. Not now.* The sick feeling returned with a vengeance in Luke's belly as the driver slowed to a stop and rolled down his window.

Dillon didn't say anything at first. He only stared at his older brother, then at the woman whose hand rested on his chest.

Luke pushed Emily's hand away, but it was too late.

Dillon nodded his head in understanding, sucking his teeth as he took in the scene before him. "Well hey there, big brother. Don't think I've had the pleasure of meeting your friend."

Luke's insides squirmed. This was the last thing he needed right now. "Emily, meet my brother. Dillon." He motioned toward his coworker. "This is Emily Pierotti. We work together."

With eyebrows lifted, Dillon nodded. "I see that you are together. Makes perfect sense." He paused and looked down at his phone. "But you know what doesn't make any sense at all? This text I got from my girl Maddie just now." He held the phone toward his brother.

He was too far away to read the text, but it didn't matter. Dillon kept talking. "She says something about the two of you—" he paused, and directed his words toward Emily. "I'm meaning Luke and Madeleine, here. I didn't realize that there was another 'two of you.'"

"Look, Dillon, that's enough." Luke stepped toward the truck, but his brother held out a hand in a stopping motion.

"Now, now, I'm just trying to find out what is going on. No need to get upset."

Luke's muscles tensed. It took every inch of willpower he had to keep from yanking the truck door open and jerking that phone from his little brother's hands. "What did Madeleine's text say?" he asked through gritted teeth.

"She says you two had a nice time in New York together, and she's saying yes to that makeover show you've been trying to talk her into."

"Anything else?" A flitter of hope rose up inside Luke, but he couldn't take time to focus on that just yet.

"Nope, but you see, that's the thing. She sounded even a tiny bit hopeful and excited about it. But now, here I am driving to The Bean and Batter to grab some coffee, and I come across this little scene." His faux-casual tone turned dark. "So help me, Luke, if you think I'm going to let you break her heart, you are dead wrong."

Luke sensed Emily stepping up beside him. "Boys, I think this has gone long enough. Dillon, we are just making plans for the show together. Producer and talent working alongside one another. Luke, we've got work to do. Let's go."

Dillon nodded his head. "Right. Producer and talent. Okay."

Luke stood frozen, staring back at his brother.

But before Luke could say anything, Dillon threw his truck into drive. "Well, then. I guess I'd better get on over to the bakery so you two can...work." And without even a second glance back, Dillon drove away, taking Luke's confidence along with it.

The race was on. He had to get to Madeleine before his brother did.

Chapter 33

Madeleine

M adeleine didn't need to look up when the door to her bakery opened. The familiar clunk of work boots on the tile floors had a cadence she'd known for years. Dillon would come right behind the counter, without asking, and help himself to a mug of coffee.

As if he read her mind, that's exactly what he did.

As always, Becca shooed him away. "Dillon Taylor, get out of my work space. I'll get your coffee for you, but you're in my way." She took the towel from her shoulder and flicked it in his direction.

He stepped back to the front of the counter and passed his mug back to Becca. "Thanks, hon. You're the best."

The little exchange brought a smile to Madeleine's lips. *Greyson Media might change the way this place looks, but they can't change the heart of it.* She knew moments like this would continue even after the makeover. As much as she hated to lose ownership, she had to admit agreeing to the buyout had given her a little bit of relief over the past few days. She just had to stay focused on keeping her bakery's spirit in place.

Becca poured Dillon's vanilla latte and added a splash of half and half to it. "Just the way you like it," she said, passing it across the counter to him.

He took a sip and smiled back at her. "You are too good to me, Becca." He strode over to the register, where Madeleine waited.

"No charge, Dillon. You know that.""Yes ma'am, I do. But I never want to assume." He pointed to her office door. "Got time to talk? I got your text."

"Sure. Come on back." She looked up at Becca. "You good for a minute or two?"

Her assistant nodded. "I think I've got this under control." She motioned to the nearly empty bakery and chuckled.

"Well, holler if you need me."

She cleared off a box of cupcake liners from her desk chair while Dillon pulled the folding chair out from behind the door and sat across from her, his knee bouncing up and down with restless energy. "Madeleine, I got your text. Are you sure this is a good idea?"

The worry on his face was clear. She'd seen it before. But today, it seemed more intense. Like the worry was actually heavy to carry. She reached over and rested her hand on his knee. "You okay?"

He twisted the silver ring on his pointer finger around in a circle. "Yeah, I'm good. We aren't here to talk about me, Maddiecakes."

She loved that he called her that. It started as a joke back in high school, since she was always baking something, but it just stuck. Once again, Madeleine remembered that the heart of The Bean and Batter couldn't be taken away, no matter what the decorations looked like.

"Well, you seem like you could use a pick-me-up. Want a brownie? It's a new recipe. I added coffee to the batter and frosted it with mocha buttercream." *Thanks, Anna Lamb, for that idea.*

He smiled a half-smile, shook his head, then took a sip of his coffee. "Maddiecakes, I read your text."

"I know. And?"

"And I've watched you and Luke together for the last few weeks. Well, aside from the four days you spent in New York."

"So?" *Here it comes. This is a bad idea, he's not right, blah, blah, blah.* She didn't want to rehash this anymore. She wanted Dillon to reassure her that this buyout would be a good idea. To tell her it was the best option. To show her that she wasn't really losing her bakery, just gaining some peace of mind. Maybe if he said it, she might believe it. Maybe.

"So, I'm worried." He rested his elbows on his knees and leaned forward, cradling his mug between his hands.

She didn't like the tone of this meeting. Dillon had always been completely honest with her, and that look in his eyes said his honest streak was ready for release. "There's nothing to worry about. I think the makeover could be good for the business." Her tone was light and confident, which was the opposite of how she really felt.

"It's not the makeover I'm worried about." He lowered his chin and looked straight into her eyes. "You already know I think this..." He waved his hand through the air. "This whatever it is, fling, or game, or flirting thing with Luke is a mistake. You're too good for him."

She knew he meant it as a compliment, to say that she was something special, but it didn't land that way.

With a sigh, he stood and paced around the tiny office, setting his empty mug on her desk. "Madeleine Amy Malone, you can sit here and pretend that everything is fine, but I know you. I know your mind, I know your dreams, and I know your heart. You may think you have me fooled, but I can see through you better than anyone else." He stopped right in front of her and crouched down, resting his hands on top of hers folded in her lap. "You're unhappy. So stop pretending. It's time to be real."

He knew. How much he knew, she couldn't be sure. But he knew she hadn't fully committed to this makeover in her mind. Did he know about the buyout? She looked at his hands clasped around hers. His calluses from working were rough against her skin. Yet, the look in his eyes was so tender and soft. How could she ever think she could pretend with him?

She worried her bottom lip between her teeth for a moment, then realized how heavy this burden had been for the last two days. It would be a relief to let Dillon carry some of it with her. To help her talk through the decisions. "All right. Let's talk."

Dillon seated himself on the chair again, but pulled it closer so their knees brushed against each other, just as they had in so many other conversations since junior high. "Okay then. Let's talk."

"First off, how much do you know?"

"I know that Luke's company is doing a show about our town. And a makeover of your place is part of that show."

"Is that all you know?"

He shrugged. "I guess. Why? Is there more for you to tell me?"

"There is."

"What else?" Concern flooded his words.

She decided the best way would be to just blurt it out. "After the makeover, Greyson Media will own The Bean and Batter." *Whew.* Saying it aloud for the first time to someone other than Luke made her feel slightly sick. And relieved. And hurt.

Dillon leaned back in his chair and adjusted his baseball cap. He said nothing, only nodded his head a few times.

She waited.

Five seconds.

Ten.

All the while, thoughts of Luke swirled in her mind. He'd started out so sweet. Never in her wildest dreams did she think she'd ever have a chance at any kind of relationship with him. But, it happened. And it had been so perfect.

Finally, Dillon broke the silence. "I can't let you go through with this. Not without telling you everything." He stopped again, his hands balling into fists. "I just ran into Luke over on Main Street."

The tone in his voice unsettled her. Her stomach threatened to empty its contents soon if he didn't keep talking. "And?" she prompted.

"How close did you and Luke get? Honestly."

"What do you mean?" Her cheeks grew warm as the memory of kisses in New York flashed through her mind.

"Like, are you two dating or just messing around or is it more serious?"

She drew her eyes into a squint. The ache in her heart swelled from a dull, constant heaviness to a thudding, intense pulse. She could still remember the softness of his lips on hers, but as soon as she let her mind go there, she also recalled how he deceived her with promises of a new bakery. One that wouldn't be hers anymore. Despite agreeing to the buyout, she still wasn't ready to completely forgive him.

Dillon deserved an honest answer. "Not that it matters now, because I don't think we have much of anything anymore, but more than friends, I'd say. It's not like he proposed at the top of the Empire State Building while we were in New York."

"Probably because he was busy with someone else," he mumbled under his breath, but Madeleine still caught it. An indignant scoff rose in her from deep in her core. She started to defend Luke, then remembered how he had already been dishonest about the buyout. Why should she believe he'd been truthful about how he spent his time in New York while she was busy with Anna at her bakery?

"Sorry, what?" she pressed, her breathing shallow and tense.

Dillon looked down at his hands and continued to spin the ring on his finger. His face was crumpled up in conflict. "He's playing you." His voice was angry. "I just saw him standing on Main Street holding on to this other woman. Emily something. She's from New York. He says she's his producer."

The air in the room suddenly sucked out completely, and she couldn't force her lungs to inhale before it was gone. The office began to spin, and her heart pounded in her ears. Surely she'd heard wrong. And did he say Emily? "She is his producer. What do you mean, holding onto?"

Dillon took her hands in his. "I'm so sorry. But what I saw definitely didn't look like two professionals in a business meeting."

Tears pricked at the back of her eyes. *How could I ever have thought this was a good idea?* She rested her forehead against her best friend's shoulder, and he wrapped both arms around her, rubbing her back with a steady rhythm. "I've been so stupid."

"Shhh. No, you haven't. You're not the first girl to fall victim to Luke's charm."

She watched her tears splash onto his dark green T-shirt and soak into the cotton.

"I was ready to turn over my mother's bakery, though. And everything I've ever wanted is here in this little building." Anger was beginning to replace the disappointment, and her heartbeat thudded rapidly in her ears.

"Yes, and he was willing to take it. All for his own gain."

"I can't believe this." She swiped her cheek, now soaked from crying, and sat up.

The sympathetic anger in her best friend's voice was comforting, but the sting of knowing Luke and Emily were still close didn't lessen. He'd been *holding* her? In the middle of Main Street? Did he remember nothing about small town life? He had to know that would get back to her.

She felt like someone had squeezed all the breath from her lungs. "I need some air. Come with me out back?"

Dillon was already on his feet following her.

She stepped outside, and the cool air hit her wet cheeks with a shock. She inhaled quickly, and wrapped her arms around herself. *I should have grabbed my jacket.*

The crisp breeze blew the leaves around, and their rustling against the gravel patch behind the bakery was the only sound.

Until tires crunched over the gravel. A black truck turned past the back corner of the building, and parked just to the left of where Dillon and Madeleine stood.

"You've got to be kidding me," Dillon spat. He stepped in front of Madeleine, his broad shoulders and height blocking her vision altogether, but she heard the truck door open and Luke's boots stepping down onto the rocky ground.

"Don't you know to stay away from where you aren't welcome?" Dillon yelled at his brother, while holding an arm behind him, keeping Madeleine in place.

"I'd say that's not up to you, is it?" Luke answered, the venom in his voice slicing through the air. "That's Madeleine's decision, so why don't you let her speak for herself?"

Madeleine put her hand on Dillon's shoulder, and gave it a tiny push. She whispered a quick, "He's right" in his ear and stepped out from behind her best friend, swiping the tears from her cheeks as she did.

"I see you came alone," she started.

Luke squinted, and he held his hands out toward her. "What do you mean? Who else would I bring here?"

"Don't play that game. Emily is in town." She stood as straight as possible, hoping she appeared strong. She'd probably failed when standing next to the bulky Dillon, but still, she had to at least look the part, despite the red splotches she knew were on her cheeks from her earlier sobfest.

Luke's eyes flicked to his brother, and the muscles in his jaw clenched up. "She is, yes. Flew in last night."

"I hear you two were on Main Street a few minutes ago. Doing what exactly?" *Heaven help you if you lie to me right now.*

"Meeting with the mayor." His voice was calm. No hint of anger or even coolness came across in his words. If anything, he used a softer tone than she had ever heard from him.

That only aggravated her more.

"Ah. I see. So, did you two get everything you needed taken care of?"

He pressed his lips together and shifted his gaze from Madeleine to Dillon and back to Madeleine again. "Can we please go inside and talk? Privately?" He stepped toward her, his hand held out to take hers.

She did not move a muscle. This was one time Luke's cool nature couldn't sweep her off her feet.

Dillon, on the other hand didn't hesitate at all. He stepped into the gap Luke was closing and swung a strong right hook, landing it squarely on his brother's jaw.

The dull thud of the hit shocked Madeleine, but it was Luke's groan that tugged her into action. "Dillon, stop!" She tried to step between the brothers, but it was too late. The fight was in full swing, and she was helpless to stop it.

Chapter 34

Luke

Luke took the bagged ice Madeleine held toward him as he sat on the curb behind The Bean and Batter. He spit onto the gravel, hoping some of the blood would land on his brother's boot. *It'd serve him right after he started all this mess.*

Dillon pressed his own icepack against his right hand, which had already started to swell and turn purple at the knuckles.

"You boys should be ashamed of yourselves. Your mama didn't raise you to fight like this, I know that for sure." Madeleine had been scolding them constantly since they'd quit fighting.

The cry of her screams were what eventually stopped Luke from throwing another punch, even though he'd had the upper hand once the fight started. But her calls to stop rang in his ears, so he'd thrown his brother to the ground and walked away.

Luke moved his jaw around, shifting it from side to side, then pressed the ice against it. *I did too good of a job teaching Dillon to throw a punch.*

Luke caught his brother's eyes with a sidelong glance, and the sorrow he saw in Dillon's eyes reflected his own. *Is this what we've come to? Beating each other up?* This had to be fixed. "Dude, we need to talk."

"Nothing to talk about."

Madeleine stepped toward the brothers, her hands on her hips. "Oh yes there is, Dillon Taylor, and talk you will. Luke, I'm not all that interested in helping you out, but I won't have you two on the rocks because of something I'm a part of. I'm going inside to check on Becca and the café. But I'll be back in a few minutes, and heaven help you both if I walk out here to find another fight happening."

Luke watched her walk inside, her hair swinging across her back with every step. A pang of remorse punched his gut, and it made Dillon's right hook feel like a toddler's slap on the cheek.

Dillon took the ice off his hand and flexed his fingers wide.

"Keep that ice on there. You'll be sore tomorrow for sure."

"I'll be fine. Your face, though. That's a different story." He knocked his forehead toward Luke's chin, a tiny smirk threatening to appear at the corner of his mouth.

"Yeah, well, I'll worry about my face later. Right now, I'm worried she'll come back out here and keep yelling at us."

"She isn't going to just let this go, you know." His warning tone didn't surprise Luke.

"You would know. You two have quite the history together." Luke ran his fingers through his hair and shook it out. Jealousy coated his words.

"We do. More than you could ever hope to have." Dillon's words were strong, and Luke felt the anger behind them rattle around in his chest.

Not wanting to give in to the anger, Luke took a deep breath. "Dillon, I need to explain a lot of things, but I can only do that if you're willing to listen."

"Why would I care to listen?"

"Because you care about Madeleine." He looked at his brother's brown eyes, an exact match of his own, and saw them soften for the smallest second. *Finally, a break.* He knew this was the moment he needed. "And so do I. We are going to have to work this out."

Dillon raised his eyebrows, then looked into the trees that lined the back parking lot of the bakery. He picked up his baseball cap laying next to his feet, dusted it off against his leg, and put it on. "Well, then. Start talking."

"I'd never hurt Madeleine on purpose." He had to make Dillon understand this. "That woman you saw me with? Emily? She's an ex. So, yes, you probably saw some chemistry happening earlier today. But I am telling you, that's over."

"Didn't look over to me," Dillon scoffed.

Luke let out a huff of a laugh. "Yeah, you and Emily both see that the same way." He shook his head. "She's having trouble understanding that clearly. I had no idea she would be taking the lead on this project when I left New York. She's managed to work her way into it."

"Fine. I'm not sure I buy all that, but for now, let's skip past that. Madeleine says part of the deal with this makeover means your company will own her bakery?" Dillon looked back at Luke. "Please tell me that's wrong."

Luke stared down at his hands, unable to meet his brother's gaze. He couldn't give any kind of answer that would satisfy Dillon.

His silence was answer enough.

Dillon huffed and stood. With a swift motion, he moved toward Luke's truck and slammed two fists down on the hood. "You're kidding me. You've made some deal to take her bakery away?"

Luke knew if he stood, it would only escalate the situation, so he stayed seated. "I didn't make the deal, dude. I've been working to prevent it."

Dillon spun on his heels, shaking his head and clenching his hands into fists again. "Doesn't sound like it worked. I'm not even sure you fought all that hard against it."

"Dillon, calm down. You have to trust me on this. That niggling guilt pricked at him again. Getting all the facts out in the open was the right thing to do, but it meant admitting his dishonesty to everyone he loved.

"Trust you to lie to her?" Dillon had stopped his approach and now stood firmly in front of Luke, staring down on him.

"No. To protect her." He stood, but stepped back and up onto the curb. "I swear. I'm doing everything I can to keep Greyson Media happy, but I also need to find a way to keep her bakery open. Did you know she is almost bankrupt?"

That did it. Dillon stepped backward and relaxed his fists. He scrubbed his fingers across his chin and sighed. "No. You're not serious."

"I am. And I'm trying to help her here. This publicity from the makeover might be enough. But it might not. And a buyout, if I can work it in our favor, might give her the financial relief she needs."

Dillon nodded his head, understanding soaking in. "I see. But there's no way she'd ever agree to this. You have to know that."

The back door swung open. "Agree to what?" Madeleine's sharp tone made Luke wince. She was in no mood to hear any of his thoughts right now, and he knew it.

He looked at his brother, who gave the slightest of nods. He also knew this was not the time to have this conversation.

"Well, at least you aren't hitting each other anymore," she said, slamming the door behind her. "What is wrong with you two? First you beat on each other, and now I find you out here talking about me?"

She handed Dillon a fresh ice pack, which he placed back on his knuckles. "Thanks," he mumbled, but she didn't stop to even acknowledge his reply.

"Let me make one thing clear, Taylor boys. You don't get to make any decisions for me. Yes, I value your opinions, but I refuse to let either of you believe that I need them."

The way she thrust the next ice pack toward Luke told him she meant business. He placed it on his jaw. It wasn't even sore anymore, but it wasn't worth risking her wrath by not taking it.

"Keep that ice on there. If you're going to be on camera in the next week, you'd better get that face ready. And right now, it's anything but." She swung the back door open and walked back inside.

I hadn't thought about being on camera. Emily's going to kill me if I delay the shooting schedule. He crossed over to his truck and peered at himself in the rearview mirror. His jaw was probably going to be fine. No bruises yet. But that fat lip might be a problem. He pressed the ice over his bottom lip and side of his jaw before turning to face his brother.

"Dillon, help me here. If you care about her the way you say, and I know you do, then you've got to trust me."

"I'm listening."

A tiny glimmer of relief sparked inside Luke. If he could get Dillon on board, his plan might actually work.

Chapter 35

Madeleine

Becca was already filling the thumbprint cookies with orange marmalade when Madeleine came back in. *Thank goodness for someone who can still think straight. At least some work will get done around here today.*

"Everything out there okay?" Becca asked, her eyes never leaving the cookies.

Madeleine sighed. "I suppose. They didn't kill each other, so there's that."

"Mmm," was all Becca murmured in reply.

Madeleine rested her elbows on the sales counter next to the register and pressed her palms against her eyes. *What am I going to do with those two?* In all her years of knowing them, she'd never seen them fight. Her relationship with Luke was tearing those brothers apart, and she couldn't be responsible for that.

"Becca?"

"Yeah?"

"What do you think about this whole makeover situation?" She needed an unbiased, honest opinion. Well, at least as unbiased as someone employed at the bakery could give. The sound of the spoon against the counter told Madeleine Becca had stopped her work. But she couldn't look up. Not just yet. She rubbed her palms deeper against her eyes, willing the tears to stay in and the anxiety to leave.

"Truthfully, I don't hate the idea. But I've told you that before."

"I know. I just wondered if you still felt that way."

"I know how important this place is to you. And I watch you struggle." She tapped Madeleine on the shoulder. "I know you're in financial trouble. Why not embrace the buyout as an option that will let you keep this place open, but without the worry?"

When Madeleine turned around, she saw Becca's kind eyes practically pleading with her to understand. She had a point. By allowing Greyson Media to have their show, she could have her cake and eat it too. Literally and figuratively. Coming to terms with losing the ownership was harder than anything, even if it was the best option on the table.

She looked at the stack of mugs lined up on the shelf over Becca's head. Her mother had carefully chosen their wide shape and extra bulky handle with the working town of Ryleigh in mind.

But so many were chipped.

She looked at her bakery with a different eye. The eye of someone who would want to change it. What she saw needed changing, yes. Especially when compared to the cheerful and modern bakeries Luke took her to see in New York. The cracked tile caught her eye, along with the dingy baseboards that could use a fresh coat of paint. The buttery yellow walls were once cheerful and bright, but now seemed sallow.

"Becca, you may be right. But I just don't know how I'll be able to turn over the ownership to a company in New York City. They don't know me. They don't know Ryleigh. What makes them qualified to own this place?"

Luke came in from the stockroom, with Dillon close behind. Madeleine had been so preoccupied with her own thinking, she hadn't even heard the back door open. She looked at the brothers in surprise, but Luke spoke first.

"I'll tell you what makes them qualified. They've got me. I'm on your side, Madeleine, but I work for them. I can promise you, I'll keep the integrity of this place for you."

She scoffed at his words, his poor choices telling her otherwise. First it was the secrecy around the buyout, then Emily, and now he had a fat lip from a fist-fight with Dillon. "You want to come in here and talk about integrity? After you lied to me about everything?" The screech of her voice surprised her, and she was grateful for a customer-free bakery at this moment. It felt good to finally let go of her careful control and say the words that had kept her awake for the last few nights.

Luke looked at the cracked tile floor. The slouch in his posture and wince in his eyes as she spouted her feelings at him pricked at her heart, but his pain wasn't enough to stop her frustrated fury.

She continued, "Whatever happened to that All-American boy who every-one in this town loved? The one who was honest and kind?"

He shrugged his shoulders at her and opened his mouth to speak, but Madeleine cut him off. "I'll tell you. He moved off to the big city, learned to care only about himself and his career, and he forgot how to take care of what's really important."

Dillon crossed his arms behind Luke, catching her eye. "Madeleine, I think you—"

"Dillon, you should know, too. You were left to help with your parents after your dad got sick." She waved a wild hand in the air toward Luke. "Your brother here couldn't be bothered to leave his oh-so-glamourous-and-self-serving-life to even come home." *There. I said it. Someone had to. If Dillon isn't willing to bring it up, I will.*

Luke's posture said everything. The verbal punches she'd just thrown hit heavier than Dillon's fist ever could.

The front door opened, and Becca greeted the customer cheerfully, breaking the tense silence. "Hi there. What can I get ya?"

A woman, tall and blonde, strode further into the bakery. But she didn't stop at the display counter to look at the pastries, nor did she pause at the register to order coffee. She moved straight toward Luke.

"What on earth happened to your face?" she exclaimed, her arms out-stretched as if she were going to take his chin into his hands for a better look.

She was almost about to cross behind the counter when Dillon stepped in front of his brother. "Excuse me, but I think you should stop right where you are."

The woman laughed, unfazed by Dillon's cool tone. "Dillon, so nice to see you again." Her voice trilled across the bakery and grated in Madeleine's ears. She turned back to Luke and glanced down at the ice dripping from his hands. "Put that ice on that lip. We can't have you go on camera looking like that."

So, this must be Emily.

Madeleine assessed the woman who might have, at one time, held Luke's heart. She was pretty, but not in a wholesome way. More in a she's-prob-ably-had-a-nose-job-and-definitely-a-boob-job kind of way. She was taller than Madeleine, the difference made even more drastic by her pointed heels. And she was skinny. She obviously knew her way around a gym.

She probably hasn't eaten a cupcake in five years.

Before Emily had the chance to introduce herself, Luke stepped forward. "Madeleine Malone, this is Emily Pierotti. She is the producer of the series and the lead on your makeover." His voice had changed. It was louder, more commanding. Even though he stood in front of her wearing jeans and cowboy boots, he clearly had put on his business persona.

No love left there at least. The indifference in his voice made Madeleine feel less threatened. But only slightly.

Emily nodded at her and held out her hand. Her smile was wide, and Madeleine realized she needed to keep this woman on her side. If, after all, she was in charge of the makeover, Madeleine couldn't afford to have her as an enemy.

Swallowing her insecurity, Madeleine shook the woman's hand. "Nice to meet you." She looked at Luke then said, "I've heard so much about you."

Dillon scoffed. "Not enough," he muttered.

"It's nice to be here in Ryleigh. I've read so much online and heard all about it from Luke that I was beginning to think this place only existed in a fairy tale. But now, here I am, standing in the famous Bean and Batter, dingy walls and all."

Dillon straightened at Emily's comment, opening his mouth to speak, and Madeleine made no attempt to stop whatever might be about to come out of his mouth. She knew him well enough that he was about to say exactly what she was already thinking.

But Luke also knew his brother, and clapped a hand on top of Dillon's shoulder. Madeleine could see Dillon's arm muscles tighten, wanting to brush his brother's hand away, but he didn't.

Emily's gaze wandered around the little bakery. "I can't think of a more interesting space to make over than this one." She turned to Luke. "What a great recommendation. You've got a good eye." She smiled warmly at him.

I'd like to punch her in the eye.

Emily must have sensed the rising anger radiating from Madeleine, because she placed a hand against the top of the display counter. "Of course, you know I think it's a wonderful business. I hear you're an incredible baker. I mean no offense, only just—" She trailed off as she traced her fingernail along the metal edge of the case. "I think this space is a bit outdated."

Luke spoke up as he moved out from behind the counter to stand next to his beautiful coworker. "Emily, there's no need to be rude. You know the history of this bakery, and, yes, while it hasn't changed much since Madeleine's mother opened it, the town doesn't always put stake into how trendy a place is. Here in Ryleigh we value people, not paint colors." He looked at Madeleine and tipped his head to the side. "I could stand to remember that more often myself."

With that one sentence, Madeleine could have forgotten the lies and anger and manipulation Luke had put her through. She wanted to reach over and take his hand. No, she wanted to kiss those gorgeous but slightly swollen lips.

But no. She'd already seen him putting on a good act before. This was just another one of his shows. One she would not fall for again.

Emily placed her hand on Luke's chest, her perfectly polished nails drumming over his heart. "Oh, of course, darling. I know small town life is different. I only meant that I'm excited to get started." She slid her other hand through the crook of his elbow and rested it on his hip. "Speaking of getting to work, Henry Greyson wants to have a conference call in thirty minutes Can we find a quiet place to do that together?"

The way Emily's confident hands slinked over Luke's body with such familiarity made Madeleine's head spin. The few bites of thumbprint cookie dough she'd tasted earlier today threatened to come back up as she watched Emily's pointer finger spin tiny, slow circles on Luke's chest.

Thankfully, Luke reached up and removed Emily's talon-clad hand off him and stepped away from her.

Becca spoke, for the first time since Emily had arrived. "Our Wi-Fi is the fastest in town. You can sit at the corner table over there. It's quiet, and no one should bother you while you work."

Madeleine's jaw fell open at that. Why would Becca offer this place for Emily and Luke to continue their flirt-fest?

Becca kept talking. "Can I offer you some coffee? Tea?"

With poison, perhaps?

Emily looked up at the menu boards. "Hmm. So many choices." She turned to Luke. "What would you like?"

Becca answered for him. "He takes his coffee black." Her deadpan tone mimicked the irritation rising in Madeleine.

Emily laughed. "Oh, I know that. We had our morning coffee together for years, didn't we? I've known for so long how gorgeous he'd look on camera. I'm so ready for him to finally get the opportunity he deserves." She grinned up at Luke, whose eyes were locked on the menu board, his jaw muscles tensing over and over.

Madeleine's blood quickly passed a simmer and started to boil. She clenched her teeth together to keep from saying something she would regret later. *Play nice. She holds the fate of the bakery's design.*

Dillon shook his head, then retreated to Madeleine's office. "I'm not sticking around for this."

Becca passed Luke a mug of black coffee. "I'd suggest a cinnamon mocha. It's got a good kick to it. Seems like your style." The ice in Becca's voice bolstered Madeleine's confidence. Maybe Becca was on her side after all?

Emily tilted her head to the side and studied the younger barista for a moment. "Hmm." Her eyes narrowed. "Interesting. Yes, I think I'll have that." She spoke with an even tone, but the coolness in it sent a shiver down Madeleine's spine.

Becca set to work on the espresso machine, and Madeleine watched Emily follow Luke to the table in the back corner.

She set her pink crocodile bag in an empty chair, then pulled out her laptop. "Grey sees lots of potential in you, and if this project goes well, he's already told me about several other on-camera gigs he's got coming up. Everything's falling into place for you, finally."

Luke looked up at her, bewilderment all over his face. Absentmindedly, he answered flatly, "Wow. That's exciting news." He glanced back at Madeleine then said, "My computer's in the truck. I'll be right back,".

Even though Madeleine's anger still boiled, a piece of her knew how much Luke wanted this show to work out.

Emily barely glanced up from her screen as he stood up and walked away. "Fine. I'll be getting set up. We have a lot to go over."

As he crossed to the back door, he locked eyes with Madeleine and knocked his head toward the door, as if to say, 'come with me'.

She didn't want to. She didn't want to listen to any more of his excuses. No more lies. When Luke had first come home, the idea of being with him seemed too good to be true. He had somehow gotten under her skin. He noticed her, made her feel special. He whisked her away to New York City for goodness sake. Romances like that weren't real. She should have seen that all along.

No. She would not follow him into the parking lot like a loyal puppy. She was better than that. But one thing was certain. She would let this makeover happen. She would take everything Luke had to offer, including every bit of publicity, money, and time he could give to this bakery. She would be successful, and then she would figure out a way to buy it back from Greyson Media. A beautiful, successful bakery owned by a strong, successful woman. That would be her new goal. And Emily Pierotti and Luke Taylor would unwittingly make it all happen.

Chapter 36

Luke pulled into the parking lot, expecting to see Madeleine's yellow Beetle, until he remembered that she'd been given strict instructions to stay away from the place for the next five days in order to keep the makeover a secret. To his surprise, the area was already buzzing with both film and construction crews. The film trailer had already been placed at the corner of the parking lot, and Emily stood near its door, clipboard in hand. Luke honked as he parked, and Emily waved him over.

So much for getting ahead of the game.

"Morning, Em," he said as he walked toward his ex.

"Hi, darling. I've got coffee inside the trailer already." She leaned up and examined his face.. "I'm glad to see that lip isn't swollen today. We start filming in thirty. Go get changed."

"I'm not your darling," he said to her with a sharp tone. "Coffee in the trailer? Is Madeleine here?" He looked around again for Buttercup, but the little Beetle wasn't around. "Who made the coffee?"

Emily scoffed and placed a hand on his back. "Don't be dumb. I had one of the interns go pick it up from that donut shop next to the motel." She led him into the trailer and sat down, before pointing to a cardboard coffee carafe set up on a folding table. "Speaking of which, that motel is horrible. I'll be glad to get this job finished and get back to civilization."

Luke rolled his eyes as he poured himself a cup of the black brew. It smelled stale and burnt, and reminded him of his younger days in the church's fellowship hall across town. "Well, I know it's not the Ritz, but it's not that bad."

She let out a tiny laugh. More like a puff of air, really. "Honestly, Luke. It's awful. The bed is too hard, the cups are paper, and the shower barely gets hot."

He sat in the chair across from her and took the pages she held toward him. He glanced over the checklist of shots needing to be filmed this morning. Next to each row was a list of who would be in each shot. Luke's name was in most of them, and Madeleine's was in a several as well. *That's going to be awkward.*

"Surely there's a better place I could stay?" Emily tapped his calf with the tips of her toes. "Like, maybe an actual house? You wouldn't happen to know anyone who lives in town who might have room for me, would you?" She lifted her shoulder up and flashed a flirty grin.

He grimaced. "Maybe Becca's got room. Want me to ask her?"

The fake pout wasn't cute enough for Luke to offer his place. Besides, there were only two bedrooms, his and Dillon's. Not that Emily would mind sharing.

"I wasn't hoping for Becca's place."

"Look, Emily. I know what you were hoping for. But that's a hard pass. Let's focus on our work, okay?"

This time, her pout was real. She put her hands in the air in surrender, palms toward Luke. "Fine, fine. I get it. All business." She pointed to the pages in his hands. "We've got a quick interior shot with your intro. We have to do that first thing before they start demoing the place. That's scheduled to be done at two o'clock, so we've got to work fast."

Luke checked his watch. 7:24 a.m. "Seems like we've got time."

"Nope. We also have to film the load-out of all the tables, chairs, dishes, and even the appliances. The plumber and electrician are already in there disconnecting everything."

Luke took one more sip of the sludgy coffee. *Becca would be horrified at this.* "Then let's get started."

"Powder up, change that shirt into the one over there, and meet me outside."

It only took a few minutes for Luke to get camera ready, but he couldn't stop thinking about Madeleine's face yesterday when she saw the way Emily flirted with him. *I shouldn't have let that happen. I should have stuck to my boundaries. We're finished. Just coworkers.*

When Madeleine didn't follow him into the parking lot his heart sank, knowing she was upset. He needed a chance to explain his behavior, but she'd stayed inside. By the time he'd come back in with his laptop, she had the keys to

Buttercup in hand and was on her way out the door. He'd tried to follow her out to the back parking lot, but she'd stopped him in his tracks with a curt, "Don't follow me. I need some space." Wanting to respect her wishes, he'd watched her drive away, despite it being completely against his typical nature.

Working with Emily hadn't been easy yesterday after that, between Dillon's truck door slamming as he followed Madeleine, and Becca's glares in their direction.

So much for hometown hero now. He checked his appearance one last time in the mirror before heading back into The Bean and Batter, where Emily was waiting next to a cameraman.

"Ready? Let's roll," Emily called.

This is it. I've waited so long, and I wish I were in a mood to enjoy this moment.

He inhaled deeply, then blew it out in a thin line while shaking out his nerves in his hands. A quick three paces away from the camera, then back to his mark, and he was ready. He'd memorized his lines, practiced in the mirror, and had done all he could do to prepare for this. Except he hadn't expected to feel so...indescribably unsettled on the inside.

Luke flashed his most dazzling smile and looked straight into the lens. "You want to know about small town charm? Well, look no further than Ryleigh, Texas's own The Bean and Batter. This little bakery is always bubbling with plenty of people, pastries, and pleased palates. Filled with tradition, owner Madeleine Malone took over her mother's baking business and rolled it into her own." He paused and looked around. "While the pastries and coffee make your mouth water in delight, the building itself has gone a little, well, stale."

He stopped and shrugged at the camera, waiting for Emily. His heart was thrumming in his chest as if he'd just jumped off a cliff and plunged into a pool of cold water waiting below. The unsettled nerves shifted into buzzy victory. *That felt good. Fun, actually.*

"Cut," she called, before checking her clipboard. "That's nice, Luke. You're a natural in front of the camera." She stepped closer to him and ran her hand down the length of his arm. "Of course, I'm not surprised."

He shrugged his hand away from her touch. A touch that extinguished his excitement like water on a campfire. "Emily, stop," he growled.

"What?"

"No, Em. We aren't—"

An airy voice interrupted Luke's protest. "Hi there. You must be Emily." A petite woman wearing blue, polka-dotted wrap dress walked into the bakery, notepad in hand. She was followed by a younger guy, who towered over the tiny woman.

Emily turned. "Oh, yes. Hello. Are you Gina?"

Gina extended a hand to shake Emily's. "Yes, ma'am. Nice to meet you." She looked over Emily's shoulder and saw Luke. "And this is the ever-famous Luke Taylor. I've heard stories of you from some of the guys around the news office."

News office?

"Yes, ma'am. And who's this?" Luke asked, nodding to the tall kid in back.

Gina nudged an elbow against her company's arm. "This is Wade. He'll be our cameraman for the story." Gina's gaze wandered over the bakery and came to a stop at the corner table. "That table over there looks good, don't you think?"

Luke looked at the two intruders. "Good for what, exactly?"

"Emily called the station and told us about the makeover piece. WTXN thinks it's a great special interest story. Airs tomorrow. But not if we don't get started on the interview." She turned to his cameraman. "So, that looks good?"

"Yep. I'll go get set up." Wade headed back out of the bakery, but quickly returned with lighting equipment, a camera, tripod, and a coil of cable draped over his shoulder.

A flurry of activity swirled around Luke as he realized what he was in the middle of: a news piece, demolition, shooting his own television special. Luke's thoughts swirled, matching what seemed like chaos around him. A chaos all masterfully controlled by Emily.

"Hey, Ms. Pierotti," called one of the construction guys. "We've got a demo schedule to keep here. You gonna be filming much longer?"

Emily didn't even glance up from the clipboard's notes she was going over with Gina. "Keep your pants on, Jim. We're ahead of schedule, and you know that." Her voice was disinterested and flat.

"Okay, but my guys will be here in an hour, and I don't want 'em just standing around."

"They won't be standing around." Emily looked over her shoulder at Luke. "Come sit down. Wade's just about set up, and we need to get this interview done before Jim comes back with his sledgehammer."

Wade had taken two chairs from a nearby table and set them next to each other in the corner underneath the teacups hanging on the wall.

Madeleine once told Luke that her mother was especially proud of the teacup display and had searched every antique shop in a fifty-mile radius to find just the right ones to hang here. *I'll take those down myself.* He was just about to ask Emily if they could find a way to incorporate them into the new design, but Gina interrupted.

"Are the teacups in the shot, Wade? They're great. Very vintage."

"And dusty," Emily muttered, before seating herself next to Luke. The brush of her thigh against his irritated him.

Gina seated herself across from the pair and looked over her shoulder at Wade. "Ready?"

Wade gave a thumbs-up and peered into the camera.

"Alright, Luke, I'm sure you're used to being on camera, so this should be a piece of cake. Emily, just be yourself."

Luke nodded. He shifted his leg very slightly away from Emily's, but she only leaned closer to him, her shoulder touching his. If he leaned much further away, he'd be pinned against the wall. He straightened his posture, and moved his shoulder behind hers.

Gina opened up. "Tell us a little about how this project got started, Luke."

He pasted on his best corporate man smile and prepared to rattle off the mantra Henry Greyson wrote for him. "Greyson Media has always been a part of the American lifestyle. While we've spent time with some of the world's most influential entertainers, it is the average American living room where we are most at home. We felt a slice of hometown USA would be perfect for our next project." He heard the words coming out of his mouth, but they seemed hollow now. Disingenuous. Ryleigh, Texas was about to become a corporate entity with each business they made over. That didn't sit well with Luke, now that he knew the effect it had on people like Madeleine.

Emily piped up, "Luke here was just the man to take charge." Her syrupy compliments made Luke uncomfortable. "Being a hometown hero himself, he suggested Ryleigh as the perfect town to showcase." She flashed a smile his way, then looked straight into the camera lens. "After all, who doesn't love a fairy tale homecoming combined with a beautiful makeover?"

"And what made you choose The Bean and Batter?"

Luke cleared his throat. "Emily actually suggested it first. She did quite a bit of research online and found this little place."

"And Luke, you've got some history here with the owner as well. Is that right?"

Heat rose along the back of his neck, and he hoped his collar hid any redness that might be creeping up. "I do. Madeleine Malone is my little brother's best friend."

"Ah, but in a small town like Ryleigh, I suppose everyone knows everyone else, right?" Gina prodded. "So surely you knew her as well?"

"True. She spent quite a bit of time at my house when we were in high school."

Gina's eyebrows shot up and her eyes sparkled. "Really? And is there any history with you two?" The mention of Luke and Madeleine's background had Gina almost drooling over the idea of a romantic twist on her special interest story.

Luke smiled. He hoped the tiny laugh he forced out would diffuse Gina's hunt. "Not really. She was too busy with her other friends."

Now Emily chimed in. " Yes, Ryleigh High's 'home-run-king' made quite an impression on everyone when he was younger, and, as you can see, he has grown into a ruggedly handsome success with Greyson Media now." She rested her hand on Luke's knee and gave it a squeeze before bumping her shoulder against his in a playful gesture. "He and I have worked very closely together for years now, and it made perfect sense to have Luke take over hosting duties for the show."

The way Emily redirected the interview back on course was a relief to Luke, but Gina didn't let go of the romantic twist she was looking for.

"Oh, I see. So, you two are close, then?"

"Professionally only," came Luke's reply, perhaps too quickly.

Emily smiled at the interviewer. "We are close. I was thrilled to see Luke get this opportunity. He is so talented and deserves the chance to be in front of the camera. He is such a kind gentleman, I'm just happy to see him become the success I always knew he would be."

This morning's black coffee sludged around in Luke's stomach. He really regretted that half cup right about now. What should have been an interview about Madeleine and the makeover show had suddenly turned into a daytime talk show interview about some crazy love triangle he was in.

Gina turned to Wade. "I think that's enough for a soundbite. Let's get some interior and exterior shots, and then we'll have what we need." She turned to Luke and Emily. "Thanks so much. I think the final cut will be interesting for our viewers." She pulled a business card out of her pocket and handed it to Emily. "Call me if you need anything else. I'll send a link to the final story tonight before it airs tomorrow. Once I have your approval, it's good to go."

"Thanks so much," Emily took the card.

Luke gave a nod of thanks to Wade then shook Gina's had before she headed outside. Despite his earlier excitement, he knew a looming deadline hung over his head. *This buyout is wrong. Madeleine should own this place forever. Maybe I could just call Grey and talk to him, man to man? Doubtful he'd listen, though. They need the good press at this point.*

Luke cleared his throat, but couldn't quite clear his head.

Emily interrupted his jumbled thinking. "Nice job. I think Gina likes you. Now go get changed so we can start filming the load-out of all these crappy decorations and tables." Emily handed the card to Luke. "Could you set this on my desk in the trailer when you go, please?"

"Sure," Luke managed to say.

The crunch of his boots on the gravel matched his angry heartbeats. How had he let Emily manipulate this situation so much? Sinking into Emily's desk chair, he dropped the card on her desk and ran his palms over his face, pressing the heel of his hands into his eyes. *There's got to be a way to fix all this.*

He took a deep breath, leaned back in the chair, and surveyed his ex's perfectly tidy desk. Everything was neatly stacked, nothing out of place.

Somehow, the extreme order of this desk only made him feel worse. He'd managed to make a complete mess of everything. He'd come to Ryleigh excited for a potential show, earned a huge promotion, and finally got the girl he'd been wishing for. This was a bases loaded and a walk-off home run type of moment. But it had turned into a major strike-out. *I let this happen. I took my eye off the ball, got caught up in what Greyson offered me and forgot what was important.* The loss of Madeleine's trust cut him deeply, but it was the loss of his own integrity that made him feel sick. *I have to fix this. No matter the cost.*

His laptop was still in his bag on the floor where he'd left it this morning when he'd arrived. *One more look at these contracts can't hurt.*

The contracts were still open on his computer from where he'd been reading through every letter of the fine print. Pages and pages of legal jargon and Latin phrases hadn't been easy to get through, but he picked up where he'd left off last night.

He started a new section of the document, *Divestiture Assets*, which at first glance, seemed like more words he didn't care to have to look up. However, he did understand 'assets', and he knew Madeleine would have an interest in all the bakery's assets. His heartbeat picked up with the promise of understanding what would happen to the pieces inside the current building.

But it was the next section, titled *Reverti ad Dominum* made him nearly leap out of his chair. If his memory of basic high school Latin was right, he might have found the solution he needed.

He picked up his phone and started making calls. There was no time to waste.

Chapter 37

Madeleine

Tears pricked at the back of Madeleine's eyes. She reached for the remote and turned off the television, disgusted by what she saw. The interview on the ten o'clock news with Luke and Emily confirmed her worst fears. Madeleine had been replaced by a skinny, manipulating, ex-girlfriend who was no longer an ex.

"Honey, I'm sorry you had to watch that," her dad said as he ran his hand over the top of his graying head of hair. "I thought it would be a nice story about your mother's bakery and what you have turned it into."

"Well, that's not what we got, is it?"

"Sure not." He leaned over and patted his daughter on her hand.

That tender touch was all it took. The tears spilled over onto her cheeks and rolled down onto her neck. *I should've known better. He always did have an eye for the prettiest girl. I can't believe I fell for his act.*

Her dad cleared his throat. "Maddie, hon, did they promise you anything about these interviews? Anything about how you or the town would be portrayed?"

She shook her head no, unable to speak.

Something like a harrumph of disapproval came from her father's chest.

The soft drizzle of rain hitting the living room windows was the only sound, and it only made Madeleine's heart ache more. The two of them sat in the quiet.

"What about Dillon? The shop's closed by now. Maybe he'd come over and watch a movie? It is burger night, and he doesn't miss that very often."

Madeleine fought the urge to roll her eyes. "Dad, we aren't teenagers anymore." But the idea of calling Dillon didn't sound all that bad, really.

"I know that, hon. But I think maybe it would be a good idea to give him a call. You could use a friend, and he's the best one you've got."

True. And no one knows better how it feels to be stabbed in the back by Luke.

She picked up her phone and dialed his number, counting each ring as it came across the speaker. Three rings in, Dillon answered.

"Hey Maddiecakes." His voice was like a river of calm over her. Nothing would make her relax more right now than to play cards with Dillon and her dad, their bellies full of burgers.

She could hear the noise of his car in the background. "Are you driving?" *Please be coming over here.*

"Yeah. Uh, listen, can I call you back later? I'm sort of in the middle of something, and I need to finish it up."

A lump formed in the back of her throat. Swallowing hard, she fought to answer. "Sure." The tears were already reforming at the edges of her eyes.

Her dad, looking at her expression, motioned for her to put the phone on speaker. "Hey Dillon, I'm grilling burgers later. Should I put some on for you?"

"Oh, hi, Mr. Malone. I didn't know Maddie was at your place."

"She is. And we're hungry. See you in about thirty minutes?"

Dillon hesitated, but answered, "Thanks for the invite, but I can't. I'm sorry to miss the famous Malone burger night, though."

"Nothing like breaking tradition," her dad muttered under his breath before heading into the kitchen.

"See you later, Dillon. Stop by if you can," Madeleine choked out, hoping she didn't sound too upset, but knowing he probably caught on anyhow.

"I doubt I'll have time." He paused a moment. "I'm really sorry."

"Yeah. Okay." She ended the call before he had a chance to say any more. "Dad?" She swiped the fresh tears from her face and headed into the kitchen. "Hold off on the burgers. I think I need to take a drive and clear my head."

He turned to her, arms open, and she was only too happy to collapse into them. The warmth of his hands on her back brought back memories of her childhood, when he rocked her at night on the porch. Sheltering here with her daddy made everything seem okay, even if it was only for a moment.

"Madeleine, I know this is hard. But remember who you are. Don't let Luke or any TV show dictate that."

She sniffled and pressed her wet cheek against her dad's shoulder. "I know. Thanks."

One last squeeze, and her dad let her go. "You're pretty upset. You sure you're good to drive?"

Madeleine nodded, grabbed her keys, and headed to Buttercup. Making a left, she turned toward her old high school and into the empty parking lot. She half-expected to see Becca's car there, since she often worked with athletes who were recovering from injuries, but the rain likely cancelled any scheduled practices. *I suppose Becca's enjoying a quiet night at home.*

The baseball field sat in the far back corner of the school's property, and Madeleine steered her way across the parking lot to the same space Luke had parked his truck the night of their first date.

He seemed so sweet that day, joking over barbeque sandwiches and recalling how he watched her in the stands. And that first kiss they'd shared was like a dream. Madeleine brushed her lips with her fingertips, wishing that day hadn't led to this one.

No. I can't only focus on my broken heart. The bakery is getting a makeover. That's the silver lining. She wanted to see the progress. She knew she was supposed to stay away from The Bean and Batter for the next several days, but Madeleine's curiosity was beginning to get the best of her. Other than her trip to New York, she'd never been away from her little business for this many days in a row. She needed to check on it. Finding some answers wouldn't be hard.

Maybe Becca's been there. I'd bet she'd tell me what's going on inside. It only took a few seconds to dial Becca's number, but she didn't pick up. Madeleine thought about leaving a voicemail, but she couldn't bring herself to sound desperate, so she hung up instead.

This is stupid. I'll just go over there. She didn't take time to think through her decision before putting Buttercup in reverse and heading downtown. The rain splattered heavily on her windshield, coming down with the full force of a Texas thunderstorm now. The Bean and Batter was only a block away, and Madeleine could see an arrangement of tents and trailers, all hiding the front of the building. But there was little activity outside that she could see.

She squinted through the raindrops now pelting her car as she eased into the lot, watching for anyone who might still be working, but it was late and stormy. She wouldn't get caught on this quick little minute of espionage. Steering around to the back of the building, a giant dumpster filled her usual parking space. A corner of sheetrock, covered in the floral wallpaper her mother had hung in the office behind the desk, peeked out of the top.

My mother chose that. And now it's trash. She had stared at that floral pattern, tracing the stems and petals with her eyes so many times, she practically had it memorized. "It will be an accent wall," her mother had explained as she hung it. "I think it will make this room more friendly. No one really loves an office, so we have to make it beautiful."

Mom was right. I never really loved working in the office anyhow. She knew I'd need it to be pretty. But that particular wallpaper wasn't the way to do it. Madeleine smiled at her mother's misguided attempts, but glancing back at the wall in the trash took the joy away.

A tent stood next to the dumpster, covering stacked towers of the café's tables and chairs. Madeleine threw open the door to her car and bolted through the rain until she was underneath the cover of the tent.

She ran a hand along one of the tables nearest the edge of the pile. The cracked corners, what Madeleine had once called 'charming and quaint' no longer looked cute. They just looked old and overused. Once again, she remembered her mother's hands holding a crinkled dishtowel, wiping down each tabletop after a customer left.

Seeing her mother's legacy piled out here in the trash and rain squeezed Madeleine's heart so much she felt it might permanently break. Her mother built this business and passed it down, all for her daughter. And now, it was discarded. Trashed.

Bitter anger seeped into Madeleine's stomach as she thought about how she'd allowed this to happen. No, how she'd allowed Luke to convince her to make it happen. Had it all really been all for his own gain? He got his on-camera job, worked with his gorgeous ex-girlfriend, and still managed to look like the hometown hero he'd always been.

Standing here, her hair dripping from rain and teeth chattering in the cold, Madeleine realized now she was nothing more than collateral damage for Luke's success. He'd never wanted to save the bakery. He'd probably made up the way he watched her in the baseball stands, and those stories of how he liked her while she was busy with Dillon were nothing but lies. He'd always been the type to get what he wanted, and he used his charm to do just that.

Dillon. She pulled her phone from her jeans pocket and almost dialed his number but stopped. He was busy. Too busy to even come over and have a burger with his best friend.

The rain picked up, now rolling off the edges of the tent in sheets. She checked her phone for a text from anyone. Becca. Her dad. Even an update from Emily would be something. But the screen was blank. An empty, lonely feeling crept into every corner of Madeleine's heart. She pulled a chair from the stack and sat, resting her head on a nearby table. The cool against her cheek shocked her, and she began to shiver. Never had she wished for her mother more than she did now.

Chapter 38

Luke

Luke's heart pounded as he read the document again. When he'd found this page on his computer yesterday, he didn't stop to think, only to send a quick email to Jake Matthews with the contracts attached. It took a quick online search to find his former baseball teammate-turned-lawyer who lived down near Houston. *Thank you, Madeleine, for that information.*

"Jake, tell me I'm understanding this correctly."

Jake's answer over the phone held all of Luke's hope. "Yes, it looks like you have some options here. If she wanted to buy the bakery back, there's a clause that would let her do that. But it's not cheap."

Luke fiddled with the pen in his hand, a list already growing on his notepad. "I know. But this plan has to work. Go ahead and start drawing up the papers for purchase. Let me worry about the money."

"You got it."

"And you are coming into town for the weekend, right? I've gotta have my first baseman on the field with me." A boyish giddiness made Luke jiggle his leg up and down. Reconnecting with Jake would be a blast, and under these circumstances, it couldn't get any better.

"Wouldn't miss it. Kristy's coming too. We'll bring the kids."

The idea of his former teammate pushing a stroller brought a smile to Luke's face. And, if he were to be honest, it was starting to look like an appealing thought for his own future. A future that no longer seemed so far off. "Can't wait to meet the little ankle-biters."

Luke ended the call and texted Becca and Dillon to check on their progress. They were already working on the plan, putting steps in motion while he'd been finishing up the shots Emily needed for the makeover. Both Becca and Dillon thought the idea of a Home Run Derby would be a great way to fundraise. A healthy competition between former alumni and current high school students to hit the most home runs would definitely draw a good crowd. If everyone in Ryleigh came, bought tickets, and contributed to the cause, it was possible they could raise enough cash to buy The Bean and Batter from Greyson Media.

Without waiting for an answer, he dialed the person he needed most if he wanted to make this work. Anna Lamb would be his secret weapon to draw people from all the neighboring towns. He'd already lined her up to come to the big reveal, but now he had to call in a bigger favor. They could charge for signed cookbooks, signed photos, autograph sessions, and even auction off baking classes with Anna in the newly remodeled bakery. Any and every idea was on the table, but her name was big enough that people would pay just to be near her.

She picked up right away. "Hey, Luke. I just saw your text from this morning. What's going on?"

"Hey, Anna. Remember Madeleine?"

"Of course I do. Is everything okay? You don't sound like everything is okay."

Luke drew in a breath. He needed to work fast, and he needed Anna on board. "Yeah, for the most part. But I've made a huge mistake with this bakery makeover, and she's not really speaking to me now."

Anna clicked her tongue. "What'd you do this time?"

"This time? You say that like I screw up all the time."

"Well, if the shoe fits. I've found men just have a way of messing things up. And you're a man, so I assumed."

Luke brushed off the slight insult to his gender. "Whatever, Anna. You're just still mad at whichever flavor of the week broke your heart."

She laughed. "True. But he was too pretty for me anyhow. Enough about me. What do you need to fix this mess you've gotten yourself into?"

"Greyson Media has a clause in the makeover contract that they will own the bakery after the makeover. Madeleine wasn't aware of that when she agreed to the show."

Anna's silence on the line was deafening. Finally, she answered. "And you were?"

He shook his head, frustrated at himself. "Yeah."

"Wow. That's bad, my friend. You're sunk."

"Not if I can help it. Any chance you could help do a little fundraising while you're in Texas this week? Maybe stay a few days and offer some classes or workshops or something?"

He could hear papers rustling in the background and knew Anna was checking her trusty journal. She never went anywhere without that spiral-bound notebook. "I can shuffle a few things around. How many days?"

He pumped his fist in the air in victorious celebration. *Things are lining up. This might actually work.* "I'd need you here Saturday afternoon, then there's the reveal on Monday, and then a few days after that for little old Ryleigh, Texas to have some facetime with America's favorite baker." *Well, at least until Madeleine takes that title after the show airs.*

"Anything to save your hide, babe. I'll get new flights booked now."

His phone buzzed with an incoming text from Dillon. "Hey thanks, Anna. I owe you one. I'll email the rest of the details to you." He clicked out of the call and read his brother's text.

Dillon: *All good. Joe's in. He's donating all his sales of barbecue for the Derby and will set up the smoker outside the stadium.*

Luke: *Perfect. I got Anna. How's it going at the school, Becca?*

He didn't expect an answer from Becca right away, but knew she'd get back to him soon. He could only hope she could convince the school to use the baseball field, plus the rest of the athletic complex for food and games. The list on his notepad was still growing, but at least a few things were handled. If he could pull this off there might be a chance Madeleine wouldn't hate him forever.

The next few items on his list were easy. Call former teammates. Pick up flyers. Call the high school baseball coach. Call Gina at WTXN News. Get Anna's publisher to donate books.

He scribbled one more thing at the bottom of the list. Batting practice. The last thing he wanted was to show up for a Home Run Derby and look like an old, washed up adult when the whole town remembered him as a fit, all-star, teenage athlete.

The high-pitched ring of his phone interrupted his momentary insecurity. "Hey, Becca. How'd it go with the school?"

"Great. They are on board all the way. Coach Norton happened to come in while I was there, and he thinks it's a great idea. He's already calling the boys on the team and getting them to come. They'll all hit in the Derby for sure"

Luke smiled. "That worked out great. Now I don't have to call the coach myself and gather the team. Thanks for taking care of that."

"It was just good timing. Did you get Anna?"

"I did."

"Awesome. I'll order another tent and table for her to set up in. I was thinking about getting Carrie involved too."

"Who's Carrie?"

"Local florist. She makes balloon arches and stuff. She might want to decorate and make it more festive."

This is out of my wheelhouse. Thank goodness for Becca. "Sounds great. Call her. Maybe she would be willing raffle off some flowers or something."

"I love it. Also, um..."

The way Becca got quiet unsettled Luke. "Yes?"

"Does Emily know about all this?"

Luke tipped his head back, pressing his forefinger and thumb over his eyes and pinching the bridge of his nose. "Not yet. But I've seen the shot list, and I'm not scheduled to be there Saturday. I think she can make do without me that day."

"It's not the filming I'm worried about. It's the buyout itself. Do you think Greyson Media is going to just stand by and let this happen?"

"Nope. But I hope by the time they find out, it'll be too late."

"So you're going to move forward and force their hand. You know you're risking your job by doing that, right?"

"Yep. But Madeleine is worth the risk."

Chapter 39

Madeleine

T he screen door squeaked as Madeleine carried the iced tea out onto the porch. She handed one of the glasses to her dad before settling into the cushioned chair. These cool fall afternoons were some of her favorites. Normally, she'd be running around a busy bakery on Saturday morning, serving pastries and lattes to the whole town. But the makeover shut all that down for this week. Today seemed as good a morning as any to spend over at her parents' home.

"Well, punkin, I've got a surprise for you," he said after taking a sip of tea.

"You do?" A twinge of guilt pricked at her less-than-enthusiastic reaction. But the loss of her bakery, Luke, and maybe even Dillon, weighed too heavily on her heart. A raised eyebrow and a shoulder shrug was the most she could muster.

"Yep. I thought you could use a little pick-me-up. I know this business with the Taylor boys, the bakery, and that Emily is tough on you."

That Emily. See? Even Dad understands.

She nodded and recited the lie she'd practiced all last night while she tossed sleeplessly in bed, her mind trying to reconcile transferring ownership to Greyson Media. "It is. But Luke will go back to the city next week. And I get a refreshed bakery. Once the show airs, hopefully business will pick up. Happy ending for all, right?" She wished she believed her own words.

Her dad looked at her and lowered his chin. "How do you feel about Luke leaving?"

She traced a finger around the rim of her tea glass. "Fine. He and Emily deserve each other," she lied. "Won't miss him at all."

"Good to hear." The tone in her father's voice said he didn't buy her story any more than she did. He took a long gulp of the tea, letting the false resignation settle around them both.

"So, what's this about a surprise?" She didn't want to talk about Luke or Emily any more than she had to, and this short conversation was already too long for her taste.

"Oh, I thought today would be a good day for you and me to go over to Southport and have lunch. Maybe grab some ice cream with your dear old dad?"

An hour's drive to Southport sounded like the worst idea ever, and her eyes rolled before she could stop them.

"Dad, I think I'd rather not," she started.

He cleared his throat before answering. "You'd rather stay home and sulk today?"

"Not home. I'd rather stay over here and sulk."

He drew his lips into a tight line and nodded. "Mmm-hm."

A restlessness stirred inside again. It was the same, unsettled feeling that kept her awake all night last night. Images of the posters hanging in storefront windows plagued her thoughts, emblazoned with Luke Taylor's name, his baseball number, and the words 'Home Run Derby.'

Typical. Once again, he's using his local celebrity status to show off for the whole town. Ever since Wednesday, Ryleigh's residents couldn't stop talking about watching Luke Taylor play baseball again. Emily and Greyson Media were probably eating this whole thing up. A chance to showcase their newest protégé doing what he does best, being charming, athletic, and endeared by all. The whole thing made Madeleine want to puke.

"Might want to stop grinding those pretty teeth, young lady. Your mother and I paid a lot to get those straight."

Madeleine hadn't realized her jaw was clenched so tightly, but she relaxed and took another sip of tea. The cool liquid splashed into the back of her mouth, but it didn't cool her anger at all. "I just don't understand why this whole town has to celebrate the ever-amazing Luke Taylor. I mean, I think everyone in town is going to the baseball fields today. It's all anyone talked about yesterday at the grocery store."

The older man squinted when he looked at his daughter, suspicion raised in his eyes. "What were they saying?" he asked, his words drawn and slow.

"Just a bunch of twittering about seeing Luke back at home plate, and how fun it would be to eat Joe's barbecue and watch good baseball again."

"That's all?" her father pressed.

"I mean, more or less." She paused and looked at her dad. "Why? Is there something else I should know?"

He looked into his now empty tea glass and rattled the ice a bit. "Looks like my tea's gone. I think I'll go get some more." He made a half-effort at standing, but Madeleine was already on her feet taking the glass from him.

"Oh, no. You stay put. I'll get the tea. And when I get back, you're going to tell me what else you know about this Home Run Derby."

"There's nothing to tell, Maddie. I know just as much as you do," he called after her as she went into the kitchen.

He probably wishes he were there himself. He does love baseball. And Joe's barbecue. She scooped more ice from the freezer into her dad's cup and reached for the pitcher of tea to fill his glass. She'd heard even more about the event. It sounded like the whole afternoon was practically a baseball homecoming plus a carnival. Emily certainly was going to get her hometown slice of life episode out of this weekend. *Good for her. I hope she chokes on Joe's barbecue sauce, right before it drips down the front of her figure-hugging designer dress.*

Her phone sat on the counter next to the pitcher, and without thinking, she picked it up to check for any missed calls or texts. No new notifications. An empty, abandoned feeling crashed over her like an ocean wave on the seawall. She didn't expect to hear anything from Luke. But not even Dillon or Becca thought to reach out to her today and check on her. They had to know she was hurting with the bakery being torn into piles of trash in a dumpster. But it had been practically radio silence from them both for the last two days.

She shoved her phone into her back pocket, picked up her own glass of tea, and carried it with her dad's back out to the porch. "I think you've got something to tell me?"

Her dad took the glass from her. "Really, there's nothing else to tell. I just heard it's going to be a big shindig, that's all." He took a long gulp of the tea, then stared down into his glass. "Your tea is almost as perfect as your mama's." He tipped up the corner of his mouth teasingly.

Despite her dreary mood, Madeleine couldn't resist the tiny grin forming. "Well, she always used to say she finished it off by sticking one finger in to add a touch of sweetness. I, unfortunately, got a little too much of your salt and not enough of her sweet."

"Well, that salt serves you well, I do believe. I think perhaps a certain television producer might need to get a taste of some of your saltiness. But for today, let's just enjoy this tea and good company."

Madeleine wanted to listen to her father's suggestion. As a matter of fact, she wanted nothing more than to sit contentedly here on his front porch, sip sweet tea, and watch the world go by. The problem was, her whole world was at the Home Run Derby, watching the man she thought she loved show off.

Chapter 40

Luke

Becca and Dillon were standing next to Luke on the pitcher's mound, and it looked like the entire town of Ryleigh along with everyone who lived within a hundred-mile radius had shown up for the Home Run Derby.

Becca's voice carried over the loudspeaker. "Wow. What a turnout we've had today." She grinned at Luke, clearly satisfied with their success. "Apparently, everyone wants to meet you, Mr. Celebrity Host," she jostled him with her elbow as she teased.

Dillon leaned over and pulled the microphone toward his mouth. "Nah. Don't be ridiculous. We all know who they're really here to see." He popped his shirt collar and flashed a winning smile at the crowd.

"Yes, we do. I see a lot of people out there who are excited to meet world-famous pastry chef, Anna Lamb," Luke announced into his own microphone. He pointed to Anna, who was seated at the front section of the bleachers. *Just below where Madeleine and Kristy always sat.*

The crowd laughed. A female voice from the crowd rang out, "Yeah, that and Joe's barbecue got us here, too."

Luke waved toward the tent where Joe's smoker sat, with Joe manning the grills. He clicked his tongs in the air at the crowd and smiled, bringing on a round of applause for the much-loved man.

"Whatever brought you here today, I want to remind you of the real reason for today's Home Run Derby. For those who have ever stepped foot into The Bean and Batter, you know what a special place it is. You also know how the

Malone family has taken great pride in building that perfect little business up." Luke shuffled his feet on the pitcher's mound, a move that was so familiar it was almost subconscious.

Dillon interrupted, "And you also can't help but love Madeleine. She's our town's real star...no offense, Joe," he said, pointing at the barbecue master.

"None taken," Joe yelled back. "She's certainly a lot prettier than this old mug."

Luke laughed out loud at that. "Yes, she certainly is." The memory of her flour-dusted cheek turning rosy pink with embarrassment the night he'd jumped her battery flashed in his mind. "But while we all know how hard Madeleine works and how much she loves each customer who comes into her bakery, there's something you might not know."

The crowd almost seemed to lean toward the baseball field to hear Luke's next words. What he had to say next weighed heavily, and he needed to get it just right. "The bakery is, in fact, undergoing a makeover. That is true, and you've seen the crews working. But, at the end of the makeover, the bakery will no longer belong to the Malone family."

A hushed rumble of dissenting comments came from the crowd.

Dillon clapped a hand on Luke's shoulder and gave him a squeeze, a reminder of their solidarity in today's mission.

"But we can change that. There's a part of the contract that says we can buy it back from Greyson Media, but the expense is more than any one person could afford. Today, you have the chance to help Madeleine buy back her own bakery."

"Where's Madeleine today?" A woman in the crowd asked.

Luke's stomach churned, and he knew he had to be honest if he wanted this to work. "She doesn't know about this option. And she's pretty hot under the collar at me for letting this mess happen in the first place." He paused and looked at Becca's reassuring face. "I guess her absence today is in protest of my actions." Luke could hear the shame in his own voice.

Becca was quick to pick up the pace, though, and keep things moving. "No, Luke. She's at home with her dad, who is in on this surprise and keeping her occupied." She turned to Dillon, who had a goofy grin on his face. "Because what's better than a makeover surprise, Dillon?"

In his best game-show-host voice, Dillon answered, "I'll tell you what, Becca. A makeover surprise combined with a buyback surprise!" The two of them gave each other a high five.

Luke rolled his eyes at their silly antics, clearly rehearsed ahead of time. The crowd ate it up, though. *They are loving this. We might actually be able to pull this off.* For the first time, he realized this crazy plan might truly work. Hope filled his chest, and he nodded with satisfaction as he looked into the happy crowd.

"Hey Dillon," Becca added to the wacky antics, "tell the good people how they can help save Madeleine's bakery from the big, bad corporate takeover."

"Well, Becca, it's really quite simple. Under the big tent over there, the quilting league has put together a fantastic silent auction."

"You don't say?"

"I do say. And then, the lovely Ms. Anna Lamb has cookbooks that she has graciously donated for purchase, and for a fee, she will autograph them. You can also purchase your very own photo package with her as well. All the proceeds from everything you buy here today go toward the 'Madeleine Malone Get-Your-Bakery-Back' Fund." He flashed a cheeky smile at the crowd, followed by a wink at Becca.

"Gosh, that's amazing," came Becca's wildly cheesy reply.

"It is. But even more amazing is Anna Lamb raffling off the chance to win one of five personal baking classes, taught by her, right here in Ryleigh this week."

"Wow, Dillon. That is quite the treat. But I have a feeling that's not all," Becca chimed in, again with her false-television voice.

"Is that all, you ask? Why of course not. Don't forget to grab a delicious lunch from Joe at the barbecue pit. And on the far side, we've got Carrie's floral shop creating beautiful fresh flower arrangements for your home. Don't miss out on the carnival games, put together by the churches in the area."

"My goodness, and all of these businesses and people have donated their time and products just to save The Bean and Batter?"

"They sure have, Becca. But wait, there's more," Dillon continued, now sounding like a late-night-infomercial salesman. "We've also got the main event happening here on the baseball field, starting in about fifteen minutes. It's the first ever Ryleigh High Alumni Home Run Derby. Thank you all for purchasing your tickets to attend this event."

"How exciting." Becca crooned. "And, say, Luke. Tell the good people who will be hitting first today?"

Luke shook his head in amazement at these two clowns, laughing the whole time. He managed to stop chuckling long enough to say into the microphone, "Uh, that would be me, Becca."

The crowd roared with applause, as Dillon wrapped up their little show. "That's right, folks. So, dig deep in those pockets, grab those checkbooks, and have some fun while we save Ryleigh's most treasured business, The Bean and Batter."

Becca cartwheeled off the pitcher's mound, and the crowd cheered again. Luke followed Becca toward the dugout, with Dillon alongside. Gina and her cameraman from WTXN beamed at the trio from the corner of the fence. "You three are fantastic. Wade caught it all on camera."

Luke smiled back at her. "I'm glad you could both make it out today on such short notice."

Gina waved a hand in the air. "Short notice is how the news industry works. You gave us plenty of time to promote this for the last two days. It looks like it worked." She gestured toward the large crowd.

Luke followed her gaze. "Sure did. Thanks again."

"My pleasure. Now, I think we will go grab some shots of the event, and maybe do a few interviews." She leaned toward Luke, a twinkle in her eyes. "I'm hoping I can get Anna Lamb to do a baking spot on Monday's morning news. If I could line that up, it would be a feather in my news anchor cap."

Luke laughed, but inside, he felt a little twist of regret. He knew Anna would be busy Monday with the reveal over at Madeleine's bakery. *If she wants to make time on Tuesday to do a small town's morning show, I guess that would be up to her.* "Good luck," was the best he could offer as Gina and Wade started toward Anna's tent.

Behind him, Dillon and Becca were congratulating themselves on their flaw-less performance. "That was super fun. I think everyone liked it," Becca trilled.

"For sure. Your idea was definitely a hit." Dillon slipped his arm around her waist and pulled her into a close hug. A really close hug. And Becca let herself press right into his embrace.

Luke almost felt embarrassed watching this quick but intimate moment between the two of them. *When did that happen?*

The sound of cleats running onto the field took his attention away for a moment, but he made a mental note to talk with his brother about this new turn of events.

The Ryleigh High School baseball team was making their way across the field and taking their places for warmups. From the stadium loudspeaker, a familiar voice carried over the air.

"Aaaaaand now, let's welcome the Ryleigh High Hornets." It sounded like Brandon Heath was still in the announcer's box these days. Luke hadn't heard that voice since high school, but it brought him right back to when he took the field as a senior.

Applause and whoops and cheers rose from the bleachers as the young athletes started stretching and getting ready to play ball. Brandon's voice boomed across the speakers again. "Ladies and gentlemen, give a warm welcome to today's special honored alumni, Ethan Walker, Kaleb Jantzen, Patrick Dakota, Brett Middleston, Jackson Westrup, Jason Carmine, Jake Matthews, and Lu-uuuuuke Taylorrrrr."

A gentle shove in the center of his back from Becca told Luke it was his turn to take the field. His former teammates were already making their way to line up along the first base line, and Luke took his place next to his high school best friend, Jake. The two men shared a manly bear hug, and a good laugh.

"Hey, man. Good to see you. Thanks for coming home."

"Are you kidding? If Kristy heard about this and knew we'd missed it, I'd be in the doghouse for sure. Glad you called me." Jake's smile hadn't changed a bit, unless you counted the neatly trimmed beard he now sported. But it was easy to see Jake was still the same guy he'd always been, kind and honest, but with a little splash of mischief.

The crowd grew silent as the local Scout Color Guard carried the flag onto the field, followed by none other than Kristy Matthews, who looked extra patriotic in her ripped jeans, blue tank top, and red heels.

Luke took off his baseball cap and whispered to Jake, "She looks exactly the same as she did at our last game together. No one told me Kristy was singing today."

Jake smirked. "Surprise. Becca called and asked."

"Ladies and gentlemen, please stand for the national anthem," Brandon announced.

And just like she had done for so many other games, Kristy's voice filled the stadium with her strong, alto voice as she belted out "The Star Spangled Banner." When she finished, the crowd went wild once again as Jake sprinted to his wife and gave her a kiss.

Nervous excitement took up most of the space in Luke's mind right now, but a tiny corner kept bugging him. *Madeleine would be shocked if she saw how many people were here to support her dreams.* He was glad Becca had suggested hiring a videographer for the event, so Madeleine could see it for herself. Maybe he'd rent out the little movie theater in town and show it on the big screen.

When Jake returned to the baseline, Luke nodded in his direction. "Everyone loves a high school sweetheart love story, right?" *I can only hope for my own happy ending after this day is finished.*

"Yep. Sure do. But yours is going to make a great story too. If Madeleine won't take you back after all this, she's a fool."

"Aaannnd now, let's plaaaay ball!"

Chapter 49

Madeleine

S pending the weekend at her dad's house turned out to be a great idea. No one bothered Madeleine there, and her dad proved to be a good distraction. They'd ended up going through some of her mother's old photo albums, and she laughed until her sides ached. Which, as it turned out, was a nice change from the heartache over everything else in her life.

Besides, her dad was a great taste-tester for whatever Madeleine baked. Over these last two days, she'd made two lemon pies, tartlets made with chocolate, hazelnut, and peanut butter, four dozen pecan sandies, and a quiche. *Maybe I went a little overboard on the 'baking as a distraction' this weekend.* The stuffed freezer in her dad's garage wouldn't hold another treat. *But they will be good for the reopening of the bakery this week.*

Madeline rolled over and looked at the clock for the eleventh time in the last ten minutes. Her entire night was nothing but an endless stream of waiting for the morning. Between the loss of Luke, the potential disaster of a makeover, and the sadness of losing her mom's fingerprints on The Bean and Batter, the anticipation for today's bakery reveal didn't allow her to sleep at all.

Eventually, she resigned herself to an early morning and padded her way to the bathroom for a shower. She probably needed the extra time to get herself camera-ready today anyhow. She'd decided on jeans, a crisp white tank top, and her favorite flowy, emerald-green cardigan for today's filming of the makeover reveal. She decided at the last minute to throw on a chunky silver necklace and hoop earrings to complete the look. A swipe of her favorite lip color, Spice Sachet, and she looked ready to go. Too bad she didn't feel ready. She was a ball of nerves.

Her dad was already dressed and waiting at the kitchen table when she came downstairs. "Morning, sunshine."

She leaned down and squeezed his shoulders. "Morning, Dad."

"How'd you sleep?"

She shot him a look that wasn't too unlike several she'd given when she was a teenager complete with eyes rolling, chin tipped downward and to the side, and a big sigh to round out her answer. "How do you think I slept?"

"Oh, okay then. No need for your salty side today. You'd better find some of your mama's sweet somewhere in there before you have to go on camera."

"Don't worry, Daddy. I'll be fine. I just need a cup of coffee and then I'll be sweet as the sugar cane in a Dublin Dr. Pepper." She poured some of the black liquid into her favorite floral mug, added a splash of half and half and a tiny wisp of sugar, and stirred. *There's literally nothing better in life than that first sip of a perfectly made cup of coffee.* "Boy, Mama sure did teach you how to make the perfect pot of coffee."

"I'm glad you like it. But you'd better get that coffee tossed down and get yourself into the car. You're supposed to meet that Emily at Dillon's shop in twenty minutes."

That Emily. I suppose that's what he'll keep calling her. Secretly, Madeleine loved that he had no hesitation about disliking the obnoxious woman, even though they'd never met.

Soon, Madeleine steered Buttercup into the parking lot of Taylor's Autobody, where Emily stood with her clipboard in hand.

"Morning, Madeleine. It's the big day, isn't it?" The high pitch of Emily's false excitement grated on Madeleine's nerves.

But she formed her most polite smile and answered, "I can't wait to see what your crew has done. What are the plans for the day?"

Emily looked Madeleine over from head to toe with a critical eye. "Hmm. I suppose that green will photograph alright."

Even Emily's jab didn't have any effect on Madeleine. "Yes, every time I wear this color, people always compliment my skin tones. I'm glad you noticed." *I'm using your 'catching flies with honey not vinegar' method, Mama.*

The slender woman barely bristled at Madeleine's response, taking only an extra half second to collect herself before moving onto her next thought. "Yes, well." She cleared her throat. "I've arranged for a van to drive you to the bakery, but we'll be blindfolding you here before you depart. Luke will meet you at the van door and escort you to the exterior for the reveal shot. Obviously, we will roll tape as soon as you are out of the escort vehicle."

Luke. Her stomach lurched. She knew she'd see him soon enough. She still couldn't decide how she felt about it. Her heart was bruised from his selfishness. She mustered confidence and replied, "Got it. How soon will we be leaving here?"

"Eight minutes." She turned to walk away but stopped and turned back to Madeleine. "Oh, and you might want to check your lipstick. You've got a little something going on."

Madeleine peered at her reflection in Buttercup's side mirror. Sure enough, her lipstick had worn off, but only where her coffee mug had touched her lips earlier. It only took a second to reapply.

"Ready steady, Maddiecakes?" Dillon quipped from behind. It was the first time they'd spoken since the night he'd declined burgers. That night seemed like an eternity ago.

She turned toward him and wondered briefly if he was upset with her. After all, no one had called or texted her all weekend. Not Luke, Becca, or even Dillon. "I guess so."

He jingled a set of keys in the air and smiled at her. "Looks like I'm your chauffer for the big reveal drive. Miss Never-Without-Her-Clipboard says we have to load and leave right now." He motioned toward a white cargo van parked near Dillon's garage. "After you, my dear."

Emily called over to them across from the parking lot. "I'll meet you over there in ten minutes. Don't forget to blindfold her."

Dillon shot a thumbs-up her way and opened the front door of the van for Madeleine to climb in. He pulled a red bandana from his back pocket and folded it into a long strip before tying it in a knot at the back of Madeleine's head. Her arms and legs wouldn't stop tingling, and her heartbeat thudded so loudly, she worried the sound man could hear it through the microphone he'd clipped to her sweater.

"Please try not to mess up my hair. I don't want to look completely ridiculous when Luke opens the van." The bandana was soft against her eyelids and she could smell a hint of Dillon's cologne mixed with the same laundry detergent Luke used. *Makes sense. They do live together.*

The instant Dillon started the van, Madeleine's heart rate ramped up to match the thrumming of the engine, and her mouth went dry. The makeover suddenly became very real. After days of imagining what she might see, both good and bad, the actual, true space would be hers for the viewing in less than ten minutes. She had practiced her smiling reaction in the mirror more times than she cared to admit and even rehearsed her camera-ready disappointed face. *I just hope I don't cry. No matter what happens, no tears.* She inhaled a deep breath as the van made what she guessed was its final turn toward The Bean and Batter.

When the van door opened, it was a familiar hand that took hers. *Luke.*

She tried to slow her heartbeat, but it was no use. Whether it was Luke's touch or the anticipation of what was about to happen, she felt a complete absence of anything calm inside.

"Are you ready?" he asked her. He stood so close, she could feel his breath on her neck. There must have been a large crowd of people outside of the bakery, because the cheering and applause was louder than she'd expected it to be. "Your dad is right in front of you. He's going to be in the shot as well," Luke spoke into her ear so she could hear him over the audience. "Emily has already called action, so you are on camera now, but this is throwaway footage. Still, don't forget to smile."

Even now, she found his coaching reassuring, a fact that baffled her. She should still be furious with him, not leaning into his confident grasp and feeling grateful for his hand at the small of her back to guide her steps. Her whole body tingled, yet she also felt completely numb at the same time. "Am I facing the cameras? Are we looking at the building yet?" *I am so turned around right now.*

"Yes to both. I need to let go of you, and we need to shoot this reveal shot." He released her hand, but it was replaced by someone else's familiar one.

"Dad?"

"Hey punkin'. I'm right here."

"Are you blindfolded too?"

"Nope, but don't ask me to tell you a thing. I wouldn't want that Emily to come yell at me for it." Even though she couldn't see his face, she knew he was smiling as he spoke about the producer, 'that Emily'.

Emily's voice carried over the crowd. She obviously had a bullhorn and was facing the observers. "Ladies and gentlemen, quiet on the set, please."

The cheering hushed, and Madeleine could sense Luke's warmth next to her. "Ready for filming?" he asked.

Madeleine nodded and hoped she didn't throw up. "Here goes nothing."

Luke cleared his voice and took a deep breath. The momentary silence seemed to take a lifetime to Madeleine. Finally, he spoke to what Madeleine could only assume was the camera. "At last, the time for the big reveal is here. Our crews have worked for an entire week to turn The Bean and Batter from drab and dated, to fresh and fantastic. Madeleine, go ahead and remove your blindfold."

Hoping she wasn't messing up her hair too much, she slid the bandana up and over her forehead. It took a few blinks for her eyes to adjust to the bright morning light, but what she saw was spectacular. Her hands flew to her mouth in astonishment as she took in the large picture window at the front, trimmed out with a pale pink paint. Inside the window, a beautiful half-wall with oval-shaped, painted sprinkles covering the bottom half. A shelf laden with cupcake stands, cake platters, and display trays sat on top of the wall. On each surface, Madeleine recognized pastries made with her own recipes, and all marked with Becca's uniquely trained style. The rainbow of colors combined with the buttery pastries made her mouth water at the sight.

The sign above the bakery still read The Bean and Batter, and Madeleine breathed a sigh of relief over no name changes to the business. But there was a new logo, complete with a bowl and whisk tumbling out of it and landing in a pile of coffee beans. The pink trim around the windows perfectly matched the color of the logo's bowl.

"What do you think?" Luke asked in his TV host voice.

His question brought Madeleine back to the filming. She had been so busy looking at the building, now painted a bright white, she had forgotten about the cameras. "It's breathtaking," she barely managed to say.

"Well, this is just the start. Put that blindfold back on, and we'll head inside."

Emily yelled "Cut!" at that moment, then turned to Madeleine. "Okay, you heard the man. Blindfold back on before we move to the interior. The shot will be the same. You can take two or three steps away from your mark but no more. Otherwise, you'll be out of frame. Got it?"

Madeleine nodded, but really, she had no idea what Emily just said. Luke was already helping tie the bandana over her eyes, and she hated to lose the view of her new storefront. *Hold off on that excitement. You haven't seen the inside yet.*

Luke led her through the door of the bakery, and the familiar scent of coffee and baked goods was now mixed with fresh paint and newly cut lumber.

She reminded herself to breathe a few deep breaths, and she almost felt her knees go weak as she heard Emily tell the cameras to start rolling.

"You okay?" Again, Luke was closer to her ear than she thought necessary, and he slipped his arm around her waist, pressing her into his frame for support.

He should be more professional, but I'm glad he's not. Madeleine leaned away from his hot breath as she nodded her head. "Yep. Good."

"I'm glad. Here we go." He cleared his throat, and she thought she heard him take a sip of water. Now came the moment of silence before filming.

But this time, it was a woman's voice she heard. *I know that voice. It's not Becca. Not Emily.* Madeleine leaned closer to the source, hoping that would help her recognize it. *Who is that? It's so familiar, yet not.*

"Madeleine, your mother gave you something really special here. Your talent for baking is unmatched, so unique. And we hope this space can now match the love that your mother poured into you, and the love you pour into your baking. Go ahead and remove your blindfold and see your sweet new cafe."

Madeleine lifted the blindfold, blinked to regain focus, and found herself grasping for Luke's arm. Or her Dad's. Anyone or anything that would hold her up as her knees buckled underneath her.

Chapter 42

Luke

Luke's arms were around Madeleine before she even knew she needed them. He worried by the way her eyes widened once she realized Anna Lamb was in her café, she might faint.

Thankfully, she didn't. But even still, he didn't take his arm away from her waist and kept his hand firmly on her hip. Anticipating her reaction, he'd instinctively swept his arm around her right before Emily cued Anna to speak. He had moved too quickly to think whether this was appropriate or not, but now that he held her, he wondered if he should. After all, he'd broken her heart no less than three days ago, setting her bakery up to be sold off, spent his time with Emily, then didn't call or text at all. If it weren't for the distraction of the makeover, she'd likely be squirming out of his grasp. And he couldn't blame her. His only hope rested with the papers Dillon held just off camera.

Soon enough, I'll see if this worked. Then maybe she can forgive me.

The way her mouth was slightly open was nothing short of adorable. He watched as her attention flitted around the entire café, then came to land back on Anna. "Oh my word, I can't believe you're here. What are you doing here?" She turned to her dad next. "Dad, do you see that Anna Lamb is standing here? In my bakery? Right here?"

He laughed and nodded his head. "Yes, I do see she's here. But maybe there's some more to look at as well?" He made a sweeping gesture with his hand, finishing toward the camera in a not-so-subtle way to remind his daughter that she was filming a television show.

"Oh, I see it. But, wow. Anna, hi."

Anna waved back and raised her eyebrows in a 'you should look around' sort of expression.

By this point, the crew members were all stifling their laughter, since Madeleine didn't even remember her new bakery. *Guess I'll help her out?* In his best TV-show-host voice, Luke prompted, "What do you think of your new space?"

He watched her scan the room, stopping on certain details and gliding past others. She ran a hand over the glossy tabletop closest to her, painted with swirling, bright blue epoxy to look like frosting, the table's edges trimmed with gold foil.

"It's beautiful. These tables are gorgeous." Her gaze wandered to the far side of the room, now lined with long, wooden benches, painted with stripes of gold, white, and pink. Rectangular tables stood in front of the benches, with pastel-colored chairs tucked underneath the front side. "I love the seating options over there, too."

He could feel she'd had found her footing again, and was ready to take off into the bakery for a closer look. He tightened his grip on her waist, hoping to keep her contained in the framed shot. *Can't have a reveal reaction on screen if she isn't in front of the camera.* "Let's head over to the counter and get a better view, shall we?"

With that, she quickly moved out of Luke's grasp and toward the counter, where she grazed her palm over the wooden top. The wall underneath matched the one in the window, blush pink with painted sprinkles, and the new Bean and Batter logo in the center. *Does she see it? Please notice the countertop.*

"Is this...?" She wondered aloud.

He smiled when she looked back at him, a satisfied warmth spreading across his chest. *She does see it.* "Yes, it is. That's the top from your old office desk. We refinished it, sealed it, and brought it out here. Your mom spent so many hours working in that office, we thought it would be nice to bring that out into the main area in her honor."

Tears were beginning to form in the corners of Madeleine's eyes, and Luke saw her swallow hard as she nodded her head silently. A lump formed in his own throat, but his on-camera persona had to ignore it, though he wanted nothing more than to celebrate alongside her.

He knew he needed to point out the next feature of the back counter, but he hesitated. If she was already this emotional, the tears were sure to come quickly.

A few more shots, then I can get her off camera and give her the good news. Luke continued his show host duties. "Madeleine, look up at the wall," he whispered in her ear. Even with the cameras rolling, he wanted to share this intimate moment.

Her mother's handwriting had been enlarged and hand-painted across the wall. Recipes and ingredient lists spread from one end of the bakery to the other. And lining the top of the wall, just below the ceiling line, her mother's collection of vintage teacups and saucers formed a makeshift crown molding.

In an instant, Madeleine's hand found his. It was soft to his touch, but her grasp was strong and almost clinging. "Oh, Luke."

The way she breathed out his name was almost more than he could take. Reminding himself they were still on camera, he bit his lower lip and swallowed hard. He wanted to pull her against him, wrap his arms around her waist, and press his mouth to hers, if only to hear her say his name like that once more when he stopped kissing her.

"This is..." With her free hand, she swiped at a lone tear that had fallen down her cheek. "Wow. I don't know what to..." she stammered. "How did you...?" She looked back at him.

He smiled. "We found your mother's notebooks in the office and used those for a pattern. I made sure to save the teacups, and our team thought it would be the perfect way to honor your mom's legacy."

She reached a hand toward her dad, who stood only a few steps behind her, just barely in the camera's frame. "Dad, this is incredible," she said, as she tugged him toward the countertop.

"I know." His voice was raspy, and he strained to keep his emotions in check. "I haven't seen your mother's handwriting in so long. I forgot how beautiful it was."

"Cut!" Emily's voice rang out over the moment. "I think we have everything we need for this part of the makeover. Luke, you were amazing. Madeleine, if you'll just step this way, we need to film the rest of the reveal."

With that, Emily broke whatever magical spell had kept Madeleine clinging to Luke. She let go of his hand and followed Emily toward the back office, where things were now tidy, organized, and coordinated in the same pastel colors as the chairs in the bakery. The design team had even hand painted a floral pattern along the back wall that was an updated version of the wallpaper they took down.

The reveal seemed to happen in slow motion, but now it felt as if someone had pressed a fast-forward button, launching them into a sequence of quick takes. At Emily's bark, everyone moved from one shot to the next, and it wasn't long before she put down her clipboard and announced, "And, we've got everything we need. That's a wrap. Thank you everyone."

Cameras were stowed, cables wrapped into coils, and lights were shut off. Madeleine's dad announced to the room as well as the people watching from outside that Joe's BBQ House would be hosting a wrap party this afternoon. Slowly, the crowd started making its way to their cars and to the party.

Anna crossed to where Luke stood and nudged his shoulder. "It's now or never, dude. She's primed and ready for you to swoop in and be your awesome self."

He looked back at his friend. "Thanks. Would you wait here while I go talk to her? And make sure her dad stays, too? He knows everything I'm about to tell her, but I'll need him here. Assuming she doesn't hate me, that is."

"She won't hate you. Not after you tell her. I promise. Now go on, and I'll find her dad."

Dillon and Becca had made their way to the antique leather loveseat in the back corner, Becca's legs curled underneath her while leaning against Dillon's shoulder. Madeleine reclined in the pastel blue club chair next to the couch, smiling at the pair as they chatted. She looked stunning today, in her bright green. He wished he had told her that earlier, when she'd arrived, but he'd been too focused on seeing her for the first time since that day they argued. His nerves about how she would react to him took all of his focus.

Even though they were all three in conversation, Luke could tell that Madeleine wasn't really listening to Dillon and Becca's banter. She looked over every space of her bakery, smiling at some parts, quirking her head to the side as she looked at others. She looked so relaxed, so contented in this moment.

Luke almost hated to go to her, still afraid he might upset her. He hadn't had a real conversation with her since the day he and Dillon fought in the parking lot. He still wasn't sure if the warmth she'd shown him today was for the cameras, or if it was real.

"Luke? Do you want to ride with me to Joe's?" Emily called from the doorway.

He pursed his lips, and never took his eyes off Madeleine as he called back, "Nope. I do not. As a matter of fact, Emily, I don't care to ride anywhere with you."

His reply garnered a huff from Emily, who stood in the doorway for only a second with her mouth hanging open.

Madeleine turned head to look at him, her eyes wide in surprise.

Well, here's my chance.

It only took a few steps and he was next to her, still expecting her to stand and walk away. But she didn't. She stayed seated, and watched him expectantly.

Becca looked between the two of them, then at Dillon. "Uh, hey, Dillon. Maybe we should head over to Joe's."

"Yup. I'll drive," he responded as he stood.

"Actually," Luke held a hand toward his brother, palm extended to stop him from leaving. "I think you two should stay. You had a large part in what I'm about to say."

The pair settled back into their seats, and Luke pulled a chair from a nearby table next to Madeleine's and sat.

His pulse raced through his ears, and his hands were sweaty. He ran them quickly over his thighs, and took a deep breath. "Okay, so I know you're upset with me, but please give me a chance to explain some things."

Her eyebrows lifted, but her lips drew into a puckered pout to one side. Not a promising start.

"First off, I'm sorry that I let Emily have that much leeway with my feelings. I never should have allowed her to be so..." he searched for the right word.

"Obnoxious? Possessive?" Dillon supplied. "Hands on, maybe?"

Becca shushed him, thankfully, before his brother's list of Emily's descriptors continued.

"Well, yeah, all of those, and probably a few more," Luke continued. "But Maddie, that was all her. She's not important to me. Not even a little bit."

Madeleine could have been a statue, she was so still. She watched Luke squirm as he tried to say all the things he'd rehearsed for days but suddenly had a case of mush-brain and couldn't remember any of them.

"I know how important this bakery is to you." *Really, Luke? Way to point out the obvious. Do better.* "And I am truly sorry I withheld the pages about the buyout plan from you for so long."

Madeleine's shoulders stiffened, and she took a deep breath, as if bracing herself for more bad news.

"But I had Jake take a look at the contract, and he confirmed something for me." He paused, in hopes she would ask for an explanation, but she said nothing. "There was a clause in the paperwork that allowed you to buy the bakery. For three-quarters of a million."

Her eyebrows furrowed, and she slowly moved her head to one side. "Luke, that's impossible. I could never afford that."

"I know. Trust me. But there is a solution." Luke rested his hand lightly on Madeleine's knee. She didn't pull away, which was the encouragement he needed to go on.

Dillon, the ever-perfect wing man, held out the file folder he'd been keeping safe all morning and passed it to Luke, who handed it to Madeleine.

"Go ahead." He motioned for her to look inside. "You're not the only one who loves this place. The entire town of Ryleigh does too. They love *you*, Madeleine. And so do I."

Chapter 43

Madeleine

M adeleine couldn't make her eyes focus on the folder. *Did he just say he loved me?* The thought seemed to be on repeat in her brain, and yet it made no sense.

Sitting in this familiar space, surrounded by unfamiliar furniture, but with the people she loved, felt completely unreal. Right now, everything seemed like it had been turned inside out and upside down.

"What did you say?" Her voice was barely a whisper, but Luke had moved so close to her, she knew he heard it.

"Which part? The solution to the buyout, or the fact that I love you?" He swiped circles with his thumb over her knee, and his touch tingled with electricity.

"Um, both, I guess." She smiled as she looked up at him, tucking her hair behind her ear.

"Look inside the folder, Madeleine." His voice was strong, now. Deep and confident. "There's your answer to both."

She looked down at the folder in her hands, and opened it. Right on top was an official-looking document, but clipped to the side of it was a cashier's check. It was made out to Madeleine Malone. When she saw the amount, she nearly dropped the papers.

"Luke, how did this...seven hundred and thirty thousand dollars?" It was a good thing she was sitting, otherwise she knew she'd have passed out. The room was already starting to close in around her. She focused on Luke's face as he watched her with a half-grin.

"I told you. Everyone in this town wanted this bakery to stay yours. And not just this town, but most of the surrounding ones too. That's everything we brought in from the Home Run Derby."

Once again, the puzzle shifted, and Madeleine couldn't make sense of it. "I thought that was just a publicity piece for the show?"

"Nope. It was all for you. Emily wasn't involved at all. Dillon sold tickets. Anna signed so many autographs, I probably owe her a spa treatment for her hands. Becca brought back lots of baseball alumni. Joe donated the barbecue. We had hundreds of people there, Maddie. They all came and were so generous. For you."

Madeleine looked over at Anna leaning against the sales counter next to her dad. She shrugged her shoulders and lifted her palms up. "Guilty. And, yes, I'll take that spa treatment."

Suddenly everything came together. No wonder Dillon couldn't come over for burgers that night, and she understood why Becca hadn't answered her texts. They were busy putting together a massive event, and all without her knowing why. She pressed her fingers to her lips, as if that would contain the gratitude overflowing from her heart.

"And we owe your dad a thanks for keeping you busy all weekend. If he hadn't kept you away from the ballfield, you'd have caught us," Dillon said.

A moment of happy indignation rose up in Madeleine's throat. "Dad? You knew about all this?"

"Sure did. You didn't think I really needed all those cookies and tarts, did you?"

She let out a short, relieved laugh. "I did wonder why you kept insisting baking would take my mind off all the stress and frustration. You just kept suggesting recipe after recipe."

She looked back at the check, still resting on her lap. "But this is so much money. I don't know how I can take it."

"You can if you think of it as a gift. You've given so much to this community, and so did your mother. This is their way of repaying it."

"And this other paperwork?" She held the pages attached to the check out toward Luke. "What is all this?"

"The contracts to make everything official. I had Jake draw those up for me." He took the papers from her, and flipped to the last page. Henry Greyson's signature was scrawled across the top line, with his name printed beneath.

The line below that was blank, but had 'Madeleine Malone' typed under it, awaiting her signature. But that wasn't what drew her attention. Beneath her signature line was another. She read the name underneath, and her heartbeat sped. The letters seemed to wiggle on the page as she tried to focus her thoughts. *His name looks so official below mine.*

Luke reached over and took the pages from her and handed them back to Dillon. "I hope you don't think I've assumed too much. But I have something for you." He reached in his back pocket and pulled out a small slip of paper. He unfolded it and handed it to her.

The check, made out to The First Bank of Texas, was written for twenty thousand dollars, and signed by Luke Taylor. On the memo line, in Luke's neat, capital letters, it read 'Bakery Investment.' She blinked a few times and shook her head, trying to clear her mind, but only confusion mixed with curiosity blanketed her thoughts. *He wants to be partners? New York is awfully far away for him to make business decisions.*

His hand was barely quivering as it rested on her knee, and his breath was now short and ragged. She placed her own hand on top of his to settle his nerves.

"You'll notice we were just short in our fundraising. But I have a proposal. I was hoping you'd let me be part owner in the bakery."

Madeleine's hands started shaking, too. She wasn't sure if it was from Luke's nervous energy or her own. She looked down at them, one hand holding Luke's check, the other holding his hand with their fingers entwined, and all trembling. "How can you do that from New York City? There are a lot of details to work out, Luke."

He took a long, slow breath. "That's true. But I hope we can work those out."

She felt Becca pulling the check from her hand, but she couldn't draw her eyes away from Luke. "Mr. Malone, did you bring that package?" he asked.

Madeleine's dad hustled over to them and handed Luke a small box, exactly the size of a ring box. "Here it is," he said, before making his way back to the counter.

The room suddenly was so very still. Madeleine's heart thumped in the center of her chest, and she squinted, trying to focus her vision.

Her dad's words from only a second ago rattled in her mind and her thoughts started to string together what was actually happening. *Here it is. Oh, right. Here it is. The moment. This is it. Here it is. Oh, my sweet sugar cane. Here it is.*

"Madeleine Malone. I have loved you since I was sixteen years old, only I was too immature to do anything about it. I admired you from a distance, wishing you were mine. You were everything I wanted back then, and you've only become more beautiful, more amazing, and I know now that I can't possibly let you slip away again. I'm sorry I've missed all the years we could have had, but I won't be stupid enough to lose any more. Henry says I can stay on with Greyson Media and work from anywhere. Even Ryleigh, Texas. Coach Norton says he'll hire me to coach baseball if that doesn't work out."

Luke opened the box and revealed a familiar, gold ring with two pink stones. Her mother's promise ring. But it now had a large diamond centered between the two stones. "Your dad was gracious enough to let me give this to you. And while I think it was beautiful, it felt a little...incomplete." He took the ring from the box and held it between his thumb and forefinger.

"An engagement ring should have a diamond."

Madeleine's entire body went weightless as Luke lowered himself out of his chair and onto one knee.

"My sweet Madeleine, will you marry me?" He held the ring in the air and moved it toward her left hand now entwined around his.

Tears streamed down her cheeks, and she lifted her hand out, fingers spread wide to accept the ring he was ready to slip on. She leaned down, wrapped her arms around his neck and pulled him close enough to be able to whisper in his ear. "I've been waiting for that question since tenth grade. What took you so long?"

He nuzzled his lips against his favorite soft place under her ear, and his voice vibrated against her neck. "Is that a yes?" he murmured.

"Oh, that's an absolutely, for sure, yes," she said, loud enough for everyone to hear. And as the room cheered, she tilted her head toward his, lowered herself next to him on the floor, and kissed him.

THE END

About the Author

Jennifer writes books for anyone who likes a good love story and a laugh. She strives to do all things in love, as that is her highest goal in both her personal life and writing career.

A native Texan, she calls the Dallas area home, where she lives with her college-sweetheart husband, two creative teenagers, and two overly-friendly dogs. She has also lived in New York, Tennessee, Alaska, Minnesota, Iowa, and Illinois. Growing up in a family who moved around the nation often, Jennifer quickly realized the value of her automatically built-in friends (also known as her little sisters). The bonds of sisterhood still run strong, as she still lives near her parents and sisters, and she delights in spending time with her five nieces and nephews.

During a long-time career as a teacher, she managed to teach all grades, from PreK to seniors. In addition to teaching, she has worked several interesting jobs. Her highlights reel would include costume designer, hot dog demo girl, Kool-Aid Man, radio DJ, theatre director, and Christmas store manager. Lately, she can be found watching documentaries on nearly anything historical, browsing travel websites, and binge-watching The Great British Baking Show. She loves Jesus, fresh coffee, afternoon naps, and colorful pens.

To learn more about Jennifer's next book, follow her on Amazon, social media, and sign up for her newsletter at www.JenniferWritesBooks.com

Acknowledgments

All glory and thanks for this book you hold in your hands go first to Jesus, who is the greatest Gift the world has ever known, given in love by God the Father. I learned first about love because He first loved me.

There's something exciting about 'firsts'. I am a first-born. This is my first book to publish. This is my first 'Author Acknowledgements' to write. Something that is 'first' implies there is more to come. That seems to be the story of my heart, always. All my life, I wanted to be a teacher. That was my first career, and I loved it. My first year, I taught first grade. That was the beginning of a wonderful time in my life, and I have memories of so many firsts – every first day of school, the first time I organized a field trip, my first book fair, the first time a student's circumstances made me cry, the first time I told someone I had been awarded Teacher of the Year, and the first time the school year started and I was no longer a teacher. But with each first, there has to come a next. This book is my 'next'.

I hope this book is the first of many written by me that you will read. And I hope it makes you smile.

Writing this part of the book is both the easiest bit and also the most difficult. Knowing who to thank is simple. Writing words to express my truest gratitude to those people seems completely insufficient. I can say, without a moment's hesitation, that without my mom's constant persuasion and support, this book would never have made it to your hands. If anyone ever needs a cheerleader who is endlessly encouraging you to follow your dreams, call my mom. Or call my dad if you need someone to quietly push you forward and gently remind you that standing still is really moving backward. A man of few, intentional words, he has caused me to become a close, careful listener.

Also, my husband and kids get all the love and thanks I have to give. Without Jason's ever-supportive, never-questioning nature, I would not have found the time or courage to invest in my writing dreams. Thank you, Jason, for opening the door to this career. Also, thanks for teaching me everything I know about baseball and helping me to love the sport as much as you do. My kids never stop asking how a book is coming along, telling their friends about their author-mom, and checking in on my progress, all while patiently giving up time with their mommy every Saturday night because it's 'write-night'. I should probably also thank the pizza delivery guy for delivering so many pizzas to my home every Saturday night while I was scribbling away at a local pub.

Writing a book is a solitary job, but building a community of writers makes it much more fun. Without my best writing friend, Stacy Wells, seated across the table from me every Saturday night, I would never have been able to reach this point. Also, alongside me on this writerly journey came many other writers and friends who helped me learn, polish chapters, and ask me about my progress. Jen Geigle Johnson, Fenley Grant, Nuha Said, Debbie Ochoa, and Mary Jolley all have their fingerprints on this book in some way, and I am a better writer for it. Krissi Dallas, Jill Cox, Heather Reid, Amanda Reid, Susan Person, MaryBeth Holm, Priya Ardis, and so many others who have walked the authorly path with me have brought sparks of joy, many laughs, great dinners, fun retreats, and more to the time spent creating together.

Many friends who asked, encouraged, sent messages online, liked social media posts, and even answered questions texted late at night while I was writing and needed help with details (I'm looking at you, Jake Norton) or story ideas all should have their names listed here. But I'm afraid I'll forget one. So, suffice it to say, if you are reading this and have ever spoken with me about this book, or even interacted with me online in a group or a forum, or we met at a conference, or if you knew anything about this book or my writing career before you read this book, this paragraph is about you. You are part of a group of people for which I am always thankful.

Finally, let me say this. I write love stories because I believe in love. It can change the world, if given the chance. It can also change the direction of someone's day, just with one small act. Look for love in the world today. Share it with everyone. Most importantly, never forget that you are loved.

Made in the USA
Coppell, TX
21 February 2023

13222132R00146